D0860075

Jan. 30, 2003

To Peggy,

From one
collector to another,
may we continue to—
gether, hansomely, and
hopefully prevail and
prosper.

Best regards,
Larry Franks

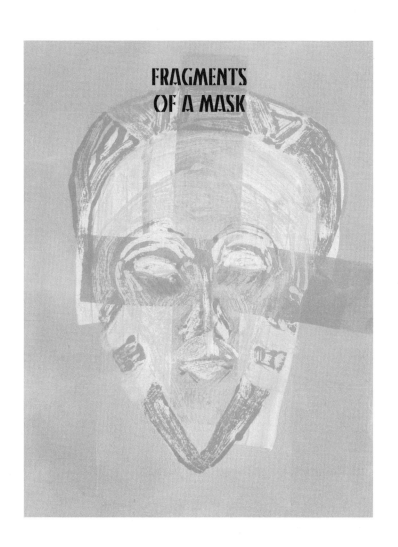

FRAGMENTS
OF A MASK

Also by Larry Frank

Historic Pottery of the Pueblo Indians
Indian Silver Jewelry of the Southwest
The New Kingdom of the Saints
Train Stops (Short Stories)
A Land So Remote (Three Volumes)

FRAGMENTS
OF A MASK

Larry Frank

SUNSTONE
PRESS

SANTA FE

This is a work of fiction. Names, characters, places and incidents either are the product of the author's imagination or are used fictitiously. Any resemblance to events or persons living or dead is entirely coincidental.

Cover Painting by Alyce Frank

© 2002 by Larry Frank. All rights reserved.

Printed and bound in the United States of America. No part of this book may be reproduced in any form or by any electronic or mechanical means including information storage and retrieval systems without permission in writing from the publisher, except by a reviewer who may quote brief passages in a review.

Sunstone books may be purchased for educational, business, or sales promotional use. For information please write: Special Markets Department, Sunstone Press, P.O. Box 2321, Santa Fe, New Mexico 87504-2321.

FIRST EDITION

1 3 5 7 9 10 8 6 4 2

Library of Congress Cataloging-in-Publication Data:

Frank, Larry.
    Fragments of a mask / by Larry Frank.–1st ed.
        p. cm.
    ISBN: 0-86534-370-5   - ISBN: 0-86534-359-4 (pbk)
        1. Antiquities-Collection and preservation-Fiction. 2. Los Angeles (Calif.)-Fiction.
    I. Title.

    PS3556. R33426 F73 2002
    813'.54-dc21   2002029185

Published in

SUNSTONE PRESS
Post Office Box 2321
Santa Fe, NM 87504-2321 / USA
(505) 988-4418 / *orders only* (800) 243-5644
FAX (505) 988-1025
www.sunstonepress.com

*F*or Alyce Frank, my wife, who
occupies the best part of my life and
who experienced with me many
favorite adventures.

*P*reface

*I*n the 1950's everything seemed open and possible. The upheaval of the Second World War spewed nationalism which spread, catching fire in countries in the throes of freeing themselves from their former colonial bondage. As a result, an ensuing surge of adventurous souls traversed the changing boundaries of an old world order disintegrating in chaos. For a brief time, the characters of this novel are caught wedged between the resulting cracks and fissures that harbored them. Now in today's realities, hardened by political and ethnic tension, it is doubtful whether the Farneys and Averys and Duskyannes could find a place for themselves in the modern world where no possible havens exist.

*I*n your collection

collect unstintingly

the marks of man

tattooed on earth's skin

and festooned

by dwellings

pegged into

our revolving orb.

In your collection

mark these signs

unsparingly as

hallmarks of

time, place, heart,

ordained by a

kindred moon,

molten sun,

stuttering stars.

1

*H*e is weightless, cruising, looking down upon the backs of eagles, the whole wonderful atmosphere his downy bed. Down below through the eagle's wings he sees the outlines of scenes of his life chalked on the ground appearing like a hopscotch maze. He knows the layout of images far below holds a special meaning, as if they signified another self and this he carries like an unsupportable weight, sinking him downward, tethering his ankle, pulling toward his marked life sprawled on fatal fields under him. He lands on a rooftop. Irresistibly he looks down and sees himself recreated in drawn squares while engaged in what he feels relates to him. In one square he is searching for something unique and attractive among wastes of endless sand. Emptiness! He stands there in despair. In another, he is in a vortex of greenness, a rich profusion of waterfalls with fish and birds attached to it. The flowering recesses beckon him. Vines entangle him, keeping him from reaching out to claim the green shimmer, the petaled jewels for himself. The beauty fades before his intrusion. He is frantic. Now, in a drawn square he finds himself running in a woods. The sun is shining but the rays don't penetrate to him. He suspects that the trees in unison are converging their crowns and sewing up the light and sky from his life below. Objects materialize-ivory masks, bronze horses, rotund Buddhas. He knows their purpose is to tantalize him. He will resist. But he cannot stop himself from examining and arranging them. They refuse him: they shift, transmogrify, disappear. He can't stand to see them out of order; they make no sense to him. He is losing his strength but if he could just touch one more object he could right the disarray and perfection would be accomplished. Perfection. He can't keep up. He can't stem the madness. He is reaching too far. Quite easily he falls off the roof obliterating his life.

Avery Judson sits up in bed. Awake, he still has the sensation of sliding. It makes him think of how once while half-asleep he had slid with this same sensation down the staircase of his childhood home. It seems a safe memory. He probes it. Halfway up the stairs he remembered the round hole in the wall covered with grillwork through which he could peer to watch the occupants in the livingroom below. He had felt sure it had been built so he could tiptoe in the dark down the stairs and without being discovered stare upon lovers on the sofa. Only his parents never loved. His know-it-all father knows nothing, is incapable of knowing a Duskyanne from a Rajah, a Katy in her sky mesas, a silver Stephanie.

There are no safe memories. He swings his legs to the floor. He thinks idly of how his dream had had to stop because it had nowhere to go but this room. For six days he has been in this room. Anyway, he has been told it's been six days. He thinks of the room as a spar to a shipwrecked man in a vast ocean, but how does that man know which way to proceed? The middle age middle of nothing is precisely nowhere.

He stares at the table with two chairs and a white pitcher. He can see inside the pitcher's rim which has a blue border. It isn't Delft but a later and cruder example of Dutch ceramics. He notes that he has noted this. So, he is recovering a part of himself with no help from himself. Recover from what? He has no alternate triumph to compensate for his destruction in Spain.

There is little else in the room except a dresser with nothing on it. The table, chairs, dresser, bed, and Avery Judson. A motley crew. They are like huge chessmen capable of tactical maneuvers between themselves. He has options. He can go to the table and back to the bed. But when he paces from bed to dresser there is Farney. Or, from dresser to closet to bed there is Duskyanne. That is all there is; he cannot shake them off. So far he can only eject from his mangled mind the events that have brought him to this room. It seems to him that each event clangs to the floor as he separates them.

A taxi took him to the Barcelona train station.

He meant to go to France, to the Rousillon.

He carries no luggage, but he had money with him.

He boarded the train and drank cups of water.

A lady passenger said that he slept with his eyes open.

He was so sick that the conductor made him get off at the next stop. He got another taxi.

The taxi stopped and he collapsed into a hotel.

He is told that he is in Antwerp. That fact is held in place by his window which overlooks a recognizable town square of tall, narrow houses standing in penguin rows.

Food is brought to him and he reasons that the hotel management knows he has money. He must still look like a man of means.

This is the data he can muster, but to no avail. According to the broken compass of his emotions he is nowhere; all roads are blasted. All he can do is push his fixations around like a simpleton sliding toy soldiers back and forth. Duskyanne. Farney. Duskyanne and Farney. Farney and Duskyanne. There are no other possible arrangements.

He stops at the table. His hand runs over the pitcher out of the habit of examination. He wants to persuade himself-as if he could know whether he had done all he could that would make life bearable-that it has been Duskyanne he has pursued over half the earth, not the Benin mask, the Ajanta wall painting. The pitcher stares at him. He pulls back his head.

God, that it had been Farney in that room! Of course, Farney. Is Farney now slipping one more bead along his abacus? A Duskyanne bead. An Avery bead. No, Farney can't do without him. That dependence is Avery's checkmate in the game between them.

"You pimp for that man no matter how loftily you would like to regard your arrangement." His father, his permanent accuser. Avery is the donkey on which his father, seeing nothing, pins tails of advice on all the wrong parts, and the tails drop off. So his father accuses the arts, accuses his mother, the defender of her son Avery, accused Darlington of starting it all.

It's the pitcher that makes him think of Darlington, the king of commonplace items Darlington had had in his shop at the end. Too common for Farney, though. When Farney's aesthetic sense went awry he knew it. What had Darlington known? For the first time it occurs to Avery that Darlington had been canny beyond his antiques. He had no conflict. Avery sees him after they had locked up the shop being met by some fleshy, over-ripe woman, endlessly in her twilight, who would hook onto him and together they would invade the night. Darlington had seemed an alchemist who could procure the fragments of ages and from them forge beauty and purpose. If he needed to cavort sporadically with blousy friends who pillowed his evenings it may never have interfered. Women to Darlington had low trade value and were worth a minimum of expenditure. In that he probably would be considered a wise man.

Avery picks up and holds the pitcher, his first determined act since he has been in the room. He lets it go in midair. The fragmented pieces scatter all over, each piece like a segment of his life. Humpty Dumpty couldn't bring himself back, but Avery could try to put the shards and bits of Avery Judson together again and make himself whole starting at the beginning when Darlington came into his life, yes, and produced a lasting impact.

Avery hadn't known what it was he'd been waiting for until he recognized it in a store window in a rundown Los Angeles neighborhood. Lofted over the window he had noted the sign: *Darlington's Art Works*-in such a block the guarantee of a junk shop. He had been putting off walking home and had digressed from his normal route to avoid meeting his father and escape a confrontation about his dropping out of college.

He could imagine his father's arguments: "The only reason to drop out of school is to defend one's country in time of war. It's peacetime, Avery. Ike is going to shepherd us through an economic renaissance. You need to have an education to prepare yourself for what's to come. You need to become somebody." It really didn't matter to Avery what the actual words or arguments were. It exhausted him to imagine the implications, much less listen to his father's dreary droning.

His reluctant feet had taken him to this stretch of tawdry businesses, a far cry from the plush neighborhood where he lived. This shop stood near the corner of Wilcox and Sunset, wedged between a featureless barbershop and a tiny restaurant where something heavy with garlic and olive oil and something rich with cinnamon and apples continually cooked and simmered. The commingling aromas were not unpleasant. Avery inhaled with appreciation, then directed his attention to 'Darlington's Art Works.'

He approached such shops curiously. He could never tell what lingered in them–why such a hideous object ever appealed to anyone in the first place, not alone sold to a new buyer; but even more puzzling one might ask the reason why in another venue a lovely piece had been disowned? But whatever objects the owner displayed Avery much preferred their unknown appeal over the contrived elegance of the interior decorators' shops his mother frequented.

She often had him tag along. Whatever she or her friends bought everything looked alike; he could never distinguish the bland and perfectly appointed furnishings from one house to another. It irritated him that the proprietors of such sterility had proclaimed it superior taste. He found in antique shops a spiritual counterbalance. If he bought something his mother attributed his act as a sort of slight cultural effervescence due to her efforts while he regarded his little collection as a perfectly prescribed repudiation of her. Moreover, he genuinely liked things.

However, this shop with the odd sign had been more than could be expected. With his face pressed to the window he saw a kaleidoscope of things he could hardly absorb–seemingly all important pieces that should be placed in museums and not just trifles like the ordinary merchandise stocked in stores or cluttering most homes.

A medieval suit of armor attracted him as it stood dramatically lit, almost alive. Avery smiled at the idea that if the knight had quietly died inside it must stink. A Chinese Buddha occupied space on one side of the armor and a Northwest Coast totem pole on the other. Beyond these Avery could make out a Gothic angel, a Navajo blanket strung up on the wall, a Chinese rug on the floor. Other dark forms crowded together. The scene didn't seem chaotic, not when each piece spoke clearly for itself. The room had a magical order all its own. Unaccountably excited he had to touch these objects.

Worried that the shop might be closed Avery tried the half-glass door. A bell tinkled over his head as he pushed it open. No one appeared. It gave him the feeling of the place being his. The shop overwhelmed him with its art oddities from the far ends of the globe, more than he could have expected.

He had despaired of ever being able to settle on a period or a culture, narrow himself to a particular aspect because various material cultures excited him and he wanted to be in command of them all. Here occurred the opportunity to review the troops. Some of them he could tell immediately did not deserve to consort with the others and he would like to weed those out. These tended to be ugly, and although real art might be unfamiliar, it should never be ugly, and even more so, irrelevant.

He picked up a Spanish Conquistador's helmet. It seemed too light, although well-worn. "Go ahead, try it on. It should look good on you. With their armor the Spanish were almost invincible to the Indians. Might be able to help you."

The voice came from behind a mound of fabrics. Next to a hanging mirror Avery quickly checked himself out-of medium height, he wasn't particularly good looking, with or without the helmet on. He knew himself to be an average-looking, slightly colorless young man whose slight, wiry build reduced him to being unremarkable. Wispy hair the color of tallow feathered across his head.

Suddenly walking toward Avery from the back of the room ambled a huge, graying man with strong features. His long, ridged nose bent in the middle. Gazing blandly at Avery appeared the roundest, most intense eyes he had ever seen. Their force seemed to belie the man's mild manners. "I didn't mean to frighten you," he said. "Often I don't hear the bell. I was cataloguing the store's inventory from behind that stack of quilts when I sensed that you were here. I guess I'm not very good at it-I can never catch up. Are you going to try the helmet on?" This introduction to Darlington had been accomplished so simply and placidly that Avery had difficulty reconciling it with the compelling presence of the man.

"Would you like to look at something else?" inquired the proprietor.

To look, thought Avery, was the perfect way to put it. To look at anything, everything, with his eyes, his fingers, his heart, and his brain. He put down the helmet. "I didn't come to buy," he said.

"No, I didn't think you had. You drifted in, but do you like what you see? I can show you more."

16

"Very much. I envy you. I think your store's . . ."

"Well, some think so and some don't. I'm Darlington."

Avery smiled at there being no need to find the word, if the right word ever existed. Darlington's great head turned to survey his domain. Obviously there is no hurry in his world, Avery thought.

Avery looked at him. "I'm ready to, if you are."

"Ready to begin, you mean. I suspect you will never end. In a way, I envy you all the excitement you'll have at this stage."

The big man indicated that Avery should follow him. It turned out to be a good-sized shop. Odd-shaped rooms opened off the main area that extended a respectable length to a back door which Avery suspected opened onto an alley. As Darlington led him along the crowded aisles he wondered if he invaded the objects or if they in turn waylaid him. He wandered among shields and icons and a Plains Indian buffalo skin painting. He found iridescent Roman glassware, a Tibetan prayer wheel, cuspidors, magic lanterns, and ancient green Korean ceramics. Each piece seemed to him to be blessed with its own unknown muse who personally spoke to him.

Darlington turned to Avery, "I always wonder about those who warn us against art possessions as crass material wealth weighing down the noblest spirit of man. When all is said and done possessions are no more unimportant than their owners, which, in my opinion, elevates the owners. At least you don't mistrust what you own, only your neighbors." He continued, "I'll make a prediction: Mankind will be judged by the quality of its trash rather than by the worth of its soul."

Avery had stayed, looked, savored, touched, until finally, with his senses surfeited the two of them locked up the shop together. If possible, he would have stayed there for the night and slept among the hosts of inanimate friends so that at 9:00 a.m. when the shop opened he could continue his tutelage under Darlington with the least amount of interruption.

At the risk of antagonizing his father Avery returned to the shop again and again. He became intrigued with Darlington's savvy, how he presented some of the best stuff and even some less than best. How did it all figure?

As routine work Avery digested dynasties and eras and mores of art as

August Darlington quietly tracked through the shop hanging his opinions on the contents: Polynesian is too often ornamentally frenetic, but the strong figures are superb; for its size, prehistoric Eskimo figures, like caveman art, have strong visual impact; Rajput miniatures are more imaginative and desirable than the stiffer Mogul ones; Pre-Columbian art, certainly prolific in quantity, has pieces of great quality like Olmec sculpture but most of it is average in quality; a few basic artifacts reach the level of art. Avery made the proper mental tag on each correspondent and later isolated the objects and scoured them with attention. In contrast to the illustrations in his college texts here the brilliant ages came alive, something he knew he could not make his father understand.

"You have never understood our Avery. You refuse to understand him." His mother's statements seemed true enough, but maybe his father really did see through him. Again, if his mother implied that his father had been too far removed from Avery then she conversely implied that she materialized as the only one who knew him; both ideas he regarded as equally repugnant. This pretension to closeness buttressed her attempts to be downright cozy. He tolerated it as far as he could, but how cozy could they be?

His mother continually cooed, "Aren't we having fun?" as if by such a reiteration it would be made true. Instead, she curdled the thin blood of his love and forced him to withdraw from her active mind and its fixation. She then became more strident and resorted to interpreting him by the little boy idiosyncrasies she had doted on, and she paraded them before her friends-how he endlessly arranged the sheets of his bed in order to quash the ugly jagged forms, 'hons' he called them-how he coined the word 'grizzer' to cover ugly throw-up kinds of messes. And how sensitively he fondled the curved neck of an inflated rubber swan he dragged around as a child. Worse, she had prattled this before the few girls he brought home. These oddities of behavior he had always linked with the fact that he had been thrown out of kindergarten for kissing girls and scratching and biting boys under the guise of being a tiger, eccentricities he considered to be signs indicative of sexual proclivity. But his teachers sternly rebuked him and his reentry to school turned out to be awkward when he joined his class, and in reverse, suddenly became very shy with his girl classmates, a condition which lingered with him.

His father's scorn for anything smacking of aesthetics naturally offended his mother who became Mrs. Aesthetics herself, but more particularly allowed her to champion her son's imaginary cause: "Compared to your kind of logic you make the boy sound batty." Yet at heart, Avery admired his father's ability to synthesize all kinds of data and put it in the hopper of an agile mind to produce succinct, logical distillations. But it went to one end only. His life was precisioned by sharpened pencils, adding machines that clicked off sums in monotonous rhythms, and the pale green ledger sheets of his well-ordered accounting firm. All his considerations involved debits and credits, red and black ink, budgets, and cost analysis. Avery figured he materialized as his father's major debit.

With some difficulty he had announced to his father that he intended to work for Darlington. His father and he both knew what maneuvers they were going to play. After all, he was his father's son. But he had been deceptive on one point; he had made his new job sound temporary when he sensed the beginning of his life would now unravel.

"For the rest of the summer, or a little longer," Avery explained. "The man's a real pro at selling. It's the best way to put into practice my business courses. You wanted me to have a job, and I got one."

"I'd meant in the firm, of course."

"But this is more in my field."

"Ah, now I begin to see. And please, tell me, what field is that? Have you finally found one?"

"I think so. Combine business knowledge with art knowledge. You've been paying for courses in that direction, too, for three years. It's time now to try it out."

"Are you offering to your employer that free spirit of yours completely gratis?"

"No, I get paid. He won't take advantage of me."

"Hmm, a glimmer of intelligence at last. I don't have any aversion to you making money, and contrary to the majority opinion of this family, I don't find money unsavory. As to salesmanship, it's half a businessman's battle."

"Actually, I'm in administration, or management, or whatever you call it."

"Do you mean accounting? You'll be handling money? Banking?"

"Yes," and Avery thought of ringing the cash register and taking out everyday spending money, the routine cash flow, and banking the money garnered from each day's sales to be stashed conveniently in a huge amphora of doubtful authenticity under Darlington's pool table. "Yes, I have fiscal control."

"Learning to deal with people?"

"Yes, many people."

"I suppose you'll learn something. If you sell that flea-bitten cargo you can sell anything." His father shook his head. "Junk. A son of mine in junk."

"Junk," his mother came in on cue. "What's junk to you is Goya to a connoisseur. Avery would never deal in junk."

Avery faced his father's contempt. He took measure of the man: his dark, three-piece business suit and starched white shirt correlated to be as correct, uninspired, and nondescript as his accounting firm. His staff dressed as clones to the firm's owner. Avery had never seen his father dressed in casual garb, even on Sundays, or when he watched the tennis matches at the Golden Heights County Club. He took it for granted his father had his pajamas starched and pressed. As a young man his father might have been game enough to try a more free-spirited enterprise with less pressure that could earn its keep and eventually come out ahead. But now he has become a financial plutocrat, and his son a marginal risk. As he expected his mother rallied to his cause but this time he welcomed her interference. It meant that the protocol for ending disputes had been set off: the argument would swing away from him and entangle his parents.

"All you care about is Avery making money. That's all you do, and it's boring. There's much more to a life than that."

"I haven't seen you giving any evidence of it."

He waited until he could leave unnoticed while his parents engaged in fighting over him, a battle that had no end.

To sit at the multi-purpose pool table presiding over cartons of chop suey with his boss Avery considered a treat beyond compare. He and Darlington talked of art, of course; they also spoke about Rocky Marciano, and the infant industry of television and its frightening potential impact on the world. They chatted on a cursory basis about Hudson and De Soto automobiles. Darlington favored the Hudson. And of course they returned to conversing about art. Avery had never had such conversations with his father.

During his apprenticeship to Darlington Avery had admitted to himself that the shop did have junk, even bad junk, and that some of the objects didn't quite add up. He didn't expect to see a revelation when he happened to enter the back room of the shop where he usually found Darlington writing or paying bills on the old pool table. But instead the big man, leaning forward, worked at a table strewn with awls, blades, spools, scissors, buckskin, sinew, and beads, bone and ivory pieces. Darlington looked annoyed.

"What do you want? Can't you see the door was closed? Do I have to put a lock on it?"

Astonished, Avery stood gaping at the repair kit before him while wishing that he could instantly vanish.

"Alright! Alright! Have a seat. I suppose it's time for you to take another step in the trade. Lesson by lesson," and Darlington relaxed.

Avery could see Darlington had realized the humor in the situation and had recovered his easy nature. The humor lay in Avery's own grave face still staring at the man. Darlington picked up a bone pendant that he had obviously taken off two woven skirts which lay on the floor. The skirts came from the upper Amazon River. Forming a necklace, he strung the pendant belonging to one cultural source, then added a bone bead from a different region. "What I am doing could squeeze by as restoration in some circles. It's called good business in others." He chuckled. "Just freely enterprising," and he popped on another bead.

Avery tried to keep his face noncommittal.

Darlington found his apprentice amusing. "You are thinking, no doubt, how captivating the necklace is now."

Not precisely, but Avery had to admit his friend to be partially right. "It is captivating," he nodded.

"Now you've learned something," Darlington responded, enjoying himself. "This is one of the few chances we have of being creative-by good works. I have made six necklaces out of a fancy skirt with incised bone trimmings. That's smart capitalism."

Avery watched, not sure how he felt.

"I suppose you are thinking that the two necklaces I'm making will not be exactly authentic for some picayune reason, just because I've changed the function of the skirts and joined two areas of Brazil together."

"I just might be thinking that. I wouldn't say they are genuine," Avery wryly agreed.

"But on the other hand the material used is the real stuff. Those bones are most probably human from men killed by cannibals. Maybe we can charge a higher price."

Darlington grinned and Avery laughed. "Still, they are fake," he half-insisted.

Darlington shrugged. "That's the nature of the beast," he smiled. "I'm a fake, in a way," he happily confessed. "I've been stringing along tatters and bits of nonsense into something quite substantial." He beamed and gestured broadly to the front room where he surveyed his art resources. Darlington had certainly accumulated enough 'good works' to allow himself to permanently reside in heaven. At the same time, on earth, his inventory would inevitably pass into the public domain, authentic or inauthentic, which tended to make him rich. No one could tell how affluent he had become since the turnover of his goods proved to be remarkable.

Somewhat ruefully, Avery had to admit that junk existed and fakes existed and both are tied up with this man. Darlington picked up a brass cuspidor. "This is what I used to peddle–junk. In fact the first commodity I dealt with turned out to be beds." He settled back in his Windsor chair, his feet up on the pool table. "We were still driving buggies around Terra Haute then. A merchant hired me to haul away a pile of old beds for five dollars. When I got the beds I didn't know what to do with them. You can't just plain litter up the countryside with beds. So I went to a junk man who stacked junk and sold them for two and a half dollars each. That's what I got. Profit of seven-fifty." Savoring his recollection, Darlington returned to his work.

Avery picked up the pendant that Darlington would need next and handed it to him. "Your accomplice, sir."

Darlington smiled. "Well, with that money I bought a few desks and bureaus and chairs from an old schoolhouse." His rhythm increased; pendants and beads now nearly filled out the necklace. "I upped my clientele and sold them to a used furniture shop that carried a few antiques. This made me a tidy sum which I parlayed into gramophones and discs and Indian baskets and walking canes and amber beads and kaleidoscopes and scrimshaw carvings . . ."

"And Brazilian skirts with etched bone pendants."

Darlington twinkled. "Eventually that too as I got smarter and read books as fast as they came out. Learned the trade, you could call it. Then I found a shack, crammed my goodies inside, and opened my first trading post. Called it 'Darlington's Dillies.'"

"No wonder you changed the name," Avery laughed. "Sounds like a freak show."

"Maybe it didn't help me any because nobody came around. So I decided to take my delights to folks instead. Bring them my circus. It's the same as selling them washing machines or the like–even better, because every house needs a parcel of beauty. I found that plain people also crave the fine ornaments of the world. I learned a valuable lesson. The real stroke of luck came when I latched on to a Whistler. Got it cheap. I moved here and set up this business from what I reaped from that painting. It's why I then decided to go for the best things but I'll always be fond of junk."

"But fakes are still fakes," Avery chided, and he smiled to himself at Darlington's self-tribute to his humble but incrementally lucrative beginnings.

Avery made his first purchase–a very credible basket. He did not regard it as junk. He thought it breathtaking–a large Yokut Indian basket from Northern California with a design of sixty-nine dark men holding hands, called a "Friendship Basket." Its high wall of gleaming textured yellow flared out at the top. Avery knew it had been loved before he owned it–certainly by its maker. But his father reacted differently. He would pass it in the hallway, slow down, and level a strange look at it. In fact, he'd automatically hook his head upward and give a tiny snort when he confronted it. His father had not acknowledged the basket even though he would more than proclaim its existence by being startled every time he faced it. Avery's mother lovingly dusted it each day.

It amused and constantly puzzled Avery to find that among the general throng who came to the shop Darlington attracted a good number of scholarly saints of the arts. "You can spot them," Darlington liked to point out, "they are phonies." To him the phonies consisted of those scholars who spotted his own phonies, the junk and fakes. Indeed, when these learned collectors assiduously dogged their way through the shop and saw a sprinkling of outright fakes, some became suspicious and dropped the 'Darlington Experience' as distasteful. But those who could be considered tenacious and not "light-weight" or "weak-hearted," as Darlington termed them persevered. In their explorations they discovered the shapes of conceivable hope in the shop's recesses which they converted into good buys of good art. One rich, active collector with fine taste but reluctant to part with cash would pay with postage stamps what he bought every time he frequented the shop until finally Darlington kicked him out.

The atonal ring of the cash register sounded continually. By now through the lessons and experiences that Avery had received Darlington came to the conclusion that his shopkeeper should be prepared to test the full value of his apprenticeship. This meant that Avery would be empowered to run the shop on those occasions when Darlington would be absent, and especially to decide what material the shop should buy.

"Beware of Armenians bearing rugs," was the phrase Darlington used to warn Avery about bad deals and how not to be taken. Darlington pointed out the roster of performers in the trade that Avery would have to contend with. Dealers often receive a ten percent discount. Agents might receive a finder's fee of up to ten percent if they brought in a big customer who bought a lot. Intermediaries were suspect, depending on who they dealt with or spied for, whether their purpose could be adverse to the interests of the shop. Worthwhile pickers got their trips paid for to purchase materials plus a small percentage of what they sold to their sponsor.

The day that Darlington told him 'he was on his own' Avery felt primed and ready to do battle. People wandered in and out: customers, clients (exclusive customers), dealers, a British intermediary, an old lady who had a brass coat rack to sell, and a newsboy. Then, a man whom he had never seen before, an Armenian rug dealer, entered with rugs on his shoulders and carrying a number of small cases. Dark-skinned with flashing white teeth, the man hurried through his wares, placing on the counter an assortment of knives and daggers, Arab brass and copper coffee pots and grinders, coin necklaces, and odds and ends of Turkish hats and silver pins.

Fearing Armenians bearing rugs, Avery bought sparingly, his education having only proceeded so far. He paid for two brass coffee pots, a brass coffee grinder, an oil lamp, and, thrown into the bargain, a rather nice wooden powderhorn covered by brass sheets, its front carved with calligraphic writing. They did not add up to trash. Darlington would consider them all salable merchandise.

Then Avery spotted three tarnished, flat animal figures in the bottom of the box the dealer commenced to fill up again with rejected material. Avery slowly took them out. They turned out to be semi-flat pieces of dark metal sculptured into vigorous animal shapes, either of brass or copper, and over twelve inches long. They were plaques and he felt they definitely did not belong among the other mediocre decorative pieces. They stood out as a wild spirited tribe of animals. He would call them awe-bearing forces. Whoever created these had worshiped and depended on animals. He expressed only his opinion, obviously not Darlington's. What would he say?

Avery had a fancy for them but he didn't trust his fancy. One couldn't sell fancy. Yet it didn't matter, he wanted the pieces for himself. He would buy them and work it out with Darlington later. He started to pay the man his asking price but at the last moment hesitated and began to re-examine them. The Armenian followed suit and craned his neck in order to peer at them. A few moments elapsed, enough for the trader to decide that he hadn't really looked at the pieces. He started to take them back. Realizing his coveted items were being withdrawn, Avery, now in a panic, plunked down into the dealer's hand twice the asking price. Calmly he picked up the figures, put them back into their wrappings, and walked away toward the back room as if the transaction had been an accomplished fact. After all, the man had made a handsome profit. Even so, had Avery by pushing his concern for completing the transaction actually jeopardized it? He glanced back. The dealer seemed to be scrutinizing his money as it lay crumpled in the palm of his hand. Avery resumed his exit.

"Hey, wait," the man called.

Avery turned around, his newfound possessions clutched tightly to him, and he realized that he shouldn't show his emotions so obviously but instead try to be casual and nonchalant.

"Okay, okay, we have a deal. Say hello to Darlington."

Avery could hardly wait until Darlington finally returned to the shop. He showed him the pile of materials and Darlington perfunctorily started to sort through the items. Avery could detect a smell of liquor on the man's breath. After picking up a big-spouted coffee pot and spreading out the other objects, Darlington pushed everything away.

He nodded his head with approval. "All basic commercial stuff. But the man never has anything of value."

Avery could just see his discoveries shine forth from the bottom of the pile. He asked if he could buy the metal figures for their thirty dollar cost just once.

Barely glancing at them, yet with a gleam in his eye, Darlington said, "I'm usually in the business of making a few bucks on each deal. It's a good practice to follow. Since this is your first stint at running the shop, I'll say yes. But be careful of your father. From what you tell me, he doesn't want his son investing his hard-earned money on my kind of junk–even high junk."

Though his parents were not home Avery locked his door before he took out his find. The coating of brown tarnish burnished into a soft, hand-wrought, luminous gold. The animals seemed to breathe. It occurred to him what he might actually possess. He had never seen anything of the sort but he quickly scanned a photograph of Scythian art in a book on ancient Russian art. The most extraordinary monuments of gold lay before him from Southern Russia, 6th Century B.C.-and he owned them. Before him ran a stalwart-busting deer with huge interlocking antlers, a leopard recoiled, and a wild boar braced to resist its foes.

It was understandable for Darlington, in a fluster after partying with his blousy lady friend, to dismiss these emblems as the ordinary flow of merchandise. None of his routine suppliers brought him anything exciting. Certainly not this one, until now. But would Darlington just shrug away his error? Not the canny dealer he knew.

In the hallway as Avery quietly prepared to leave the house he encountered what he considered a personal holocaust. His beloved basket laid before him destroyed. He gaped at its once pure rim, now shredded into a jagged outline like a broken straw hat, part of its tapered side caved in. Against its smooth, precise weave the sixty-nine little men no longer held hands, but jiggled and jumped crazily out of step. Avery had not been a witness to the basket's destruction but he knew what had happened. His father had yanked the basket rudely from its roost, most probably tearing it, and as he became further vexed and frustrated he had thrown it on the floor. He picked up the corpse and placed it on the diningroom table.

Avery arrived at the shop early. He didn't feel good about yesterday's deal. He hadn't done anything wrong or dishonest, but he hadn't been totally honest either because he did not single out the pieces and discuss them at length with Darlington. He had intuitively known how good they were. His fancy provided the only thing going for him and he should have told Darlington what he really felt about his acquisitions.

Avery immediately confronted Darlington with his discovery.

"Well," he fiercely regarded Avery, "now that you know what you know then that puts our deal in a different light." He quickly glanced at the objects, his eyes piercing like a heron about to spear a marsh creature.

Darlington waited. Then he placed his hands firmly on his Windsor chair withholding any further response, waiting for Avery to return the treasures. Avery hung back. Unconsciously Darlington began to rub the arms of the chair and each stroke became more vigorous. Finally he just leaned forward in the chair. It became obvious that Avery had resolved to keep his prize. Yet still Darlington lingered. To Avery he appeared smaller.

"You won't make the proper gesture. You won't offer those items back. You won't square with me. Then I guess I will have to properly handle the matter for you. You have certainly learned much. That's good. You've learned that I was careless. You knew that. Now you're on your way with what I have taught you. You don't need me and I don't need you. Goodbye." Darlington went to the rear of the store.

Avery watched him disappear behind the huge bronze Buddha. Being suddenly alone shocked him. He discovered himself in the position of having graduated from high school, coasted through three years of a state college, and now he had been kicked out of a different kind of institution. No, that wasn't entirely true. He now could claim to be the owner of at least several thousand dollars worth of Scythian gold masterpieces that had been funneled to him, plus a Darlington Ph.D. on art and high and low junk.

Before him appeared his father's face, large and distorted, much as it looked when as a child his father suddenly stuck his face down toward him revealing all its features grimly magnified. Mr. Judson glanced at the mangled basket and then his eyes swung toward Avery who looked utterly fascinated.

"Avery, I hate to be irrational and I must admit I did an irrational act, but I think we can resolve this in a reasonable fashion."

"Father, I'm sorry we couldn't have worked out our differences earlier, but now it's too late. We have a fundamental impasse."

"This should not get out of hand. Yes, Avery, your basket and I collided. It didn't belong here, not in this house. I could not live with it or bypass it. I don't think the basket represents you, but some lesser soul. I would like to say I am sorry. I have always contained my anger."

"So have I until now. There is no use being polite and civil any longer. You've taken care of that. My basket-what once could be considered a basket, a damned good basket, poses a threat you can't understand, you can't control. All you could do is smash it. Certainly you handle your office affairs more cleverly. I chose that basket and I assure you it represents me. It was mine-really mine. What you did was kick me."

"Perhaps we all need a kick to wake us up," his father advised, "but I want to be fair about this. I will pay for whatever the basket costs."

Avery now perceived how uncomfortable his father felt, a unique condition for him to let show. But he didn't see any reason to make it easier on him.

"No, it's not a business matter of equating numbers on each side of the ledger-balancing a loss with a gain. I am the only one who has lost. You wouldn't understand a matter of ethics." He slightly regretted his last statement, particularly since it rang true. But now he intended to trample across the threshold of his father's heart.

"I am leaving home and going into business for myself."

"It wouldn't surprise me. I want your mother to hear this," and he opened the door and called her in. "Your son is going into trade. He is merchandising 'his internal sense of aesthetic order,' as you call it, like the ratty bundle of sticks he brought into this house to annoy me. Just precious nonsense. I hope he can make a living at it."

Avery's mother replied, "Now that you have forced him to leave this house are you pleased? You have insulted me. Does that make you happy?"

"No, it does not. I didn't make him this way. But I can tell you this, Avery. If you leave here to sell what I regard as debris that should long ago have been burned then you can forget me, and my expertise, and my business, and my capital. Making money obviously disinterests you. I want to stop you before you ruin yourself." His father gruffly slapped Avery's knee as if to knock him back to his senses. As he reached the door to leave he turned and addressed his wife, "And now you two can have each other."

As he left the room Avery called to him, "Father, rest assured I'll not bother you with my welfare any longer. You have left no room for me in this house. Goodbye."

Avery realized throughout the whole miserable session the fact that Darlington's name had not been mentioned, even though in reality his name had been silently interwoven between all their words. Avery knew that Darlington lurked at the bottom of his father's emotional well. Darlington wielded the threat that his father had not been able to overcome. But his father did not suspect that his son had already left this charged issue behind by also leaving Darlington. Truly, Darlington once had a major influence over Avery. Once. He would not tell his parents what had happened with his employer. Not on his life.

Avery followed his father out of the house in order to avoid his mother's consolation.

2

*F*or several days Avery proceeded cautiously and carefully to select his next course of action. He arranged a schedule for himself which precluded an encounter with either parent. He rented a cheap room and took all his meals out. He spent his days in bookstores poring over expensive, handsome art books until one proprietor after another fixed him with baleful stares of unwelcome that intimidated him to abandon the books and leave the stores. At city libraries he resolutely continued to study the encyclopedias of world art at leisure unfettered by bookstore owners. He also combed the financial and business sections hoping to find support for the plan that began to take shape and solidify in his mind. He found no pat formula but he came to a decision.

On the seventh day following the confrontation with his father and his week-long avoidance of both parents Avery went to the bank. He withdrew the $20,000-plus-interest left by his maternal grandmother and incautiously walked with it to a different bank two blocks away. He did not want to risk the safer and wiser course of a transfer of funds from one bank to another; his father's nose for his son's financial affairs would have sniffed out that transaction. The inheritance money had long been in the same bank where his father did business.

As Avery deposited the considerable wad of cash into his new account he thought along the lines of poetic justice. The money in fact had been left to his mother who in turn immediately gave it to Avery in a gesture of a doting mother's privilege and largesse. "After all," she reasoned at the time, "your father is a successful man and growing more so each day. Spend it wisely, dear." Avery smiled to himself and nurtured his thoughts of poetic justice; his mother didn't realize just how soon he would spend that money. Wisely.

Avery moved out of his parents' home. He happily avoided his father's scorn and his mother's tears. He wrote his first check for a down-payment on a small, slightly rundown shop in an affordable area that had a back room where he could sleep. With subsequent checks, none very large, he bought inventory for his new venture. He assembled mostly small California baskets and Southwestern pottery, a dash of Eskimo ivory and bone artifacts including a nice group of small animal and human figures, some nondescript Plains Indian beadwork, a good Tibetan skull and prayer wheel, a number of African brass weights and ivory bangles plus some wooden head-rests and stools, a few Asian Buddha figures, and Oceanic containers and New Guinea boar tusks with shell ornaments. In all, a smattering of fairly eclectic and affordable pieces. The shop had one large room that would serve as a gallery. It never occurred to him to have business cards printed.

The shop didn't amount to much. Its articles displayed taste within a middle price range, and Avery manned it with solemnity and dedication. He sat at a desk that commanded the room. There he could survey his host of visual treats haphazardly illuminated by one electric bulb and whatever outside light managed to pierce through the windows. At dusk he liked to sit in the gloom and feel the presence of the intimate throng of incandescent objects about him, surrounding himself with peace and harmony. He declared this the only comfortable home he ever lived in. Of course he realized that a distinction existed between his special roommates and the people outside his private world, like his parents. But he much preferred the former.

As to people, he could view them from inside passing by his window where he felt coolly detached, and yet curiously involved. His mind swooped on and dallied with the crowds of onrushers often selecting those he thought might be worthy to be his guest inside. Occasionally one would peer into the shop window. Avery would hold his breath and imagine great insights were taking place within the beholder by such a singular exposure to his taste, and that the total effect would affect unknown lives with his world of wonders. But mostly he hunkered alone. The few potential customers that wandered in he lectured to or offended and effectively scared out. Once a man came, a dentist, who wanted to buy an incised, thick Oceanic wooden club with a good-sized ball head as a drumstick to beat a drum with. Much to the surprise and even a bit of amusement registered by the dentist, Avery sternly refused to sell the club to him because he would frivolously pervert its original purpose as a club.

Avery leaned back and perused his collection. Although he had the joys of being a contemplative shopkeeper he erred in being too contemplative and too little shopkeeper. Shopkeepers to his right and left and across the street certainly did not share the stress and strain he felt. If the ghosts or spirits of those who owned this shop before him had likewise suffered in common they gave Avery no extrasensory sympathy. He still had to pay this month's rent and next month's rent and eternities of rent with no impending sales. He could no longer afford to not react. Unconsciously he became restless.

Looking at the crowded street again he noticed perhaps for the first time that the hulking stream of humanity coursed on quite naturally without any need for him. Maybe that's the way it should be. But at this moment he knew that he needed the populace, especially a live-wire client with an extensive amount of artistic judgment and an equal amount of art oriented financial reserves.

Standing in front of his window and checking his address book loomed a gray haired, middle-aged man nattily dressed in a plaid suit. He persisted in remaining there, finally peering into the window. With his hands up shading his eyes he pressed his nose to the glass. After another minute of immobility the man entered the shop; the imprint of his nose bonded to the window. He barely nodded to Avery and busily concentrated on the art objects. He stepped up to each one, gaped at it as if he intended to outstare it, and then disjointedly broke away. The limbs on his gangly frame did not seem to operate simultaneously. He flung one long arm toward an open display case while the other banged a fragile coat tree beside him. Avery feared for the safety of his merchandise. The man repeated this distracted behavior until he had completed his tour of the room.

Avery knew that this dolt could hardly be the designated savior coming to his rescue. The visitor came abruptly to a halt and rechecked the address he had written down. He had a tall, thin, bony frame with a sunken chest and he walked with lurching movements.

"You're new here, I've been told."

"Yes." Avery connected him with a man who had been in Darlington's shop representing some foreign interest, an intermediary. He would be careful.

"You're the man, alright," he announced in a British accent, plus the fact that he introduced himself as Mr. Dalton Smedly.

Avery asked, "Have you come to the right place?"

"Yes, I believe so. This is a fine place," he enthused, and then looked vainly around the room again as if trying to gather evidence to corroborate his statement. "You are Mr. Avery Judson, I presume? I say, your gallery is open to sell merchandise; I mean you are in trade, are you not?"

"The shop is open for business," Avery brusquely remarked, "but only for real business. Do you want to buy a number of pieces?"

"No, I instead want to sell. Of course, a thriving business needs to replenish its stock. I represent a concern that has a great number of guns and other weapons for sale, all antique." The animated, rapid delivery belied his pasty, expressionless face. To add to his offensive behavior he had a mannerism of leaning on the desk.

Avery had generally considered weapons in a category of non-art, a judgment that Darlington also held, although some exceptional pieces could be considered art.

"As you can see, I do not have weapons and similar artifacts here. Never acquired them. I'm afraid that . . ."

Extremely exasperated, Mr. Smedly began to shout. "Do you not understand that what I mean by weapons cannot be put on the same plane as artifacts? Mere artifacts. We are talking about swords and daggers and maces encrusted with jewels. We are talking about art."

"Aren't we always talking about art?"

"Yes, that is why I am here. This collection is the finest display of weaponry on the market, or for that matter that ever existed."

"What kind of inventory are you talking about?"

"My client has all kinds, you name it: swords, knives, gorgets, cutlasses, armor, batons, bows and arrows, lances, rifles, pistols, and even artillery. The sword of Caesar."

He must command an arsenal, Avery thought. Even though weapons never interested him he believed they created a solid demand among certain collectors, bringing high prices. He considered his fortunes. There seemed to be no way he could accumulate even rent money unless he deviated from the steady uneventful course he teetered on. He had to blast out of the rut in which he had placed himself to try for the moon and perhaps land on a mountaintop. He needn't take a fatal risk, but a plunge, yes. Then an insane streak of foolery overtook him. "What if I decided to take the whole works? The entire collection," he blurted out.

"What? Everything? You mean that? Heavens! Even the artillery?"

"Yes, of course, the artillery. But first I must contact my investment backers. If you give me enough time I will take the stuff at a price you deem fair, if it is within reason." Avery knew he was safe so far. Although he really had no investors naturally Smedly assumed he did.

"I expect you can obtain the necessary funds," the man said in confident tones. "Then, splendid. My time is at your disposal. When do we proceed? But I must say, shouldn't you look over the boxes and cartons of weapons? There's a storehouse full of them, you know."

Avery agreed. The man proffered his hand and Avery formally shook it. They arranged to meet that evening at a warehouse in the Chinese district. As Dalton Smedly left Avery dropped into his chair, sank back, and watched the awkward, angular man wedge into the traffic and get taken up and lost.

A simple idea jolted him: what if he theoretically owned a mint of weaponry? Crazy. Where could it all be put? Even though his father could handle a situation like this he obviously couldn't bring him into the deal. But he knew no one else well enough to ask for help.

One name surfaced: his father had dealings with Randolf Farney. Among dealers and collectors Farney's name prevailed as one of the foremost, and Avery occasionally followed his exploits featured in the newspaper. His father dismissed him as a businessman who had a penchant for flashy, unorthodox ventures that for some reason often turned out to be good investments. Inherently Avery's deal seemed just as flashy, or perhaps fishy. Although he had never met the man, he knew–instinct told him–that Randolf Farney fit the bill. He would pursue the Farney possibility pending his inspection of the weapons.

Here and now, Avery wondered why he became the target of this odd, balding intruder-this Smedly. He puzzled over the matter until his mind went blank.

"On time," Smedly chirped and pretended to look at his watch. There in an old warehouse Avery beheld the stacks of crates and containers piled high that Smedly had mentioned, many with their lids off. Avery quickly identified columns of rifles, revolvers, scimitars, sabers, spears, iron mail, shields, and three cannons. Guardian of the room of riches, Smedly produced a dash of laughter coupled with a slight flourish of his hand. "Add up the value of each weapon in all those boxes and the fortunate potential owner has made a great investment, but at a price."

"Incredible. There's a box of medieval helmets."

"One of many," Smedly exclaimed, "indeed, a treasure trove. My client wants to sell this collection and you are the lucky one to buy it," he said patly.

Thoroughly impressed, Avery inquired, "Who owns the collection?"

Smedly's cheerful face went awry; his lips puckered. His boundless enthusiasm ground to a halt. "What? What does it matter? Are they not beautiful? I will guarantee their ownership."

"But you have to explain-show me proof," Avery responded.

At that moment a sharp, authoritative female voice demolished the uncertainty. "This collection needs no explanation. I trust you have noticed the box by your side. Please open it and inspect the contents. You won't be disappointed, I'm certain. Your mouth is hanging open. Most unattractive. Do close it. Please, open the box."

Startled, Avery shut his mouth and glanced about the dimly lit, shadowed warehouse. He could see no female shape, nothing to house the disembodied female voice. "Who are you?" he shouted unnecessarily. "And where are you?"

The female voice grew irritated. "It doesn't matter who or where I am.

I am not for sale. The items in these boxes are. Now, please, open the box by your side."

Avery promptly removed the lid and took out a dirk. He held the handle covered with breathtakingly precious jewels, radiant gems exquisitely clustered together. He took a breath when he saw many dazzling kindred pieces underneath fashioned by the finest craftsmen. He caressed the dirk, turning it over and over in his hand.

"You've managed to close your mouth, good, but now perhaps your eyes are hanging from their sockets? Do pop them back in so that you may adequately examine what you have in your hand. Is comprehension now setting in? The dirk you are holding would fetch at today's market value a minimum of $40,000. Gemmed daggers and cutlasses of great kings certainly require no explanation. Those eyes of yours can surely tell you the collection is genuine. And for your edification, it will be legally guaranteed. Now, Mr. Judson, you can return the weapon to its box." Her pungent speech was at once authoritative and amused.

Avery leaned down as though to replace the dirk. "Not until I see you," he said with more conviction than he felt. "Then I will be your humble servant."

"Humble, no; bumble, yes." She emitted a good entrance line as she stepped from behind a high pile of packing cases, her hand extended. But she did not offer her hand in the traditional greeting Avery expected. She deftly took the dirk from Avery and replaced it in its box.

Her white suit against a dim room, the buttoned jacket that opened revealing strong hints of delicately contoured breasts tied to her fiercely impressive entrance easily upstaged the array of fabulous riches. Avery admired her; Smedly trembled, plainly cowed. She confronted them both on more than even terms. She stood disturbingly close, a superb creation herself made to be touched. If no woman had ever interested him before he began instantly to atone for that former neglect. The words, 'I saw a lady passing by and I shall love her 'til I die' came to him, a ridiculous and romantic jingle. For the uninitiated Avery it read ridiculously true.

Her Lizabeth Scott pageboy just touched her shoulders. She fixed Avery with a blue-eyed stare. The hint of a smile crossed her wide mouth. She raised her eyebrows, pushed Smedly out of her way, and with authority picked up the box of gemmed weapons to take with her. Without a word she turned from both men and moved quickly toward the entrance. Avery had time to note the smoothly muscled legs, taut stomach, and lean hips. Then she disappeared.

Subdued, Smedly rallied and addressed Avery. "Is it settled? Yes? We have no more problems. Now we will arrange for the financing. I will be at your shop tomorrow afternoon at four."

Avery still dangled, buffeted in the wake of a female storm. He would have asked Smedly about her but he saw that the uneasy man quickly left the premises. He wondered if she came with the deal. Hoped so. Now he had more incentive than ever to buy the collection, and the collection itself truly incredible was reward enough. He would play for both stakes. So far he figured he had nothing to lose if he could not raise the money. But now he could not afford to lose everything.

Normally, Avery would have thoroughly checked out the collection but under the wildly unnatural circumstances he didn't think it feasible. He simply blundered. Yet he did manage to agree to meet Smedly.

In his shop Avery's circle of art objects no longer held for him the same serene and uplifting spirit. Instead the weaponry and the girl became fused as one in his mind and tortured him like a double-edged sword. He now somehow considered himself in arrears for at least the sum of a quarter of a million dollars. It would easily require that much to secure the collection. However, he thought of Randolf Farney and again Randolf Farney, and now came the time for all good men to come to the aid of his country–Avery's cause.

He called the man. A secretary enquired who he was and he drew a blank. Who was he? Quite unaccountably he decided and referred to himself as the son of Mr. Maynard Judson. Then Mr. Farney came to the telephone and said that he knew his father. When Avery explained that he had discovered a collection Farney consented to see him at his house.

Avery drove his hand-me-down Studebaker (another gift from his mother) toward Randolf Farney's Bel Air home with a heightened sense of something new and unfamiliar, and deliciously unpredictable. He considered the circumstances unbelievable, impossible. He drove, oblivious to the devices of gardeners mowing and weeding lawns and gardens from handsome Edwardian homes built when his own father was born. He could think only of how he had readily, most easily, used his father's name. By throwing out principles he held dear he had committed an original sin by compromising himself as he attempted to free himself. Nevertheless, in spite of this miscalculation, he exulted that the first phase of a sketchy plan had worked. Now to proceed.

Standing in the vestibule of Randolf Farney's home gave Avery a certain feeling of accomplishment; at least he had arrived this far. Farney would be out to greet him at any moment and until then he could only speculate about the gentleman.

Gazing down the hallway Avery immediately observed that Mr. Farney had taste and money but he puzzled whether the emphasis leaned more on the latter. His Queen Anne furniture pieces with a few Georgian items he considered superb but uninspiring as a unit. They appeared a little too perfect, too pat, more likely chosen as some Platonic ideal of the most complete set of period English furniture assembled. Nothing breathed; each article had been designed and set stolidly one next to the other in rows of staid groupings.

Farney must have made a deuce of an effort to track down the various items. He romanticized that Farney personally had found some of them. As he glanced around and saw the other decorative touches he thought that here Farney had scored successfully. Along with a large ceramic, prehistoric Chinese jar and a painting of luscious red apples by Corbet, all eminently respectable, there stood a Victorian stuffed toy lion, a painted magic lantern, and a large canvas of a nude from a western ghost town, grand and comic; Farney's acts of irreverence. If his taste proved wacky, tentative, and superficial, at the same time it remained imaginative and playful. It could not quite be called camp though. No Art Deco or gumball machines or merry-go-round horses intruded. He felt the man to be sincere, even if no gauge existed for one to ascertain what each piece meant to the owner or to each other. If he was a Sherlock

Holmes and could diagnose the culprit from the pertinent clues he had investigated he would say that his absent host seemed complicated; uncertain in some areas, but one who also had the sweep of a relentless and restless soul with intriguing hues of bias. Although Farney's enthusiasm kindled keen his eye did not select the extraordinary art piece. End of deduction. Now the man may appear.

And he did. Randolf Farney strode quickly up to Avery, apologized for being detained, and welcomed him into the library with a gesture that proved to be at once graceful and expansive.

Farney looked the quintessential patrician: a finely chiseled man with narrow tapered features and thin dark hair that glided back immaculately from his high forehead. Seigniorial to the hilt he even possessed an elegant sinuous nose. His charcoal suit had an expensive and custom-tailored read. To Avery the cloth looked like cashmere. Across his trim, vested midriff, a gold watch and fob-antique, of course-appeared stunning against the rich dark fabric.

Farney seated himself in a handsome armchair and indicated imperiously to Avery that he should be seated across from him. To be treated in such an open manner tickled Avery. Behind Farney a library of old manuscripts served as a background and from a fine hi-fi system a motet by John Dunstable poured through Avery like a rich liqueur. He appreciated the opportunity to experience Farney's taste. He felt increasingly confident that he could more than cope with the situation and even be of service to Farney.

As Avery unfolded the story of his discovery to his host he became conscious of performing his tale with sureness and charm. In fact he thought he had exceeded himself because of the way his listener registered interest, grunting and wagging his head in affirmation. He sensed that he did not have to insinuate the slightest point.

"So you feel a quarter of a million dollars will buy this collection," Farney summed up the matter, "and you have come to me to back your project. I must say it intrigues me. It's hard to encompass; all the pieces do not fit. It's like supervising an excavation; only at the bottom strata of the digging lies the key to unravel the whole story."

He paused a moment and looked thoughtfully at Avery. "I regard this as adventure. And if I undertake it my reason will be that I want to fully savor some intangible mystery behind the scene. In fact what beckons me to go anywhere is not only to obtain art, although art happens to be my elixir, but it's the very same intrigue and suspense that you are bringing me. Art is only part of that total experience."

When Avery mentioned that he saw a number of weapons encrusted with gems, Farney shrugged. "Ah, what would you expect? Obviously, a supply of this sort could only come from a kingdom and its ruler, an emperor of sorts. If the collection turns out to be as fine as you have indicated then the price is imminently reasonable." Then he launched into a "session of logic" as he called it, "to scout out in advance what's coveted." It is vital, he stated, to know the name of the responsible seller and not just the front man like Dalton Smedly. One didn't want to invent trouble but the booty had to be properly secured. "No green jade eyes taken from a jungle idol to haunt you," Farney amused himself. Also the problem of government customs officials and how the material entered the country had to be examined. "So who is behind this masquerade and for what?"

Avery felt elated; he had accomplished his wildest expectations. He had no one to go to after Farney and now he could foresee no obstacle in sight. Besides, he became immersed in the jets of energy of this singular man who displayed himself marvelously in so many directions. Both of them he knew were possessed even though their approach to art collecting varied. It surprised him that Farney seemed as pleased with the shrouded state of affairs as with the idea of obtaining the collection which Avery saw as his own primary motivation.

Farney paused again and assumed a stern expression. "I don't know if you should get involved with me. Now take note of this. I must warn you I drive hard for what I want and you will have to abide by my rules. I run the show. But if you are still willing I will lend you the money. After the collection is sold you must pay me back before we split the profit." He leaned back satisfied; he would begin to unravel the mystery tomorrow in Avery's shop.

In the course of their talk Avery played his theme of art, one in which he believed. He tried to proclaim in his own way that he had a rare eye and ran it over rare and compelling art. Whether he impressed Farney with his sense of aesthetics he couldn't tell but he certainly hit the right chord when he mentioned that he enjoyed the music of John Dunstable.

The captivating strain of the conversation delighted Farney. "From Dunstable through the seventeenth century English music seemed to roll on its own native wheels," Farney elaborated, "but then it got mixed up with that German, Handel, admittedly an excellent baroque composer, but for all practical purposes English music seemed to cease shortly after the Renaissance until it made a belated reappearance around the twentieth century."

Avery agreed but hadn't determined why. Again, he seemed to align himself to Farney's tangent. Avery complimented him on a fine, early bronze that he figured came from either India or Nepal but finally attributed it to India.

"You are right," Farney declared, "congratulations." Then, he proceeded to explain briefly the difference between East Indian and Nepalese bronzes.

Farney pointed to a long wooden tubular object with a front end shaped into the head of a bird and a small horse-like figure perched on top over a hole. "And that? Do you know what it is?"

"Oh, a Sioux Indian flute."

"Good."

"But why on a Pennsylvania Dutch chest?"

"I see that bothers you. Never mind if either the contents blend together or simply clash as some decorator's concepts of banality. Each piece I like and each carries its own weight. This house is a box for them. Of course I make mistakes in judgment and that is where I could use some outside advice."

Avery's ears became antennae. 'Outside advice' to Avery meant that he had a role to perform for Farney.

Farney added, "Quite honestly my eye is not creative; it needs direction."

His frank admission touched Avery. He felt that the two of them had similar interests, but even more, they had been consumed with an incorrigible inquisitiveness to acquire, to travel, to know continually more and feel more, to grace life with prime marvels of art. They seemed to mesh together and form a strong pattern.

But a pleasant distraction occupied Avery's attention when a striking woman paused at the hall door, then came into the room. Avery thought that no woman could have better matched Farney's mien and bearing; he figured she had materialized as some special decor created in order to fit his moods and mental landscapes. In one visual gulp he gleaned her willowy frame and the way she walked with smooth strides which produced the vibrant, billowing effect of her long gray, shimmery skirt. She nodded at him. Age? Most probably ten years older than he and many years younger than her husband. Farney said without rising, "This is my wife . . ."

"Yes, I am Stephanie."

Avery stood straight and received communion; he mentally bowed before her oval, perfectly spaced white face with brown eyes and a slender arched nose, all set off by stinging black hair with streaks of silver. He said yes or no or some kind of correct phrase, he hoped. He thought that within such a short span of time he had met two magnificent women almost back to back. One small, delectable, exquisitely formed; the other stylish, slender, and classically handsome. Somewhere interspersed in the emotional baptism she had bestowed upon him he heard Farney introduce him as 'Mr. Judson.'

He saw her studying him, even with a lilt of amusement.

She said, "I hear you men are thoroughly engrossed in planning some nefarious scheme. What is it?"

She is superlative, Avery thought, and it pleased him that she had placed him together with her husband on the same lofty plane.

"We have been reviewing an assortment of mischief, mayhem, and mystery which we plan to get to the bottom of," Farney said matter-of-factly.

"Yes, we are after the green jade eyes of a jungle idol," Avery fabricated to amuse her.

"It sounds as if you were at least having an entertaining time, if nothing else. Mr. Judson, do you deal in idols with green jade eyes?"

"I am planning to," he smiled.

"I have here, my dear, what may be considered the essence of Mr.

Judson, a Mr. Avery Judson." Farney pulled out a paper from inside his jacket and riveted their attention to him. "An official dossier, I suppose it might be called, pertaining to his brief business life." Then Farney skillfully unraveled the contents of the dossier he had compiled on Avery. He did not interpret; he clinically spun out the damning data on Avery's unfinished university career, his break with his parents, his association with a second-hand curio shop with a dubious reputation, and his current stint as a shopkeeper. At the end he pointed out that Avery's shop did no business, and it would just be a matter of a little time before it closed. So Farney had predigested Avery and at the same time pretended to be uniquely sympathetic to the young man.

Farney seemed to be through when he put away the file but then he commenced to produce another document. From Dunn and Bradstreet he devised a report on Avery's father, the financially successful senior Mr. Judson, who because of his admirable financial reputation, Farney confessed that he allowed himself to meet Avery. One more fact Farney stressed–Maynard Judson had disowned his son. Then Randolf Farney put the papers down in a neat pile.

Floundering in consternation, Avery felt that by some diabolical stroke he had strayed into the wrong house. He realized Farney had buoyed him up and then deliberately demolished him. Instead of his being ridiculed, Farney's every word and gesture had seemed supportive. As a whim, or better a ruse, they underlined Farney's peculiar manner of diversion; to Avery he committed an inexcusably hostile act.

"Your dossier is just a congestion of words," Mrs. Farney broke in, "far from complete, in fact, just plain boring, and surely one of your silly maneuvers. This is another of Randolf's tests he continually devises for his friends."

She also has gracious instincts, flashed through Avery. "Yes," he said, "a test I apparently failed."

Avery detected Mrs. Farney glance at her husband, check with him, and start to rise. Gratefully Avery followed her lead and declared his intention to leave. A noise of endorsement came from Farney who strode up to see Avery out. At the doorway Farney called out, "Remember, young man, we meet Smedly tomorrow afternoon at your shop. Please arrange for that."

Avery smarted. He resented being patronized. Surely Farney knew he couldn't forget. As he trudged to his shop he savored one triumph all his own. He had withheld from Farney the event of his meeting the amazing woman in the warehouse, the best part of the riddle about which Farney knew nothing and therefore couldn't control.

3

"I wouldn't say that this is the place for an interior decorator to visit." Farney looked around in Avery's shop.

"Exactly," said Avery. "I throw all interior decorators out."

Heating a pot of coffee on a hotplate near the desk, Avery offered Farney a cup to drink and a place to sit in the only other chair in the room.

"No, I'll wait," he said to both offers. "I would like to check out your shop and see what you have here."

Good, Avery thought, he would just let him wait-that's more than he deserves after last night's humiliation.

Farney examined the art items hanging on the walls and displayed on the tables, picking them up and closely scrutinizing them. "Small and relatively expensive, but delightful, a real charmer," he would talk to himself, or "I can see why you chose this one, amazing detail and yet uncluttered," and further, "but evidently I can't fathom this; nothing I know can encompass this-what is it?"

Avery decided Farney to be sincere in wanting to know more, even in his childishly open and impatient way. "It's a lime container made of a gourd shaped like a fish by New Guinea natives," Avery told him. "They used the white lime to decorate their ceremonial carvings."

"I see," Farney mused, "but still, it isn't terribly good?" he earnestly pleaded.

Avery shook his head decisively. "No, it isn't terribly good, but it's worth the price. The patina indicates it has been removed from the wet, humid climate about fifty years ago or else it would have rotted."

Avery noticed Farney unsuccessfully try to suppress a smile. He knew he was fully satisfied; he had seen, doubted, asked, learned, and along the way his faculties had been sharpened. Even out of his milieu he had not been wrong.

"Now for the business at hand," Farney exclaimed enthusiastically, and turned to Avery. "I've done my homework. I'm prepared for Mr. Smedly."

"As prepared as you were with me?" Avery asked with a bitter edge to his tone.

"Quite a bit more," Farney replied. "I've been thinking. This outfit that has the weapons must be a strange group, almost like amateur operators."

"How come?"

"It's Smedly. My research indicates he will stick out like a sore thumb. Someone must be pretty desperate to use him."

At that moment Mr. Dalton Smedly arrived at the shop, opened the door, and stepped in. When he saw Farney he came to a halt with his hand still on the doorknob. Avery put down his cup of coffee and moved forward.

Smedly addressed Farney. "What's this? Who is this?" and then he faced Avery. "We're supposed to meet here alone. This is a private matter between us."

"I want you to meet Mr. Randolf Farney," Avery quickly replied.

Avery saw a frown of resentment on Smedly's face. He considered Farney an intruder.

"Still-well?" Smedly showed his impatience.

"Mr. Farney will be my partner in our venture," Avery resumed.

"Well-of course, meeting you is my pleasure." Smedly immediately approved. "You want your share of the quarter of a million dollars weapons collection, the price you know, Mr. Farney. I should have expected there would be another partner."

"I guessed the price," Avery praised himself.

Smedly took some papers out of his jacket. "I have here the necessary papers for all parties to sign. Let us look these over," he said in high spirits.

To Avery's surprise Farney had so far disengaged from contending with Smedly, perhaps as part of his strategy. But now he did so.

"Smedly, you are not from England so why do you pretend to be?" Farney struck.

Dalton Smedly reacted almost comically. "What? What you say is not true. Certainly, I am British. Why do you say this?"

Farney pressed, "It's your accent. It is East Indian or Egyptian. You are not an Englishman. I haven't dealt in Egyptian cotton exports for nothing. And, furthermore, after checking you out I've found that your name isn't Smedly and you are in no position to deal with us."

Avery almost sympathized with Farney's victim. But it also amused Avery to see Smedly so utterly deflated under Farney's buffetings. Smedly found himself the chair and sagged into it.

"Whoever I am, I beg to differ with you, sir. I can assure you that I am perfectly authorized to represent my-client-and to make our transaction."

"That's exactly it," Farney confronted him. "We deal with your clients only and not with an ex-British subject on a temporary visa in this country. Why, Mr. Smedly, if you are here smuggling illegal merchandise certain United States authorities would be concerned. Just whom do you represent?"

Silence ensued-then the telephone rang. It surprised Avery because it rarely rang.

Smedly had sunk further into his chair when the ringing caused him to give a little jump and stare fixedly at the instrument on Avery's desk. Farney had broken away from Smedly and started pacing the shop, again picking up objects.

The telephone rang three more times. Finally Avery lifted the receiver and tentatively said, "Hello." He felt at this moment any news would be bad news when the response shocked him. It was her voice. She! The woman in the warehouse. He felt her voice to be different, even somewhat disguised. He tried to hide his emotions for the woman from Farney.

Avery handed the telephone to Smedly and told him he had a call. Smedly nervously took the receiver as Farney commented, "Ah, we are magnetic; we already fascinate someone enough to telephone us."

Smedly did no talking except for uttering a "yes" and a "yes" and then a "no." When he hung up he confessed to the listeners that he was afraid that both of them had been correct. Now that Mr. Farney had come into the picture complicating the situation he has just been informed that he did not have, after all, the right to represent his client. This would all be explained to them shortly in the person of his superior.

Farney slapped his knee, eyed Avery, and laughed. "We are cajoling the tiger into our den. Maybe I am causing a little trouble for them. I knew our friend here would have to bow out once the deal developed any snags. Obviously, this place has been under surveillance since I came in."

The change of events thoroughly confounded Avery. "I thought business deals for the most part are direct and simple," he directed at Farney, "particularly when two parties have made up their minds to do business." It surprised Avery that Farney had made his remarks openly in Smedly's presence.

"Not this deal," Farney snapped, "and here's our impending visitor."

A short, olive-skinned, rotund man in a shaggy overcoat walked into the shop. He removed an ill-fitting fedora that revealed a round, pink, balding spot, with a surrounding fringe of white hair so luxuriant and so white that Avery thought momentarily it had been pasted in place like Santa Claus hair. The man opened his overcoat revealing the center of his body firmly anchored to a wide, solid belly.

Smedly fidgeted as the tension increased and the man saw him. He drew himself up taut and whispered, "I didn't count on another party being here." The stranger pushed him aside and he wilted away.

The short man shook hands and offered pleasantries. To Avery he did not appear nearly as formidable as Smedly had led them to believe. He introduced himself as Dr. Artin Pasha, Egyptian. He considered himself a historian, he explained, and not a true doctor, but he is often called upon anyway to cure the ills of his people. He had assembled and procured this assortment of weapons, the purchase of which he hoped Mr. Farney would approve.

"Does Dalton Smedly work for you?" Farney asked him.

"He is in my employ."

"Who owns the collection?" Farney continued.

"I will personally vouchsafe the validity of this sale if that is what Mr. Farney means."

"No, that is not what I mean. Who owns you? Whose employ are you in?"

Dr. Pasha tensed. "The weapons themselves, are they not sufficient for you?" He spoke with quiet, steely reserve in felt-coated tones.

"No. To have the weapons is fine but they are mere items. I require more than just to simply possess them."

"You persist too far-in poor taste," Dr. Pasha glared harshly at Farney. "You are apparently not interested in what we deem a remarkably good business deal. If you lose what you are seeking you will be more headstrong than responsible in your game. Yes, to you a game, using what you said, 'mere items,' to serve as your playthings to amuse you."

"Oh, they are more than . . .," Farney interjected.

"But you do not know better," Pasha cut off Farney. "You do not know the power that such an assemblage representing generations of collections shrouded in history commands over our perishable lives, and what integrity it represents."

The man is completely impassioned, Avery thought.

"Yes, our country's past-Egyptian and Arab-comes back to haunt us. The dead from the ancient tombs and the living presence of the mosques, still in grandeur, look at us with contempt."

As Dr. Pasha emotionally carried on Avery watched Farney tapping his foot with impatience.

Dr. Pasha rushed on. "They remind us of the feats of our ancient civilizations compared to our abysmal backwardness of today. Who are really the 'mere items,' Mr. Farney? We or they?"

Farney intervened, "Would you please come to the point, Dr. Pasha?"

Dr. Pasha's eyes again flashed intensely. "Yes, to the point, of course. Unfortunately, our client is in delicate financial straits and is in no position to dicker and delay. Thus I am forced to put up with fools-a dilettante zealot," and he indicated Farney, "and a young amateur collector who I must say has a flair for adventure. Consequently, the favorable venture for you and this reluctant explanation."

At least he treated me more kindly than he did Farney, Avery thought.

"How did the illegal arms shipment enter this country and from whom was it stolen?"

Dr. Pasha strained to control his anger. His round face reddened. "You realize you should not have made such an unnecessary and insulting remark since I have guaranteed the shipment's entry to this land. Obviously I have sufficient proof. You do want to ruin this negotiation, I believe, Mr. Farney, as you will if you keep going on so . . ."

Then Avery watched both men withdraw into a locked stance of opposition resembling a frieze of figures in stone. They did not budge. Almost imperceptibly the hard, fixed look of Dr. Pasha began to let up and soften. Finally a feeling of resignation shuddered through him. "It is the royal collection of my King . . .," and he paused.

A king is involved raced through Avery's mind, a real king. No wonder everyone kept it a secret-the King is in trouble.

"His Highness does as he pleases and wishes to dispose of his collection. An American citizen brought his collection over here in perfectly routine fashion-the duties paid for. She has worked for our government before. Everything is in order. We have the papers."

Avery winced and it seemed as if his blood boiled inside. 'She,' blurted to him; 'she has,' stifled him; 'she has worked for our government,' swarmed him.

Farney told Dr. Pasha that he received his answer with satisfaction, and under the conditions Pasha referred to he would accept Pasha's offer to sell the collection. Although the Egyptian agreed to Farney's terms he cast the figure of a sad and defeated man. Then Farney resolved the various arrangements to acquire the collection. Farney voted himself to be in charge of the transactions with proper sureties given by Dr. Pasha and both scheduled to meet at Farney's bank. Copious goodbyes echoed throughout Avery's modest shop. Mr. Smedly had been rejuvenated and brought back to smiling, and he and Dr. Pasha stepped out in harmony. The tumultuous events stunned Avery with excitement. He couldn't seem to realize that the deal had actually been consummated. It occurred to him that Farney had never seen the weaponry and had relied entirely on Avery's own judgment.

In two days Randolf Farney bought the collection. He drew up an agreement and he permitted Avery to split any profit derived from the enterprise because he had discovered the collection.

Each partner allowed himself the opportunity to acquire one object before the collection would be sold. For historical reasons Farney chose the baton and sword that Napoleon had left on his Egyptian campaign. He had always admired the Little General.

Avery selected a full-sized golden Egyptian cat that he found alone in a corner of the warehouse. What Farney called "a golden dividend." Sitting on its haunches and rising up regal and supple it suggested the one great eternal feline. Farney said that he knew the cat had more aesthetic value but he had taken what he wanted.

The cat served as Avery's talisman of personal triumph. Antiques and weapons dealers marveled at the booty snagged by the purveyors of the collection who managed to disperse it to domestic and foreign markets for a considerable fortune. As a result a controversy erupted as to whom the collection rightly belonged, the nation of Egypt or its ruling monarch. Due to the resultant scandal which added to the mounting opposition within the country the anti-monarchists prevailed and toppled the King of Egypt from his throne, ending the dynasty of kings.

Avery cherished the golden cat. Often he wondered if he could have possessed the woman with the weapons too. It made for interesting speculation, while the months slipped into a year. Avery celebrated the first anniversary of the sale with an uncustomary bottle of champagne. He toasted the "weapons woman" often during his evening of revelry, and in a flash of comprehension that a certain amount of alcohol can sometimes trigger he realized her roll had been a key factor in selecting him to be the main agent to buy the collection. He remained in her debt.

4

Randolf Farney went to Europe leaving his wife behind. She formed her own decisions; she could travel freely, but only occasionally did she exercise the prerogative. She waited for him, and in the meantime, she represented him and superbly executed his domestic interests which for Farney amounted to prolific and taxing work. Mrs. Farney constantly illuminated the 'news of the day' and Avery avidly followed her activities. She made numerous appearances at board of director's meetings (she had power of attorney to sign for her husband), important openings of more important places, numerous cultural activities and art exhibitions. Mrs. Farney accomplished a great deal and prepared for Farney who always came back.

Avery saw Mrs. Farney a few times in the course of his art pursuits, but only at a buffet in honor of ancient Maori art did he manage to detain her for an instant. Avery withheld his natural desire to go right to her because he did not know how she would receive him. It could go either way, open or closed. But as he hovered next to a Maori shield Mrs. Farney sought him out.

"Mr. Judson, Mr. Judson," she called out. "I have been trying to speak to you but you continually get tangled up among the clutter here," and she held him. "We have not seen each other since you helped trigger an Egyptian upheaval and have become famous."

"Thanks to one Randolf Farney," he said seriously.

"Oh now, it took the two of you to brew up that much trouble. Randolf rates the whole experience highly; he always chuckles about it."

"Are you busy after this-function?" he asked.

"You know Randolf is in Europe," she reminded him. She laughed. "So, let's have another time of it."

He examined her.

"Soon," she said, and she took off.

Avery accidently met Mrs. Farney once more (he knew he would cross her path) without having to call on her. She naturally attended an afternoon lecture on ancient Japanese Haniwa sculpture given at the university and Avery caught her finishing a cigarette in front of the lecture room just before the speaker began. She provoked the eye even by merely taking a few nervous puffs. She swung her electric black-blazoning hair about as she detected the sparse attendance. Her body turned and reacted to the slightest hint of activity, and her figure, slithered into a gold knitted sweater, moved with a charged awareness that delighted Avery. She greeted a number of people while at the same time equally dismissing them with a note of finality. When Avery walked up to her she dashed her cigarette to the floor and joined him.

"I am glad you came," she said with relief.

Avery chided, "Are you hiding your husband?"

"No," she grinned, "and I am doubly glad you're here. I've been bored."

They sat down and as the lecture commenced Avery took her hand and she let him for a moment before she girlishly disengaged. Avery saw her flush as she laughed. Under the circumstances Japanese Haniwa red earthenware sculpture stood up nobly; yet the projected slide show punctuated their waiting with impatience. Somewhere during the lecture they managed to agree that they should have a late lunch or an early tea.

He took her to a small cafe he knew had good mutton stew with green chili. She did not notice or preferred not to mention the small quarters with seamy linoleum tablecloths and vein-lined dishes. She literally overwhelmed the room with her color combinations of her white skin against her vivid hair and a gold lamé blouse set off by a flouncy black skirt. Avery watched her energy spill over.

She looked severely at him and said, "I think my husband owes you an apology. A year overdue. I would like to make it for him."

"An apology?" he queried.

"Yes, for that dossier he had compiled on you. I minded the brutal way he sprang it on us–he was horribly rude . . ."

"I confess that I felt woefully squashed, but I did get you to defend me and that made it worthwhile." She did not seem to hear him probing into her feelings about her regard for him.

"It bothers me that he could consider us so trivially-with sheer disregard," she reflected.

"I don't know if it was that bad. He was devising his strategy to try and make the best deal for himself by putting me down. After all, we had been fencing around for an hour or so before you entered. He aimed at me."

"No," she spoke doggedly and in fixed phrases of conviction. "We did not count but the deal did and that's what's the matter. He didn't care. He used me as the means to completely humiliate you."

She shuddered and Avery realized that she had placed herself in Avery's shoes and didn't like the fit. Her utter candor touched him.

Her anger gradually subsided and Avery suggested that a walk would cure their chili-corroded stomachs. "I'm on fire," she agreed, and she jumped up and downed a cooling glass of water.

"You'll always remember that we had a hot date," he teased, and with a flourish they left. Then he thought of a shop nearby that often showed primitive art, and as he explained it to her he led her to the shop.

"No," she jested, and when she detected his eagerness, and simultaneously his concern for her, she consented. He turned her around. "You're punished because you're with me," and he pushed her through the door.

The interior of the shop beckoned to them. Mr. Rumford attended to a customer and waved to Avery. As Avery nodded at the dumpy old man his eyes pierced the room for the perennially rare and beautiful while he caught Mrs. Farney stopping and noticing his sudden absorption.

"You're just like Farney. I suppose it is true that business and women do not mix," and she gazed at the shop's proprietor who ardently pressed home his point of business to a prospective buyer. "They are an indifferent mixture. If a woman tries to help the business she gets mixed up with the ego behind it. If the woman doesn't try and leaves the business unintangled and self-sufficient, it's she who is likely to get mixed up as unfulfilled and disconnected. It's the woman who, after all, gets messed up."

She studied Avery; he had not listened. Rather, he had just pushed off from her and located himself around a cluster of small objects from old thimbles to snuff boxes of horn. Amid a rash of little bone spoons lay an elaborately carved piece of ivory. Avery's hand shook as he reached for it and he knocked over an ivory pie crimper. Seeing Mrs. Farney approaching he withdrew his hand and waited for her appearance, and awkwardly smiled off his suppressed excitement. She tipped her head sideways and tiny curls of a smile spread as she followed him with curiosity. To show his unconcern he nonchalantly returned to the hunt and leaned over and deftly plucked out the ivory piece from the case. Then he clinically inspected what appeared to be a carved web of mellow elephant ivory, a lacework of tiny men wearing funny hats joined together, five of them. Puzzled, Avery rubbed his fingers over the figures and then wetted them. He straightened up, tensed his shoulders, and tried to calm himself. If he made the correct analysis he held the key to a universal masterpiece.

Gesturing at his happy discovery to Mrs. Farney, the bemused beholder, he said offhandedly, "There's some logical madness to this; it does make sense." After thus declaring to her that he could be quite sensible he casually strode up to Mr. Rumford, held out the ivory, and asked, "Mr. Rumford, how much for this?"

The owner quickly estimated, "Twelve dollars."

Avery took out his wallet. "For a fragment, too much."

The man shrugged his shoulders and accepted the money.

"By the way," he diffidently resumed, "where did you find it?"

Mr. Rumford recollected, "Bunch of small gimcrack I bought from a dealer in New York–about a week ago–why, we swapped some material."

Avery edged away. "Do you remember where–the man's name and address?"

The man blinked at the too-quick rejoinder while Avery holding his breath burned in silence. "Maybe the guy has more pieces to this broken one," he tried to soothe the shopkeeper.

"Oh," said Mr. Rumford, "his name is Mr. Sophio Ramón. He's in the book. Encantado Museé's the name."

Avery looked for Mrs. Farney but she had left-she vanished, away. He shouted "thanks" as he ran out.

That night Avery took a plane to New York and he remembered Stephanie. Farney's Stephanie laughing warmly at him. But not his. She had been so enticing to him. To possibly obtain one hypothetical and yet coveted item he had botched acquiring another more real and important one. Fantasy's Farney's Stephanie. But he rationalized there's always a Stephanie, not really, but perhaps to be with another time. Perhaps. At any rate, now he must delve into the source of art. What he sought, if it could be had, couldn't wait a fractured second. Then he pondered about the getting of Stephanie, whether he possibly could, now or later. Yes and no. Could she be disenchanted with Farney, even slightly? How much regard did Farney have for her, and did she crave more?

But at this point art held him in its magnetic field. Maybe he could make a significant amount of money, certainly not anything like Farney, or even earn enough to impress his father. He dredged up haunting images of great art from the gallery of man's imagination and became literally consumed with these specters. He had no choice but to bed down with mistress art.

When he landed in New York he checked the directory; the shop was on 64th street. He took a taxi there and looked out and studied the place in the moonlight. Here a splendid Museé materialized for him in the wrong section of New York, an obscure shambles of clapboard and siding but a veritable Museé, anyway. As he stared at it a light turned on from within and yellow jumped out of the window cracks. What he had wildly hoped for took place. The shop stayed open at one in the morning. His outrageous zeal plus a wisp of chance had produced this possibility. Avery glanced slyly at the cab driver who didn't seem to be alarmed or even cognizant of this historic revelation. The taxi man yawned and Avery hastened to pay him.

Avery knocked on the door and a dark complexioned man, possibly a Puerto Rican, opened it.

"You're open so late-how come?" Avery blurted out.

The man, surprised at being bothered and then badgered, responded, "Why are you here?"

Avery stalled. "I want to buy some gifts-I have to give a present to someone tomorrow." He waited to be rejected.

"Well, then come on in. I live in the back of the shop and came up front for some matches-I'd run out."

Inside Avery noticed that the owner stood barefoot, a relatively young man with combined Spanish and Black features. The shop didn't have much, a few ugly Pre-Columbian Aztec pieces, stiff, frenetic and unrelated, good Lapland folk art, and a number of stunted bronzes from India, garbled Shivas, and Buddha heads, a far cry from the best examples. It had the taint of his former shop, an uneventful cell, except for a salient group of African carvings which gave it a different quality. The Africans! He brushed by the man and gazed at the delicately fashioned masks and pieces of wooden sculpture, some Baule, mostly Yoruba. The best stuff! He caught his breath. The man undoubtedly had an affinity for African material and had access to it.

"How much for the Yoruba mask?" he inquired.

"Mister, I want one hundred seventy-five," returned the man.

"One-fifty?" Avery countered.

"No," the man maintained.

"Alright," Avery decided and handed him the money, "but tell me where you got it."

"Why?" he asked.

"As a collector I like to know the background of the piece, and I might want to sell too-someday. It's real, isn't it?" Avery interjected.

"Hell, yes, it is!" exploded the man. "You didn't come in here to ask that-or you can close the door behind you."

"You know I want the mask but why can't I know where it came from?" Avery inquired.

"No reason," he paused, "it came with the others from Africa-from Johannesburg."

Avery took out the little African ivory fragment. "I bought this in Los

Angeles. Rumford said he got it from you on a trade. I'd like to know if the mask came from the same place–and who it came from."

"I thought so," the man concluded. "You didn't just walk in here to buy a gift for your mother. You a cop? I don't need no trouble. I wish the hell you never came at all!" he looked suspicious and bewildered. "Why don't we forget it; you give me the mask and I'll give you your money back," he proffered the bills.

"No, the mask is mine, but we can end this if you'll tell me who is the dealer from Africa. What's more, I'll give you back your mask and you can keep the one hundred seventy-five. Then you'll have nothing to worry about."

The man puzzled over the matter. "I'll play your game. Give me the mask."

Avery gave it to him.

"I got the bit of ivory from the same man in Johannesburg. He can get you what you want. Name of Heinrich Jabbo."

Avery felt satisfied but hung on. "Is he German, a Boer?"

"He didn't tell me!" the man fumed.

"I'll close the door tight behind me," Avery quipped as he went through it. And immediately afterwards, out in the night air, he wondered what good the mask would have done him anyway. He had "bought" an excellent fake.

Wending his way through Johannesburg Avery enjoyed the bright pavement stalls and muti shops of Diagonal Street. He also fancied a tour through "Egoli"–the City of Gold–to see some historical buildings dating from the founding of the community in 1886. But he startled himself out of pursuing any further diversions when he realized that he could have the wrong information. If his informant had lied, he could be pursuing a fantasy. He isolated what he considered to be pertinent.

The recently seen African material had to be faked by someone knowledgeable. All the quality masks could only be Yoruba, neighbor to Benin, his own area of vital concern. The shopkeeper had already mentioned Johannesburg before Avery presented the ivory piece to him, and so most likely the African material came in one group from the same source. And after all he had found Mr. Jabbo listed in the directory. Also the New York shopkeeper had no need to fear him since he left the fake with him and it couldn't be used as incriminating evidence.

Avery knocked on the door and a pasty-faced woman with her hair rolled into a large bun answered. Yes, she said, he had the correct residence and he stood before Mrs. Jabbo. Avery felt rewarded. When he asked to see her husband she told him Mr. Jabbo was not in, not at home, or not to be here for some time since he had left two days ago for London.

Avery stepped inside. "Why? For how long? Where can I reach him in London?"

The woman started to titter pleasantly. "You are just like the other man," and she explained that the other day she had had the same kind of visitor.

"Another visitor? And he's gone?"

Mrs. Jabbo seemed to absorb Avery's peculiar behavior well enough and proceeded to say the man waited for her husband from morning to night and kept on talking to her. The man was always excited. When her husband came home the man took him away and they closeted themselves in a room for a long time. Then her husband came out and said he wanted to go to London right away, and she guessed this other man had talked him into going. Avery reminded her of the other man, she said-too many questions.

Through her obscure German accent Avery could detect in her a cunning stubbornness that he supposed complimented her husband. But if he couldn't mastermind events to serve his ends he felt he could at least learn more about Jabbo. Further question: what profession did Mr. Jabbo have? She answered that he bought all kinds of things and sold them, like stuffed animal heads, hunting rifles, and precious stones that had been mined, and occasionally he brought forth what the natives made and used, old and dirty, which she didn't see why anyone would want them.

For some reason, perhaps by her gestures, Avery figured she had been all along indicating that in the next room Jabbo stored his merchandise. So he walked to the room, opened the door, and looked in. There, seemingly, he couldn't see much of interest but he felt fortunate to get a good look because she came up, pulled him away, and closed the door with a burst of energy. But he did have enough time to see a number of banal modern wooden sculptures where the natives clumsily stereotyped themselves, and then scanning the room further he spotted the unmistakable feature he could identify, a handsome Yoruba figure, and this time old and brilliant. Jabbo certainly filled the bill as his man. Right beside him in a corner a wooden planter box stood filled with a jumble of canes from which he could make out one in particular whose gold handle held the insignia of the Nazi swastika. Then Mrs. Jabbo came.

"I think you should go away now," she said to him.

"I will, but only if I can ask you one more question."

"Ach, no, I can't think no more."

"Your husband . . .," he began.

"He left so fast we had no time to make plans."

"I know, but how would you reach him if you had to?"

"You will go away then?"

Avery nodded.

She told him that after his trips up north her husband often brought a variety of skins, horns and tusks with him for a certain taxidermist in London to work on. He is a good friend of his and a man who had done business with her husband-at Mr. Henry King's Taxidermy. The end. She would answer no more questions and he had to leave now.

Avery obliged her.

5

Avery bought a Guide Michelin and thus armed, pored over the book during the entire flight from South Africa to Heathrow. He surmised from the guidebook that to find lodgings in the Tottenham Court Road area would provide a location which would enable him to move about with a minimum of effort during his stay. And he wouldn't be far from the British Museum.

Once in London he found what he wanted–an inconspicuous hotel just off Tottenham Road. With the help of a chatty taxi driver he also found the taxidermist's shop. The place displayed a huge ugly pelican, quite menacing in bearing, and a rare Himalayan snow leopard in the front window. The door held a sign which stated that the management would be gone for the morning and would be back at one-thirty. He speculated that the key to penetrating the shroud covering the ivory fragment would be traced to that shop.

He took tea at a nearby shop and observed the English clientele seated around him. They seemed to be conservatively dressed people disposed to an orderly conduct of life, at least that is what he preferred to believe. Avery felt he needed this climate of law and order and rationality to counterbalance his own voracious urge to hound the quarry of art to the remotest crevices of earth, and perhaps to split himself apart. Avery's watch showed ten-thirty. He paid for his tea and quickly hailed a taxi for the British Museum.

Avery stood at last before the Elgin Marbles. He shook his head, laughed aloud, and enjoyed himself thoroughly as he stood before the Marbles. His obsession for formal, refined beauty became momentarily sated as he encompassed them. In no hurry he gradually moved away, proud of his emotional restraint. He did not genuflect.

Avery next chose the Egyptian room. He viewed the cold Egyptian art:

imposing figures massively conceived as sacred creations in honor of kings who attempted to outlast death with their monumental tomb monuments, but whose silent remains only emphasized the fact of massive death. Still they stood, the grand royalty so preoccupied with immortality that they froze spontaneity in their crypts.

When he reached the end of the hallway a museum attendant and a woman walked out of the rear offices. Passing across his view Avery sniffed at the official, and as the party descended the stairway he erupted. The women—she was the girl! Smedly's girl or Dr. Pasha's. The weapons girl. He dashed to the stairs. He knew she had seen him because suddenly she hurried, leaving the astonished official far behind. As Avery sped over the flight of steps she reached the bottom and began to run. He thought it droll that to the same degree he wanted to be with her she obviously didn't want to see him. At the museum's entrance Avery caught her and tightly viced her arm. Impressed by his urgency she did not make a scene but steadfastly continued her way out. She made a few more paces and turned to him.

"Will you please be gone! You are nothing but annoying," and a cold hostility slithered through her words.

Avery released his hold. "So, I am. But this is my way of wooing you."

The woman stopped short, overwhelmed by consternation. "What are you saying?"

"That when a girl runs from a man there are dynamic possibilities to be explored," he offered.

She gaped at him. "You are incredible," and she started to leave. He held onto her, and she said curtly, "I will be late for an appointment and cannot be concerned with you," and she walked away.

"A most pressing appointment, no doubt," he retorted. "Well then, let us walk it together."

Avery stuck with her, sometimes dropping behind, but ambling up in spurts. She proceeded in tandem for a short while before stopping and facing him calmly. "Well, what do you want?"

She appeared quite as he had imagined, perhaps better. From head to feet, he rhymed to himself, here's a descending description of my sweet. Her face, not beautiful, but arresting, engaged in its lilt of appealing fineness and fierceness mixed; russet hair stopped just short of her shoulders which seemed small and yet surprisingly solid; and her torso cascaded downward undulating to a strongly indented waist which then flounced out along firm, tapering legs to its exquisite end.

"Well, it's hard to have a talk with you just standing like this. You must be tired. Could you shuffle your other appointment to make mine?"

"I can arrange that," she said. She headed for a cafe and entered it. A waiter intercepted them. She sat down prepared to dole out a small measure of her time as if she supervised a clinic. She ordered nothing and he had coffee. He savored her in her brown wool dress. She simply percolated excitement for him.

He began pleasantly. "It's over a year since we crossed paths-as brief as it was. That turned out to be one helluva year."

"Yes, you did very well by it, did you not, Mr. Judson. You have come up in the world. It certainly amused me all the same."

Avery cooled off some degrees. "I seem to remember your being involved with a motley crew-just a casual association, no doubt."

"No, I mingle freely with the motliest of creatures-in fact, anyone. Why, I am presently with a Mr. Judson."

"A Mr. Avery Judson, if you please," he proffered and smiled over his trouncing. "Let's try again.. How nice to see you once more Miss or Mrs.-whatever. Are you enjoying London, and could I personally add to it? I can-just by removing myself? Well, bless you. You are staying at the-Westminster Abbey? The crypts are comfortable? Excellent. I shall pick you up and we can have drinks. Holy water."

"You are an idiot of the first order-thoroughly motley," she injected her first note of levity, "and now I will have my cup of coffee," and she ordered it. While the ice remained not altogether broken between them it began to thaw out and allow them to enjoy their repartee.

Avery continued in the vein he had established. "Is Mr. Dalton Smedly living here in this dear homeland, or in an Egyptian mummy? What greatness."

She smiled and flicked away a wisp of hair that had trickled down into her line of vision. "He was a simpleton, wasn't he? Still, he performed some tasks well. He blundered into you."

"Luckily he made me a marked man willing to be executed. But why was I so honored?"

"We selected you because of your inexperience-being new to the business. You didn't know much and you wouldn't ask a lot of questions, and for that matter, you didn't. Also, you had good connections-we knew of your father."

Would you believe it, Avery reflected, my dear father always appears as a blessing in disguise. "It's like father, like son," he chuckled.

"But unfortunately you did not quite fulfill our purpose," she added. "We should have gone to a professional dealer-perhaps a major one. Certainly not you."

"Why, that would have ruined this lovely game we are playing," he pouted. "It would have been like my not being born, thanks to you. What is wrong with me? You seemed to have accomplished everything you wanted."

She smiled. "Yes and no. The method of bringing about the sale was as important to us as the sale itself. We wanted it to be kept a total secret. You surprised us with Mr. Farney. Once he got involved he exploited the situation to his own advantage which was not to ours. The publicity turned out to be most unfortunate, in fact, disastrous. To many of us-we still consider you a disaster," she laughed.

"You use freely the royal 'we' and 'us' as if you were one of them." Avery no longer took her lightly. "Perhaps your friends are connected with the King's entourage, and maybe the King's lackeys, and all that's quite charming," he said facetiously. "Forget that crap. How and why did you get involved with them?"

Her voice sobered. "Another year and you and I can go into that-at our next reunion."

Avery heard her. He knew that he needed more time with her. He invented some nonsense. He looked at his watch, then jumped up. "Hell, I have to go. I'll pick you up tonight for dinner. Where?"

"The gentleman is leaving the lady-most mysterious-after our long separation. No, I can't meet you."

"Then I won't go. I'll stay here forever."

"Then you will miss your appointment."

"Then I will just have to and that's all."

She weighed her words. "Meet me tonight at Kettner's in Soho, nine o'clock."

He searched her face. "You really mean it?"

She deliberated and resolved the matter. "Yes, I'll meet you there."

He stopped on his way and considered turning back. The thought stabbed him-what's her name? He chastised himself for not knowing a single figment about her. And again he worried, will she show up? Would she be worth too much for him to leave? Certainly she would be, and he knew it. Leaving beautiful women had become a habit. But he made his "appointment" and rejoiced that the taxidermist remained open.

Dusk had settled strongly and the street lights began to fuzz to a yellow murk. The shop seemed locked, but when Avery knocked on the windowpane a boy in his early teens showed him in. He introduced himself as an apprentice to Mr. King and explained that he needed to work overtime to prepare for mounting a giant kudu. Huge, sharp horns and stripes on a head told of an animal that could have been first invented as an imaginary beast on a Renaissance crest. Avery glanced at the other stuffed specimens, even a giant Komodo dragon glaringly replete. Mr. King, the boy informed him, would be in after eight in the morning. Avery asked if the shop received a steady shipment of wildlife from Africa and the boy nodded yes.

"From Mr. Heinrich Jabbo in Johannesburg?"

The boy blinked. Why, Mr. Jabbo had just come to London and had been to the shop yesterday, the boy told him. He had brought a number of animals with him, including the giant kudu.

"Who is the head for?"

The boy didn't know. He had never seen the customer before, but he wasn't from London or England for that matter.

"Had Mr. Jabbo known the customer before, perhaps as a friend?" Avery pursued.

"Whenever Mr. Jabbo visits the shop," the boy related, "Mr. King becomes very busy and keeps me busy, and I can't keep track of the customers."

Avery persisted. "Did the same man accompany Mr. Jabbo to London?"

The boy opened his mouth and shut it again. A shiver of uneasiness rippled over him.

"Ask Mr. King yourself, tomorrow. He's the owner," he said stiffly. He immediately involved himself with the stuffed kudu. Avery watched him for a minute. Then the boy looked up and darted a glance at something behind him and slightly nodded his head. Avery wheeled around and a figure flicked out of sight. He rushed out the door but saw a swirl of a wisp of nothing in the dark. He hesitated before leaving. He had detected a swish of clothes, an odor, a presence, all unmistakable, known, and yet bewilderingly furtive. He looked up at the now cynical expression of the boy focused on him and he felt caught and foolish.

He reached the restaurant slightly late but he couldn't find her there, and according to the head waiter she had not appeared. But maybe he could be wrong. He, himself, had been late. Avery waited. Then he walked outside. Returning to the lounge, he regretted leaving her, rued the enormous fatality of having done so. His tie needed continual adjustment. He didn't want a drink but walked to the bar and ordered one and didn't drink it. It was late enough not to wait. He went towards the telephone booth but didn't know who to phone. As he decided to drink his drink she hurried into the place. Instantly he felt that she did not rush to meet him but rather to plunge away from someone else. She seemed distraught, her clothes slightly ruffled and in disarray. She looked pale.

"I am sorry," she stated weakly. "I . . . I am simply late."

Avery gently showed her into the dining room. She instinctively shied back. "Could we stay here for a second, or stand outside a little while? No, it's better here!" She was softly urgent, tentatively pleading. She unbearably appealed to him.

"Of course," he strung words together but he meant them. "As long as you and I are here it doesn't matter," and he became conscious of his ardor. He noticed the glass he held. "Would you like a drink?"

"No," she said, "not now, but we can go ahead and eat. I'm alright."

They picked a table carefully even though an empty room with no diners awaited them. Just to be with her, his pleasure rang personal and deep. He avoided any confrontation.

"I don't really know why I am here and what I am doing–in London," he said airily, "but somehow everything's working out. However, wherever I go seems to be fraught with a bizarre tension. Some obscure motive governs every happening."

He noticed she had nervously finished his drink that he brought in from the bar. Her color had returned with an awakened vitality.

"The excitement is here, Mr. Judson," her voice sliced with charged meaning, "and you are also here, and invariably two magnetic forces combine. Let us hope you do not explode; your excitement is flammable."

"You manage to put danger in my activities."

"Yes, it is possible in London for an impetuous young man to stray and get in trouble."

"And what–or whom–were you dodging from–evading–when you scurried in here?" He launched the question at her and surprised himself.

Avery saw her lose control. She hadn't expected an inquisitive rebuff.

"Did my lateness bother you?" She smiled faintly and leaned away with a rustling motion.

Avery prickled inside. He had recalled the same intangible flutter earlier; the verve of her movement sparked the impression he had of the person watching him, unseen, at the taxidermist's. And the distant scent and odor crystalized of the same starch. She had seen him.

"Yes," he acknowledged. "I didn't think you would meet me here."

"Avery, because of you I came. I was delayed and I could do nothing about it." She shuddered.

"Why are you in this city? You seem out of place just as I am."

"No," she spoke wearily, "I have been here many times and so London has become one of my homes–a familiar ground."

"But you were not born or raised here. You were born in the States."

She paused. "It's no use to put patches together. But no matter. Yes, I am American but so what?"

He leaned toward her and probed her eyes with his own. "You have no idea how often I have thought of this as a quandary. I, finally, ultimately figured it out over a bottle of champagne. Between the bottle and me I made toasts in honor of the absent you. How you worked in Egypt with our friends of weaponry and they in turn worked for the King. You had to be the vital American they needed to channel the goods into the States. Yes?"

"Yes," she answered.

He was almost abashed at the briefness and sureness of her "yes." He had intended to field a forthcoming explanation or apology but none came. Rather, she uttered complete acceptance. He came to a halt and shifted his ground.

"Why did you run away from me when you first saw me?"

"Because I realized you would ask me a lot of questions."

He nodded. "I guess I am an expert at that-the king of questions. But you have no name but Miss Unreality. I seem to be able to reach you only with questions." They had not finished their dinner, but she rose to leave the table.

"Can I take you home?" he offered.

"Thank you but I think I'll take a taxi."

"I'll go with you," he said firmly.

"No, I am tired."

"Yes, made sufficiently tired by watching me go into the taxidermist shop," he shot at her.

She bolted a surprised look at him.

"We are not so purposeless as you pretend, my dear-what is your name?" He started to close his hand over her arm.

"No, please, I've had enough for today of struggling. I'll tell you if you will leave me alone. My name is Duskyanne Reef."

"And your address? We have various interests in each other which seem to overlap," but he said this gently.

Her voice trailed off. "The Flemings-on Half Moon Street."

He realized her state of exhaustion, that Duskyanne Reef had reached the end of her endurance. He had what he wanted.

"Alright," and he took her to himself and kissed her. Firmly he caressed her. "Chalk that up to his youth," he said, and walked away.

She did not resist or move. He wondered if she had the same taste for it that he did.

Eight o'clock found Avery at the taxidermist shop. The reputation of the owner, Mr. Henry King, he understood to be one of London's finest taxidermists, and here before him stood the very same man expecting him. Mr. King behaved like a self-satisfied man in his fifties, smartly dressed and established. Moreover, he seemed delighted to behold a presentable young man before him. He became talkative, even garrulous in Avery's judgment. Bobbing his bald head up and down he showed Avery a spotted hyena with a huge jawbone designated for a museum, and an enormous, special ostrich egg set under glass which a woman had ordered as a shrine. Avery didn't know what the shrine immortalized, but the egg came from Mali as indicated by a card inside it. Mr. King digressed and effused about animals, London, and the galaxies of people who whirled in and out of his shop. He lauded his profession (really an art, he insisted) for preserving the world's array of animals for future generations to appreciate, what he called the significant contemporaries of mankind. "Who would otherwise remember the animals?" he wailed.

Then Avery asked where he could find Mr. Heinrich Jabbo.

Mr. King considered for a moment, and then spoke as if illuminated by a new thought. He knew a Mr. Jabbo, but not where he lived or could be found. He deemed the matter closed, and in his sprightly, chatty manner, indicated that he would be immediately, extremely occupied if any resumption of the subject continued. He massaged his bald pate.

But Avery clung on. "I have something of interest to give him."

Mr. King again deliberated, seemingly weighing a newborn curiosity with what Avery suspected to be a growing fear. Perhaps he has a personal dilemma with Mr. Jabbo, Avery thought. "It is impossible to reach Mr. Jabbo," and he apparently felt he had to elaborate, "for he lives in Johannesburg and only occasionally visits here."

Avery countered, "Your apprentice mentioned that Mr. Jabbo just recently came to London and had been in the shop to see you."

Mr. King frowned. "But that doesn't prove anything. If he walked in, he also walked out. I do not know where he is." As his anger rose it broke into his modulated tones.

"He also said that another man accompanied him from Johannesburg," Avery bore down.

Mr. King reached the limits of his self-restraint. "Enough. I've squandered my time." His voice had a ragged edge. "I must go back to my work. My work, do you understand?"

Avery understood. He also realized his probing had gone too far. He had presented no credentials but only vague innuendo. Mr. King obviously had attempted to shield Jabbo, and the second man, whoever he was. Avery knew he couldn't topple the defensive barrier at this time. "Well, see you later. I'll be back to see Mr. Jabbo. Give him my best," and he left the shop.

On the street, Avery realized it would be futile for him to try to construct some sort of logic out of events when he remained just as ignorant of these puzzling occurrences as he had been before he began his search. He did not understand the man's reluctance to discuss Mr. Jabbo with him nor what made him so controversial. Every link on his trek so far had been severed with surprise and contradiction, and no relief loomed in sight.

As he rounded a corner he caught a glimpse of a well-groomed man across the street walking quickly ahead. Preoccupied, he seemed to be leaning forward, pressing against some kind of invisible resistance. Surprisingly, it could only be Farney. Farney in London and going fast. This seemed plausible. Farney's affairs took him everywhere, and Stephanie said he would still be in Europe. But this incident bordered too close to what Avery himself considered his own redoubt of interest-inviolate, territorially his. So, as incredible as Avery's behavior would appear even in his own eyes, he halted, hid, and backtracked, sleuthing Mr. Randolf Farney, while all the time he planned to stop his sleuthing nonsense and greet his friend. He wanted to find out what he was up to.

And Farney rewarded him immeasurably for his bizarre conduct by slowly approaching the taxidermist's shop and entering. Avery neared the shop and gazed across the street as Farney receded inside. He could see straight through the doorway. Henry King slammed down the receiver of a telephone and advanced distraught upon Farney, gesticulating and jabbering. Farney listened, sat down, and started to glance back. Avery shrank into the foyer of a cafe where he could partially watch unseen.

Then, unbelievably, impossibly, from some other planetary ethos, a voice called to him. "Mr. Judson, you have saved me the effort of searching for you." Avery whirled around. Before him Duskyanne sat at a table.

He gawked, tried to recover, and did manage to greet her.

"Get away from the doorway," she commanded. "We have a view of them from this table. Come here."

Avery felt compelled to do what he wanted to do in the first place. Through the window he could see that Farney and the taxidermist strenuously engaged in a heated conversation.

Avery refocused on Duskyanne. "I guess we have a courtship going. My ardent efforts have brought me good results. It's nice to be wanted," he said with delightful confusion.

She appeared to him lusciously efficient now; to her, simply efficient- to him, mostly luscious. Her two-piece suit exclusively spelled out a small and sharply delineated midriff. A comic strand of hair had slid over her face and hung there while she in mock exasperation puffed and blew it away.

"If you will watch closely you will soon see another man join them. He is the indispensable Mr. Jabbo that I heard you asking about. He is the cornerstone to all dealings with Henry King," she said appraisingly.

"Did you always know Farney was involved?" he asked.

The silence she reserved for him seemed stern and consuming. She continued as if uninterrupted, "If you want me to finish telling you what you should want to know-for your own benefit-then you must promise to stop questioning me. No questions whatsoever."

"What I want to know and what is for my benefit are not just contained in that lousy shop over there, but I'll promise . . ."

Enlightening the two of them, the other man abruptly appeared and went inside.

"Yes, now we can go on." Her tones impatiently jarred him. "King and Jabbo are partners in a business-Jabbo working Africa with King his representative and distributor. King used to operate in Kenya where he obtained for big game hunters an illegal number of animals, selling them stuffed specimens or ivory tusks for trophies-an international poacher.

"Jabbo worked as a scavenger. He poked around and grabbed or looted whatever he could-occasionally a low grade diamond mine or false goldfield. He would hang around a tribe and by means of his corrupting influence he managed to infiltrate it and take over its ceremonial wealth. He would turn native against native, bribe some, tell lies on others, masquerade as the government, and with his most efficient weapon bore into the priest cults as a sexual deviant. The religious leaders of many tribes are allowed sexual liberties as part of their acquiring insight into various worlds. With insight and vision they have a power. Jabbo latched onto this practice and through the priests he would grab the ritual art of the tribe. The government would then have to cope with the hostility that Jabbo had aroused. Whole areas would go berserk with natives who realized they had been violated, and they would try to recapture their religious property.

"King went to London and set up shop. Jabbo sent him his illegal traffic concealed in animal corpses, and King as a taxidermist would smuggle them out of the country as big game trophies. King knows the markets-he has a lucrative trade."

During her briefing Avery's attention broke away from her to check on the shop and its three occupants, and then went back to her face with its pert beauty.

"How did you know them?" he queried.

"They, too, were in Egypt, in the Sudan," and her hand darted out and whisked away fallings of her hair until they slid down again. Her eyes rolled upward and she made a face.

"And you too worked in Egypt," he said, disgruntled.

She assented in silence.

72

"Where does Farney come in? Does he know?" Avery peered through the window.

"Your former partner knows, and knows. He most probably met King and Jabbo somewhere in Africa, perhaps in Egypt, and for this particular venture they undoubtedly contacted him and asked him to come and personally pick up the article. One too important to export by ordinary means, don't you think so, Mr. Judson?"

"And how do you figure in this?" he demanded.

"Remember, I work for a king," she prattled on purpose, "and not a Mr. Henry King. End of questions!"

Avery scowled, caring. "Come off it now. Why don't you try to get the article away from Farney? What about Farney?"

"I have tried," she confessed, "but he has succeeded in stopping me. His price remained too high."

He tried to muzzle his emotions. "I wonder what your price was–what you did and didn't give? I am sure that Randolf Farney plays for the largest possible stakes."

"Do you want to know your course of action?" she exploded. "And will you stop verbally pawing me in your ridiculous manner! It's a simple matter for me to leave."

Furious, but thwarted, he said, "Go ahead!"

"You have only to blackmail Jabbo and King. Farney is involved with them deep enough so he can't do the same. They can't afford to be exposed," she stated with dispassion.

Avery ashamedly stammered, "I don't–certainly don't–mind the blackmail part but how do we stop their entire corrupt activity?"

"WE do nothing. You may crusade for decency between dealers and their art, or art and their dealers, but YOU will be doing it. In fact," and she tapped on the window, "Mr. Farney is leaving that den of iniquity right now which gives you the opening you need. Mr. Farney isn't planning to leave London for at least a week."

"How in the hell do you know so much about Farney?"

"Right now, Mr. Judson, I said is the delicious instant for calling unexpectedly on your potential clients, or should I say, targets. But only at once!" She could not be reached.

He got up to go and then hesitated. He couldn't leave her.

"While you are staring at me you might as well know one more piece of information even if it won't help you in what you are about to undertake. The night I met you at the hotel you guessed that I was disturbed. You were right. Jabbo caught me in the shop trying to take the Benin mask. Yes, the Benin! Don't look so stupid. And yes, I tried to steal it. Only he returned before I could get out. He attacked me even though I gave the mask back to him. I barely made my way out with my life."

"Do you expect me to believe this?" Avery asked incredulously.

"My dear pious boy, do you think that I am in the habit of inventing horrid stories about myself? Of course it's true. I wanted to crush Jabbo and King, and even Farney. I have no scruples about stealing from thieves. Since I couldn't stop those plunderers let's see what you can do to blast them and get the mask."

"Now it's my turn to dictate terms," he said in a mock-gallant voice, a ploy to keep her amused and interested. "I will endeavor to win for the lady the boon she has asked for only on one condition. She must promise to remain here so I can give her a kiss. Do you promise?"

She did laugh as he had hoped. "Miss the drama unfolding? No, it's been too long a road for me not to see it end somewhere. Yes, you can count on my being here." She sat there as if she waited for him to take the lead and do the deed, and then come back to sweep her away.

"It shouldn't take an hour," and he leaned toward her. "Thanks, I'm on your side." He pressed her hand, and suddenly swished away the hair that had cascaded over her brow. "Now in town, I won't let you down," he sang as he left.

Across the street stepped Avery wearing the feel of the woman's eyes on his back. He realized he hadn't somehow mentioned the ivory fragment to Duskyanne and that he had his own ongoing joust with Jabbo independent of her. He reached the shop while its partners seemed to be arguing. Avery could hear their voices jangle together and indistinctly some of their conversational drift. He heard fragments like "the offers" and a reference to "all the trouble today" when he effortlessly broke up the scenario. Mr. King saw him first, momentarily shuffled forward as if to bar the door, then halted on his heels. He quickly pointed out Avery to his companion. Mr. Jabbo stood stolidly still.

Mr. Jabbo could only be judged as a shock of a man: middle-aged, red-faced and red-bodied, knobby and boney. Glasses bored in on a face that matched a hawk's. Mr. Jabbo calmly swallowed the atmosphere and swung his arms around in spider-fashion. "Well, how do you do, my name is Heinrich Jabbo," and his half-open shirt drooped downward. Small projections of cartilage popped out of a misshapen chest whose pink skin lacked a shred of hair. His speech consisted of shrill, sliding sounds coated with an affected lisp.

When Avery presented his name, Mr. Jabbo, in jest, went through the mimicry of being delighted. "Naturally we expected you, a fine young lad."

Avery proceeded on course. He brought from his pocket the small piece of age-stained-yellowed ivory that he had purchased from Rumford in Los Angeles. He studied the figures caught in an ivory mesh and handed the fragment over to Mr. Jabbo.

"This carving Mr. Sophio Ramón from New York bought from you along with other objects. Mr. Ramón deals with you," Avery mechanically stated.

Mr. Jabbo scrutinized the piece with a trace of continual laughter overlaying his face.

"Mr. Ramón is mistaken," he claimed. "This piece never passed through my hands. Perhaps he became confused with the rest of his merchandise." His eyes continually flashed and pierced and his high, irritating voice spilled and dashed along as accompaniment. He seemed to derive sustenance from dropping and loving each of his words, and to Avery he wallowed in the swill of his own self-infatuation.

"Along with the other articles Mr. Ramón showed me on the bill of sale he had from you were a number of outright fakes–African masks and figures," Avery lied. "Of course, you did not list them as such when they officially entered the United States, and they were not described on the bill of sale. Besides, I wonder where you obtained the Nazi officer's baton which I saw when I visited your wife and home in Johannesburg. Probably directly from the S.S. Elite."

"I am surprised you bothered to travel as far as South Africa, Mr. Judson. Do you really believe your project to be worthwhile? Please, tell me how is my wife, the fat, dear thing?" He gloved an edginess in a tone that held each word with equal emphasis.

Dispensing with Mr. Jabbo for a moment, Avery sought Mr. King. "You have an equal stake in this, if not a larger one, since you are the shield for this sweet enterprise," and he flourished his hand at the two of them. "Imagine if an informant were to find out about you and then spill the beans on your corrupt activities. It's a sure thing his Majesty's government would totally dismantle you and your illegal operations–contraband goods from South Africa smuggled into the United Kingdom, and then further disguised and parceled out of the country worldwide, not to mention the production of fake art. I suppose this would be worthy of a lifetime jail sentence."

Mr. King's bald head glistened wet and its wrinkles creased deeper as he made a distorted, half-flailing motion of his hand toward his partner. "I hope this time you don't exceed the boundaries. Don't go too far," he said plaintively to Jabbo.

"Will you just shut up!" Jabbo's mouth venomously opened and closed as he jabbered. "His talk is only talk, stupid talk. Don't you see? His words become unpeeled into nothing. Keep wagging your tongue, Mr. Judson."

"Thank you." Avery advanced, and he faced the rows of stuffed animals ready to be shipped. "I suppose that inside that warthog is a Dan mask, real or fake, and how fitting it is for this animal mold of nature to house the masked spirit of man. I am sure the natives you stole these masks from, if they are authentic, would have heartily approved. Here's a small animal, most probably extinct, a Strand wolf, illegal to hunt. Perhaps inside are votive offerings of Ashanti brass weights. And what could better match the giant horns of an ibex head here than a fake Bambara antelope mask underneath with its own long horns? There's a half-century of prison right in these bundles alone, and that is true only if there are no small gold Ashanti heads inside the wolf. Then we can make it a century." In a feigned display of concern, in caricature, he exclaimed, "Where, oh where is the Benin ivory mask?"

"You see!" cried Mr. King. "It doesn't do any good to just stand there to oppose him. Can't you tell? He knows!"

Mr. Jabbo leaned on the desk and regarded the ivory fragment, and as he did so a necklace of incised dog teeth spaced with beads poured out of his shirt. Smiling, he scooped out the necklace from his concave chest and pronounced, "From the Admiralty Islands. Pretty, aren't they?" Then he tucked them fondly back into his shirt and they disappeared among a few ghost hairs. "You apparently are interested in a Nigerian ivory mask from a Benin Oba's reign in the sixteenth century-one of a handful. I have one. But it is already bid for," and a tissue of a smile stuck onto his mouth.

"Let me see it," Avery said.

Jabbo went to the head of a wildebeest and from inside lifted out a package. He held the package and unraveled it. Avery watched the wrapping partially dissolve into a strikingly elegant headdress several rows deep of what resembled ivory ruffles. The front row showed little men with strange hats forming a chain with each other.

Avery stepped toward it and examined the carved tiara of human faces with double-layered hats, like cakes, that extended down the sides of the mask and passed under the chin forming a complete circle except for the interruption of ears. He instantly detected the piece the mask lacked. Although the tiara clearly missed a critical piece, Avery in order to be sure still had to scrutinize the mask. Below the ears a separate chin necklace formed a base to which the miniature people served as a ruffle. Above the ears the gauntlet of men perched on a kind of netted cap, like the finely-textured wig of an English judge. It looked complete except for Avery's small missing piece of the fretwork which now he felt screamed out its absence to everyone.

Avery swiftly applied his fragment to the gap in the tiara and it joined the merry band of little men into a whole unit-a perfect fit.

"Yes," Mr. Jabbo flicked crisply, "you have the correct piece that is missing, but isn't it a shame that someone else has all but bought the Benin mask by offering the right price."

Avery stood back and absorbed the mask's brow inset with metal, and underneath, eyes bulging with molten intensity-the curved nose with flared nostrils under which in perfect symmetry rested two thickly arched and pendulant lips. Here existed an affirmation in triads: intellect, sensitive heart, and vigorous aesthetics. Nothing else had perfectly brought together the physical spirit of a human, whether this black Oba king, a Chinese courtesan dancer, or a splendid Greek youth. In the mask the humanity of every continent classically merged together.

"My price," Avery stated, "is in proportion to my ability to destroy you which is considerable."

Jabbo parried, "A price. Mr. Judson, a price. Not rotten vagaries or you might as well take yourself out of here."

The mask had a skin to wallow in, Avery mused: jade, satin, and silk could not rival its round mellow ivory surfaces striated by finely formed dark hair-lines..

"Price? I will not turn you in to the authorities from all the countries you have violated. I will not bring an irate mob of witnesses who would impale you if they only had the chance. Plus, I will not arrange to bring you back to certain vengeful African tribes who have an admiration for your death. Why, your death would be a remarkably pure sample of justice.

"On the other hand, I will buy your Benin ivory mask and thereby automatically become so involved in your stench that I will be rendered harmless to you. I have a cashier's check for twenty-five thousand dollars," and he placed the check next to the mask.

Mr. Jabbo laughed with great force, and Mr. King stepped nearer to the table.

"When I said 'price,' I meant it exactly so, a legitimate offer and not a farce. You haven't come a fourth of our way–a shoddy display of amateurism," Jabbo rebuked him.

Avery desperately plunged on. "I will leave the money here for a minute, and if I do not have the mask by then I will put the money in my pocket and crucify you. Watching right now is a competitor of yours, Miss Reef, who is thoroughly familiar with your company. And–I had a partner in the United States, Randolf Farney, who could be used to blackmail . . ."

"Heinrich!" screamed Mr. King. "What are you trying to do? Fight against us? Take his damn money and let him have the mask. He can harm us more than the money can help us." Mr. King ended in a beseeching fit.

By now Heinrich Jabbo had completely ground down to a halt. He looked at his hysterical partner with scorn. He stood there unnerved, still intractable, but Avery could see that he realized he had no other alternative. He opened his mouth, closed it, and opened it again.

"Then take the mask. Needless to say, you don't need a bill of sale. Take it and get out!"

Avery did precisely that. He grabbed the mask, put it into its wrapping, stuffed its slightly over nine inch bulk into his coat pocket, and quickly left the shop. Just outside he called back, "You can keep the wildebeest." He looked inside and saw Jabbo tearing his hair out.

Proud and enormous in accomplishment, he rapidly strode to the cafe where he had left Duskyanne. One point impressed him: her name registered with effect on Jabbo and King. However, it had taken him more than the hour he promised her to carry it off.

He rushed into the cafe. She had left. He couldn't find her at the table nor in the restroom, and when he asked the waiter for a message or note the waiter told Avery that she had given none. The lady had departed immediately after he did.

Her hotel turned out to be a reality, but not Duskyanne. The lady had checked out in space and time. He had the mask but at what price? He had lost out again. In his collection he did not have a Duskyanne-perhaps an article impossible to obtain. Perhaps.

6

The hotel seemed drab and grubby to him in a London where he now viewed lives as gray, gloomy, and shuffling endlessly between the city's battering ramparts. He comforted himself by displaying the mask on the fireplace mantle. He sat down in the suite's small sitting room to seize the ruddy afterglow of his success–to revel in a studied review of his treasure. He considered what would be the proper pose and attitude for veneration. But he was never allowed the rich, contemplative desserts he deserved.

From the bedroom he heard a shuffling noise. He leaped up to confront Mr. Randolf Farney emerging from the room. Avery froze, shocked. Farney instantly glanced at the mask on the fireplace mantle, proceeded directly to it, and began to inspect it without giving Avery a sign of recognition.

"Get out of the line of sight of my mask. Dammit, you're blocking my view. I can't see through you. Get out of the way," Avery growled.

Farney moved back. "I didn't know you were here. You took so long in arriving that I fell asleep on your bed. However, your late arrival allowed me time to speak at length with King and Jabbo on the phone." Farney allowed himself a smile. "You left those two in quite a state."

Distrust of the man overcame Avery. He arose and took down the mask, clutched it tightly, and instinctively moved away from Farney.

Farney laughed indulgently as if he could out-wait his peevish friend. He shook his head. "I have never underestimated you, but how the hell you knew about it I will never know. Stephanie didn't even know."

"So what! Who cares!" Farney galled Avery. "How did you find me here?"

"No problem. When I was informed that you had the mask I checked hotel registers. Fortunately I recalled your penchant for first-rate art and second-class accommodations. I investigated second-class hotels, first, or it would have taken longer to find you." He appraised the room. "This is about what I expected."

"Who gives a damn what you expected."

"You're the winner. You own the mask." Farney shrugged benevolently. "Why should you be so petulant?"

"Farney, you're obnoxious. You try to be a King Midas or some kind of a law like gravity but you don't control much in this universe. And I'm not one of your dregs. I'm myself and you can't help but be yourself, so let's accept the miserable fact."

"Precisely. I'm here because you are exactly you, and I want you to enlarge upon the process of your life through me. But the fragment? Stephanie saw you buy it. Then New York, Johannesburg, Jabbo, King, and Reef. Incredible. Even more so is your uncanny luck. With due respect for your scampering talents I would like some of it to rub off on me."

"You and your luck," Avery snapped. "What luck did I have?" Avery still remained sore.

"Why, for all your dash and perseverance you never would have bought the mask if at the last minute you hadn't mentioned my name. You simply didn't have enough cash, and nothing else would have budged Jabbo except my name. I'm a key player here."

"What's so great about that? Forget you."

"Let me ask YOU a question. Why did you use my name?"

Avery thought a moment. He dared not involve Duskyanne. "I don't know. I had to come up with someone big and important, and I had just seen you so I gave your name."

"But you must have been aware that I sought the mask–had bid for it since you inferred that to Jabbo. As a player you knew I was involved. And yet why did you use my name when I was the buyer? It could only have caused the wrong effect."

Avery smiled at his Duskyanne secret. "I don't know. I didn't think it out clearly. I had to come up with a clincher. I didn't have a reason."

"How could my name put any pressure on them when I picked up Jabbo in Johannesburg . . .?"

"You were the other visitor!" Avery said, astonished.

"Yes, I picked him up after he contacted me. I flew him to London for the sole purpose of obtaining the mask."

"I should have figured that out sooner," Avery speculated.

"So you can see that as your opponent and Jabbo's financial supporter I was not the best calling card to give out. Still, you managed to blunder into saving yourself. When you mentioned my name they thought you were an agent of the government, and that I was also employed to bait them into getting caught in the act of illegally selling to me. Although they suspected you, they thought you had become corrupt since you were blackmailing them. And then you offered that ridiculously low price. You were so tight you almost lost the deal. But Avery, I never tried blackmail, and instead I offered them a huge sum of money. They felt I tried to entice them into a trap."

"So they were afraid?"

"Sure they were," Farney snorted. "Either through you or me they think the government's on their track and so they'll have to suspend operations, at least in England."

Avery beamed. "Then I've kept a promise. I really achieved something," and he considered his absurdity, "without really knowing how it would come out . . ."

"A promise to someone and a contract with me. I would like to form an indissolvable business partnership that would bind you to me, and me to you–what amounts to a Faustian eternity."

Avery looked askance. He visualized the same dapper, crafty Farney, just freshly arisen from a nap and striking out rudely unannounced and unwanted in order to gain the upper hand. Avery snapped apprehensively, "Farney, why would the all-powerful need me? Why pick on me?"

Farney sat down, settled comfortably in his chair, and prepared for a frontal attack. "I hope I never really know what I can potentially do. But I certainly know what I cannot do. That has saved me many times. Never to presume when you can't perform."

"You seemed to have been in the midst of the chase, caused all kinds of waves," Avery parried, "you did alright."

"But you did better. No, my background is all wrong for art dealing. I have the wrong training. When I first collected I was concerned with hatching a deal and seeing how far I could outsmart my rival. I did remarkably well. I read up on a lot of subjects and became sufficiently knowledgeable in buying bargains. By then I had enough money to pay what something was worth, but I didn't do it. I delighted in practically stealing items, although I didn't always like what I bought. But that didn't matter, I had made a bargain."

"Why are you telling me this?"

"Because you have to know this. It is true, even to the smallest detail. Once, I spent more than three years trying to buy five Mimbres Indian picture bowls–pictures of animals and native domestic scenes painted inside them. I figured the pots worth seven times what I offered the owner who lived in a small California town. He didn't really know that, but each year he turned me down because he stuck to the blind, dull instincts of the pedant–haggling for a little more because that is what he does. What were the Mimbres prehistoric pots to him? For three years I hammered at him with no results. The little town he lived in gave him no exposure to knowledgeable buyers. Then I said I would offer him less the next time around since no one would ever buy his pots except a fool, and I was doing him a favor. In the fourth year I broke the little peddler. He had even begun to think he had been unfair to me. He almost begged me to buy them. I got them the way I wanted them."

"And you screwed yourself in the process. You eventually lost out to future dealers."

"Yes, but I didn't realize it then. Since I wouldn't pay for an object's true value–I thought there's no sense in that–the dealers turned their backs and wouldn't sell to me. They tired of seeing their goods downgraded. So I lost many treasures although I managed to find others."

"Farney, you don't need anything–myself included."

"No, you're wrong. It all breaks down to performance. One day I went to my storage room and looked at what I had won so hard, and my little dominion clearly appeared ugly to me. Utterly without taste. What I had purchased often turned out to be letter-perfect in the book, in form, but wrong at the core. I knew then that I needed another mind to take over where I had failed. And Avery, you in a fashion were born for me."

"But were you born for me? No, Farney. I respect your resourcefulness. You have actually made art pay off. Partly due to you I'm almost a financial success." He put on a silly smile. "Also, I like your wife, but that's as far as it goes with us and no more."

"Wait a minute," Farney quipped, "you're not as financially successful as your old man," and he laughed. "He's a millionaire several times over and you need my resources to be his match."

Avery looked up, surprised. Farney quickly continued. "What counts is that we cooperate in order to quit nullifying each other. I have too much to do to have to watch you. I'd rather take you just as you are and let you do precisely what you are going to do anyway. Only I want to be sure you're on my side. No longer can we be opponents because in my proposition whatever we acquire belongs to both of us."

Avery spoke cautiously. "I don't know. I don't want to be a pawn of yours, locked in some sort of cage like the animals in South Africa's Krueger Park. The animals can prey on each other and be preyed upon–create life and death scenes, but only under the control and supervision of the Lord God park warden who allows the game of life to go on. You are that park warden."

"In a manner," Farney conceded, "but the park fences surrounding the animals fade away in my offer. I am setting up a trust fund consisting of you and me as the sole trustees. A foundation will be formed to finance and house the collection of art works we amass, and it will be endowed to carry on with its purpose regardless of what happens to us. So you can see there are no cages or fence masters over you. Your only responsibility is to buy what pleases you."

Avery grunted, "So we as frail human pillars will serve as the foundation for a Foundation."

"Yes," and Farney became cagey. "But as Macbeth says to his wife concerning King Duncan's coming visit, 'He's here in double-trust.' It is imperative for us to set up a reliable trust that can be doubly trusted. Now Avery I want to know your thoughts."

Avery did not speak for several minutes and during the silence he realized that he had been tightly cradling the Benin mask, guarding it from Farney. Finally, he said, "My thoughts, certainly. But Farney, we should first have a bottle of brandy so we can celebrate. The occasion calls for it."

Farney raised his eyebrows in surprise. "Dear fellow, you rarely drink. But if you really want to commemorate the occasion–and it's surely worthy of commemoration–we should carry it out properly. Dinner at the Ritz this evening. The Foundation will be pleased to pay for the first 'working dinner' between its partners."

"No, no," Avery protested. "I didn't bring appropriate clothes for dinner at the Ritz. And I think we should drink a toast right here in this little suite. It's fitting, somehow–my second-rate accommodation, as you call it, to launch a first-rate enterprise. But I wouldn't know what to get. Would you do the honors, Farney?"

Farney shrugged his shoulders and muttering something about "finding a decent dram shop in this neighborhood," left Avery's second-rate lodgings.

Avery didn't want dinner at the Ritz. He didn't even want a drink although he suspected he probably needed one. What he did want required a few minutes by himself away from Farney who could addle his mind just by his presence.

Actually Avery didn't need time to think about whether he should or shouldn't enter into Farney's enterprise. Farney had hooked him, and Farney, having been asked to make a purchase of an appropriate libation with which to celebrate, realized it. Moreover, Farney knew his man. He might as well have said, "You can't afford to turn down this deal," and Avery couldn't.

But Avery did need time to think about something else, a nameless factor just outside the parameters of Farney's verbal offer. Avery would have to be very careful, very cautious in the months and years to come. The animals in Krueger Park came to mind again but did not particularly frighten him. What bothered him seemed to be rather elusive, and potentially more dangerous. What had Farney said? Something about a "Faustian eternity . . . an indissolvable business partnership that would bind you to me, and me to you–what amounts to a Faustian eternity."

Avery sat down in the one comfortable chair that the room offered still clasping the mask tightly to his chest. His hands felt moist. For many minutes his mind spun and tumbled, one thought hurtling headlong into another.

A Faustian eternity. He knows. He knows he can have me, his whore. And the price is right, the price is perfect, damn him. My body for his money, or even more to the point, what his money can provide. Avery shuddered. Well, not exactly, he thought. It's worse. First, he's going to addict me with his opiates so that I'll slaver before him, beg for his favors, anything . . .

Avery stopped himself before another of his hodge-podge allegory/analogies careened out of control.

"Now, wait a minute," he said aloud. He relaxed his arms and the mask slid into his lap. He lifted it, held it at arm's length, and spoke to it.

"You know and I know that only by a fluke I got you. And-I-want-more-like-you. Lots more." He shook the mask slightly as though to make sure it understood. "And I can't crave any more beauties like you without him. Or damn few. No more ivory masks, no Scythians, no gold cats. Curse YOU, Farney!"

He rose and paced, the Benin mask once again clutched across his breast.

"Avery Judson," he addressed himself to the empty room, "he will draw you into his great Farney maw and swallow you–won't bother to digest you, and he'll spit you right back up whole again like Jonah and the whale."

Avery fumed. He had utter hostility for the man and fury reserved for himself. Totally weak, he knew he had already acquiesced to Farney's offer. He stopped pacing momentarily and moved to the small bedroom. He halted before a mirror.

"Listen," he said to his image. "Hold on here. You can buy a few pieces of priceless art in your lifetime. Only a few more, because you won't sell any of them to buy more or even to pay for rent and food. If you continue on this track you'll end up an old man in a shabby FOURTH-RATE rooming house somewhere eating a meal a day from a soup kitchen, but surrounded by . . . by what? A few more collected things, a paltry few, one Benin mask, one golden cat, and a par-tri-idge in a pear tree." He sang the last phrase.

"BUT!" He released one hand from the mask long enough to shake a finger at the Avery Judson in the mirror. "But," he repeated more softly, "you go with Farney, you collect for the Foundation, and the pieces unfortunately can never be yours, true enough. But you can look at them, be with them anytime, almost live with them. Yet they would be yours and not yours. And you won't starve, you'll live rather well, in fact, and maybe . . ."

Avery turned from the mirror not trusting himself to look into his own eyes as he spoke the next thought that occurred to him. "Maybe-once-in-awhile-you-can-buy-something-for-yourself-with-Farney's-money."

Spoken in a run-together staccato medley, he as hastily put the thought aside lest it gestate, take shape, grow and stand full-blown to greet Farney upon his return. Although it had been born in his mind Avery knew that on this score Farney would never allow him to collect privately.

His heart beat hard and fast and his hands trembled. He moved back to the sitting room and replaced the Benin mask on the mantle for fear that in his condition he might drop it. He sank into the chair exhausted. "I've sold my soul to the devil and I'm about to drink to it," he said. "I hate the son-of-a-bitch." The eyes of the ivory mask bore down judgementally into his own. "Oh, not from you," Avery complained.

Farney opened the door and looked quizzically at Avery. "Talking to someone?" He glanced about the room.

"Only myself," Avery recovered. He went to the mantle and retrieved the mask.

"Damn you, Farney, but I'm for it-your deal," he croaked. "What am I doing buying objects that cost a fortune?" He indicated the mask. "I can't afford to keep this." He placed it on the mantle once more. "I'll just go bankrupt because I don't want to sell it and I can't keep on buying forever. There's no way I can really get started. But with your help I can buy what I want even though it's not totally mine. In a way it still becomes my collection."

Avery paused and reconsidered. The stunning mask would still, somehow, be partially in Farney's foreign hands–and Farney would be foreign to him–would always remain a stranger. The shadow of Farney would shroud his acquisitions. Avery should be his own man. He could make out. Or could he really? "It comes down to this, Farney, it seems like your deal is made for my salvation."

"Agreed," said Farney, "the financial part has already been executed and the draft of our agreement I have here with me," and he gave it to Avery.

"Do you mean you were so positive I would agree that you came armed with a contract?" Avery wavered. "You were so cock-sure you had me."

"It is to your credit you are so necessary to me. I will be a good partner . . .," Farney vowed.

Avery tallied up the man: quite serious in fulfilling his purpose, bristling with a dubious businessman's integrity, and most important, brilliant . . . and cunning. Plus evil? Avery toyed with the thought but then dropped it. Yes, Farney would make a 'good' partner if 'good' did not mean anything more than the fact that he would indeed be enduring, like a mountain, a permanent support.

Avery read the contract rapidly and signed while Farney uncorked a bottle of fine Napoleon brandy. From his coat he extracted two shot glasses. "From the pub, opposite," he explained. "Told the owner they were critical to finalizing a business transaction." Farney filled the glasses to their brims and each man raised his glass slightly to the other. They drank.

"What about Stephanie, what does she mean to this?" Avery asked.

"Oh, don't worry about Stephanie," he said with authority.

"I'm not about to worry, but . . ."

Farney ended the matter. "Stephanie's mine, the mask is part mine, and Miss Duskyanne Reef will soon be mine. Goodbye, Avery. I have a flight to catch to Florida."

Avery burned while Farney closed his briefcase and left. No matter how he chose to construct an image of this man it could only be in terms of an implacable adversary. Where does art stop? he thought. He picked up the bottle of rich, fine liquor, opened the door to the suite, and walked down the hall to the common loo. He yelled, "Stay in Florida, Farney, it needs you." Then he poured many English pounds worth of the rich Napoleon brandy into the toilet. "Screw you, Farney," he shouted as his words and the brown liquid gurgled down to the sewers of London while he pulled the chain overhead.

7

The Foundation's working capital provided for Avery's return trip to the States. With Farney in Florida Avery saw Farney's lawyers and deposited the Benin mask in the vault of Farney's bank as legal property now belonging to their Foundation.

In Los Angeles Avery called Stephanie and she invited him to the Farney residence for dinner. Mrs. Farney greeted him and he thought she appeared thinner and more nervous than ever.

"Did you see Randolf?" This, her first utterance, dented Avery's pride and caused him to spurn her eagerness just a bit.

"Yes, I saw your husband in London."

She flushed. "I fall into this condition when he's away for some time," and she checked herself, "but I have always thrived on a state of uncertainty," and she smiled through her concern. "Still, tell me about him."

"Farney is fortunate." He regarded her fondly. "I invited your husband to my hotel in London where I rudely wrenched his hand behind his back and forced him against his will to become my partner," he chattered. "I drive a hard bargain."

"Not so!" She seemed thankful for his diverting nonsense. "I received the news from our lawyer. I had to sign some papers which included a note from Randolf who said he got the greater object, a Mr. Judson, and you were intolerably difficult."

By this time he seated himself and Stephanie served his scotch and soda which she didn't share. "Part of my tale I didn't fabricate-I was rude," he conceded.

"If you were rude you were provoked," she sided with him. Randolf can anger anyone, and especially me. But how is he?"

"Who-me?" Avery parried.

"No, not you. Randolf!"

"But you know about him-you knew about our partnership."

"That note he sent to our lawyer is all I know. Can't you tell? It's weeks since I've heard from him."

Avery became somber and thought about what he could say about Farney. But he didn't have to say anything.

"This is outrageous vanity, but did he mention me?"

"He said somehow-something like-'Stephanie is mine.'" Avery would have rather faced Jabbo than to have to outfox her.

"That's nice, even though it wasn't told to me," she said. "And so I'm his, and he's his own self's, and you Avery are locked to him, I guess as 'partners for life' in the very same paddock with me." She ended with a pleasantry. "In a paddock without another drink and food to eat. Goodness, what hospitality. Come to dinner. It's ready."

In her "paddock" he would go, he conjectured, since he was allied with this good woman who will always be a loyal friend.

At the table she showered him with attention now the common business about Farney had been dispensed with, and he, too, doted on his hostess. Before him lay a dinner spread for participants who would be absorbed in the elaborate ritual of shuffling dishes, rotating courses, and choosing the correct instruments of attack designed to be balanced with social intercourse, grandly polite, righteously correct, all pointlessly deployed. To delay his desire for her, to forestall his fantasized result for the two of them would of course be in order, even if tedious order. But instinctively he applauded the delays. He would not try to control their drifting.

Perhaps Stephanie liked him because he had been catapulted into the family circle and served as a good substitute for the evening; perhaps she could steadily grow to like him. Perhaps, just Farney. Still, how ideal it would be for Avery to take this lithe, sweeping lady to eat the same meats and fruits with him, and at the right bite to submerge himself beneath her sumptuous Mandarin housecoat and aptly be enhanced. And then to be refreshed with dessert. But it would have to be otherwise. He had to be content with having her at arm's length involved in a sort of personal theater with no climax enacted. Worse, he had compassion for her beyond his thwarted aspirations.

"What are you thinking about, Mr. Judson?" she bantered as Avery again centered on the Farney-shrouded woman and her reality.

"Let's adjourn to the next bump on the road and I'll tell you," he responded.

After dinner they moved to the library. A servant brought an assortment of vari-colored liqueurs which they sipped from miniature silver goblets as they talked. She had little to say about herself at first. Her activities she discounted as the 'daily chit-chat of living between big events' which he deemed typical of her. He for his own part assiduously avoided London and the Benin mask because the subjects seemed somehow irrelevant to them. But in passing he referred to some Spanish Majolica tiles lining her fireplace which resembled the ones inset over the front door of the house where he had spent most of his boyhood and where he cherished a large fossilized fish that appeared to swim on the flagstone entrance.

His recall of such a trivial detail ricocheted and immersed her in her past. She, too, had once been occupied with fossils, but as a collector. She fingered back into the long lax rope of years, being mesmerized into relaxation. If she collected fossils she could ask her zoology teacher lots of questions. Naturally she had fallen in love with him at her private school. She had been to countless private schools: in Chicago, Philadelphia, San Francisco. Being precocious, her parents allowed her to explore her depths, apparently in regard to her personal freedom which they furthered by affording her an superb education. She traveled, tested a battery of the finest minds and bodies of a few strays, and later Farney garnered for her a university of life experiences that had solidified her thoughts.

Avery gathered that Farney had caught her right-impulsive, daring, shimmering, multi-powered, and Farney had caught her wrong, before she could realize her own image of herself. She said Farney often behaved like a romantic schoolboy–the only beau she ever had who displayed an imagination for the absurd, who swore to write novels, play polo, chin himself sixty-seven times, master left-handed ping pong, and invent a simple bolt to plug up the universe which would make him millions. Farney filched her because he made her laugh, skewered her with laughter, and she adored to laugh. He would limit her to seven laughs and she would exceed her limits by bursting into laughter in the middle of the morning before her lipstick wore off. He would carry her down steps, sometimes stumbling and nearly dumping her; insanely drive slowly into a blank wall, not caring, while kissing her with the engine idling; and entice her to enjoy punching him.

Farney played a favorite game of asking people to choose from various alternatives, insisting upon a choice as if their lives rested on their decision. "Which would you do without if you had to-the mountains or the seas?" he would ask. "Would you, if necessary, rather lose completely your sense of hearing or your ability to speak?" Farney intoned, "If your life had to transmigrate into one of these animals which would you select-a coyote or an anteater?" "If you must be on a desert island with either your mother or father which would you pick?" In spite of the amazing nonsense the questions generated, after a day's playing of Farney's game the answers seemed to add up to the sum of a player's definitive personality, like a crazy Rorschach test.

Avery found it difficult to fathom the Farney of Stephanie's description. She presented a Farney given to flights of fancy and whim, elements he now controlled in a vice. Avery thought, tongue-in-cheek, of the man who he had faced as a guest in his house as perhaps being flexible and open enough to permit his guests a respite from the stringencies of listening to the early music of John Dunstable on the hi-fi and thus allow for the playing of a slightly later baroque piece, a deviance Farney would consider pure frivolity.

But as Avery knew, it came to pass that the absurd turned real and true: Farney had raked down his imagination to business deal-level attainments. The fanciful bolt changed to a commercial screw that tied onto anything and never unscrewed or slipped off; he had patented it for millions of dollars. A silk screen process applied to men's ties and children's books with illustrations animated by actual sounds and even fragrant smells furthered his fortunes. His perfection of a cheap way to procure gold ore caused a revolution in gold mining and reactivated thousands of mines throughout the world. He composed a popular song, actually a prescription of how he later viewed love, that blazed for six months in every juke box, and blazed more money for him.

'I'll love you
If you'll love me
I must have this
Guarantee
to love;
If you'll love me
With no love returned
I'll love your love for me.'

And he still devoted time each day to reading his favorites, Milton and Hawthorn. His humor changed. It crackled less of unrelated foolery and bore down on the straits of his fellow beings. But who can gauge humor or would want to?

What exactly happened to them both Avery felt would be impossible to decipher. That Farney's world broadened extraordinarily and his passion for all things intensified is certain. Correspondingly, Stephanie's place of importance contracted allowing less room for Farney to feel her smoldering self. But Avery counted on the vast aptitudes of both of them to include him.

Stephanie's talk shifted to the Foundation and Avery's plans. "Your parents must have been responsible for your interest in art."

Avery became serious. "You are right but in the wrong way. I don't think I would be here with you if my father hadn't hated this business of art so much. To him a son should follow his father and make money. Because of him I vehemently refused to. The pursuit of art I felt meant the opposite of money—and directly counter to what existence meant to him. I suppose I should be thankful that he got me here."

"I am especially glad," she stated, "but what will your next joust be with adventure? After all as your best fan you should tune into your hometown audience."

Avery had not the least inkling. "With ample money and a Foundation for my roots," he said matter-of-factly, "I want to sit down in some room and not go anywhere. Nowhere. And if I do go somewhere I want to go for different reasons," he said wistfully.

"Where?" she pressed him.

"On a picnic tomorrow with you in a boat, or on top of an inaccessible mountain."

Somewhat to his surprise she happily accepted. "Avery, you have yourself a date," and the evening ended with both of them jubilantly anticipating the morrow.

The following day Farney telephoned them. He had returned earlier than expected. That would be Farney, who, in effect, of course usurped his date and called off their excursion.

Alone, Avery lingered and lurked in the city. He paid homage to Darlington and he could hardly believe the mediocrity of his art. Either his old mentor had slipped onto poor times or Avery had sprouted new eyes, or some of both. The man had suffered a stroke. He hunched with a steeper bend to his stoop and walked with the lagging gait of an old man.

Darlington greeted Avery testily and the shopkeeper muttered that he didn't find material as easy to come by as before. Avery saw an Ethiopian Christian painting which he recognized as one of his former possessions that once inhabited his forlorn shop and now had found its way to Darlington.

Darlington posed one question for Avery. "Do you still have the Scythian gold beasts? For if you do I'd like to buy them back from you-at your price. You know I have the money. And that way we would make things even at the shop."

Avery hesitated. "I would like to."

"You can do it," he said hoarsely. "Yes?"

"You know about the Foundation," and Avery knew that he knew. "The figures are legally consigned to it-the Foundation now owns them."

"It was an oversight," Darlington said tersely. "It could have happened to anyone."

"Yes, anyone," Avery limply said.

"But it happened to me. Could I see them? Wherever they are."

"In our repository. I can try to get you in."

"Thank you. It was an oversight," and Darlington moved away.

Avery passed his old bank where his father still kept accounts, and unaccountably, through the glass windows he saw the man making deposits at a teller's window. He stopped and watched his father as he processed his business and found him the same, definitive, and clearly impressive man who still maintained his authoritative bearing. Every act his father performed, even the most perfunctory, seemed to be a solitary one, isolated from all other beings with their cares and concerns. He stayed invulnerable because he remained a little Godhead of business orbiting as his own satellite, except that unseen, behind him, lurked Avery, his weakness, his unfinished business. When his father completed his banking and started to exit from the bank Avery panicked. He slipped away and hid inside a drugstore and watched Mr. Judson walk by swinging his briefcase in abrupt, jerky movements. Why could he not face him? Not yet. Too soon for a confrontation. He would wait for the future, and he knew clearly the future would wait for him.

Still, Avery meandered through the city. Across and away he went to the boyhood block in which he had been nurtured, a trenchant fortress of houses rubbing shoulders a mile long and honeycombed between with seedy lawns and gardens. He sought the house where he had lived for so long, the first in the block and next to an alley. He decided to climb onto the roof of his long-remembered house. On the other side of the alley lay the land that encompassed the La Brea Tar Pits and where in his youth thrived rabbits, gophers, and dirt dunes. Now all had succumbed to chic apartment tracts which in time depreciated sufficiently to be open to common human traffic. His rabbits and rodents had been bulldozed out of their burrows and run over on the adjoining paved streets, and the prehistoric animals, he reflected, had long been mired in the tar pits during the ice ages; both had vanished to epic change. While the ancient animals had been preserved through their boney monuments the others stayed preserved in Avery's memory.

He turned now to his city block and scanned the rooftops, still a gauntlet of roofs with few gaps in between. He stifled an urge to scramble across. At nine years old he had navigated the rooftop of every house on his side of the block, making a passageway successfully bridging from one end of the block to the other, even though at times he had to climb down from the heights and snake across rickety fences or crumbly walls or trees (now dismembered) in order to ascend to the next rooftop. This remarkable childhood odyssey, he thought, this once towering achievement he accomplished without touching the ground. Not touching the ground! A feat that Tarzan and Columbus and

Lindberg had never attained. But his father had construed the boy's caper (his father had received a complaint) as sheer opposition to his wise insistence that Avery should perform constructively.

His parents, he sighed, had long moved away to superior climes but he had emotionally clung to this large, yellow, two-story Spanish-tiled house of his childhood. There he would spy through the round window-opening in the stairway upon his parents in the livingroom below. An ongoing recollection lingered with him that he would wait for them to draw closer to each other, to sweeten their voices, perhaps to kiss or even go further. They didn't. The best they could manage was to be polite to each other. Whatever love existed drowned in the politeness.

They had a problem and perhaps he did, too. His mother longed for a doting husband who would pay particular attention to her particular details, and equally indispensable, would be an enormous financial success. His father craved a surrendering woman who loved him when occasionally he came home from the office, and who would still be as loving while he stayed continually away from her. They had the inevitable, a mixed dosage of considerable financial success and an occasional tendril of love.

But himself! Here he sat meditating his wherewithal in the limbo of his favorite rooftop. Should he find a retreat in the Himalayas? He really had no choice. He would be led where mistress art led and would sacrifice himself to her altar. To run after art, his tantalizing tart, the same rhyme, the same dynamics, the same essence, so elusive it gave him a headache. He hesitated. All roads lead somewhere but not this one of the mind-a boyhood maze on the rooftops; he would not climb up again. He got down from the house. No, he would move no more in this city.

Before he left he received a letter: "Dear Avery, your father and I are happy whenever we read about you and the Foundation. It's the best reading in the newspaper. I wish you would come to visit us. Your father works too hard and needs some relaxation. I would like to come see you wherever your work takes you. Perhaps New York City? But I don't want to leave your father here alone. Please think of us. We think of you a lot. Love, Mother."

Avery didn't respond.

8

*H*e decided to drive to Arizona heading toward New Mexico where he had heard there existed a collection of early Spanish American religious art which he knew nothing about. He told Farney nothing-he didn't care. Avery stopped to pick up a lanky, bearded hitchhiker. The rider told him he'd like to continue in the same direction and did not give Avery his name, although Avery asked. But during the ride Avery discovered the man to be a fledgling anthropologist in his middle thirties who had his master's degree in something. He spoke of an old car that couldn't take a long trip.

"Are you going to the dance?" he asked soberly, and looked at Avery with a clean cut, outdoor-hardened assumption.

"What dance?"

"Oh, the dance."

Avery waited.

"It'll be a good dance."

"Yeah, what dance?"

"The dance I'm going to," he frowned. "I missed it last year."

"But you won't miss it this time."

"I wouldn't miss it if I had to go sleepless for two nights which is just about the case. An important dance!" he pronounced solemnly and glanced away.

"Then you've seen it before," Avery gathered.

"Three times except for the last time I missed it, and that won't happen again," he stated. "I shouldn't have missed it."

"What?" Avery quipped, deciding to tease the trip along with jaded banter. It helped to while away the long miles.

"The dance."

"Oh, the dance, the one I am going to," Avery baited him.

"You're going to the dance, too?" he reacted, agitated. "To the Hopi Niman dance?"

"No, I am going to the debutantes' ball," Avery told him with a straight face. "Where did you say?" he questioned.

"At Hopi Pueblo, a vital dance. Get with it.".

"You're right," Avery vowed. "I guess I should go."

"Listen, I'll make it simple. The dance is for the departing Kachina gods who leave Hopi for the mountains after helping plant corn and beans."

"Anything else?"

"Yes. The dancers wear masks and become the Kachinas-gods themselves."

"Is all this important?"

"Sure it is. That's what I'm trying to tell you. The center of the world can be found there and the dance helps to stabilize the world."

"Do you believe that?" Avery queried.

"Typical dumb question," he snapped scornfully. "Do I believe in your heaven and hell? Do I believe in all the wonderful progress your shiny car stands for and all the garbage your rotten civilization spreads across the country? Do I believe in a Hopi Indian who chooses to live isolated on a mesa and live with the dirt and the stars and the eagles?"

"The eagles?"

"Naturally the Hopis have eagles," he bristled. "They are important because after their deaths their immortal spirits as messengers accompany the Kachinas to their sky homes in the mountains."

"Okay, but what do the Hopis mean to us?"

"It's like this," the hitchhiker said condescendingly. "A small group of people have for hundreds of years lived on a few mesas and never left their original position of heart and mind. Through their Kachinas and the natural forces they represent the Hopis have danced and sung and prayed their way intact-in peace and sanity. Now the Western world wearily watches itself choke with spiritual rigor mortis. Perhaps its eyes will be drawn to this enclave of dynamic contemplation."

"You know, " Avery bantered, "I wouldn't have known about the Hopis unless you clued me in. I had to meet you by accident in order to find out."

"You mean you wouldn't have known?"

"And all these cars and people on the highway driving our same direction are most probably not going to the Niman dance, incredible as it sounds. In fact, they might not even have heard of it, as astounding as that might be."

"How would you know?" he retorted, and his eyes turned suspicious. "More people know a lot more than you can imagine. Do you think I don't know what I'm talking about-that I'm just bullshitting? If you do, I'm sorry for you!"

"No, I think you're on a good track and I'm glad I met you to tell me about the dance. I'll be there for sure since you set me up."

They remained quiet for a long while. The rider sat rather disdainfully and Avery became tired. Finally as it turned dark the man ruffled their edgy silence and indicated that he wanted to get out. Avery stopped and the hitchhiker parted with some advice. "Remember, Hopi isn't just another place. Treat it with reverence."

"I will."

Avery drove a little further and pulled over and went to sleep. He woke up to an illusory third dimension revealing the countryside with rearing bluffs and tawny columns of cliffs and buttes. Reds, yellows, and white shimmered from sandy surfaces in a sea of summer. A brisk, late July morning unfolded. He ate at the Keams Canyon Trading Post where sallow waitresses and kitchen hands dolled out pasty food. He saw a rack of yellow-fatted meat that he heard identified as horsemeat. Here stood a commercial house flourishing with a separate market, cafe, and trading room of Indian goods, rather than the ingenious old-fashioned operation of the one man trader that did most everything. It struck Avery that the daffy anthropologist had the right idea about modernity spreading all over; this impersonal, grubbing, garish aluminum store stood as an anomaly among the huge fortresses of rock and stone that encircled it. A scattering of Navajos and Hopis came and went. They depended on the post just like he did.

Avery drove into Hopi land and after some several miles approached a high mesa with a flat-top of earth. Protruding ever so gently from its heights he could see low, stone-structured buildings, their slight, merging outlines blending in with the rock outcroppings and the dun-colored cliffside. It would be easy to pass it by which the Hopis must have been pleased to have their enemies do. At the base from where the dirt road wound sideways to the top stood another trading post of brown blocks of stone built in Hopi tradition. The pieces of masonry wedged and pieced together, Avery thought, could be the first dwellings of mankind, like in Celtic Ireland. In these houses Avery felt there must be a certain degree of finality. The generations that had passed through them testified to an eternal life that created an eternal death.

Inside the store Avery found modern Hopi ceramics: attractive bowls and jars made out of a creamy yellow clay, decorated with black and red symbolic designs. A young girl managed the store. She appeared to be typically Hopi, short with small bones, black hair and amber skin. Although slight, to his personal satisfaction her slender figure supported pronounced breasts and buttocks.

Avery addressed her. "I might want to return and buy a few gifts on my way back to Keams Canyon."

"Today we are closed. I am about to close the store," she said in shy and yet straight terms. A thick Hopi-woven red and green sash wound between a blouse and skirt.

"Why? What's the occasion?"

"There's a Niman dance–a Hopi dance at Shipaulovi on Second Mesa. I'm supposed to be there," she explained.

"Can anyone go?" he knew the answer.

"To most Hopi dances, yes."

"I'll be back after the dance," he said. "I want to see it and I may have some questions to ask later."

"But the store is closed," she protested.

"I'll be back," and he went to his car.

When he had climbed the sloping ridge and turned off at Shipaulovi it surprised him that there was not a dance or a congregation that he could locate. The inhabitants spread willy-nilly everywhere to the confines of their rock-raised enclosure. The clouds had percolated suddenly and now fulminated into silver and gray sheets. The ethereal colors twined around the stone-jammed houses and turned them into magic hutches in a dry rock kingdom.

He would not presume to ask anyone to explain the lack of activity because he might receive the answer there would be no dance, leaving him stranded. So he wandered about and saw a large kiva with a ladder climbing up from within its deep underground ceremonial chamber. He crossed the rectangular plaza rimmed with sagging adobe houses and a few sapless, sagging wooden benches and instinctively lifted his head abruptly to confront a thrust of eagles. The eagles glared. They hulked there and they flapped their wings and blazed their eyes–a group of eagles on the rooftop–the crucial Hopi element mentioned by the hitchhiker.

He had encountered the omens and they had spelled the place. The eagles appeared black, grey and black, brown, and one had a feathered nodule on its head. When the wind stammered and ushered a fierce blast the great birds' wings inflated and their huge, ponderous bodies surged upward pounding and thrashing the air above the roofs until the wire bands tied to a leg of each bird pulled them rudely down to the dirt roof. The birds shuffled about, tore madly at the wire with beak and claw, and then rekindled by the bristling wind they hopelessly attempted again to mount the sky. For a moment Avery wanted to free the eagles, to cut the wire bands and release them. He looked at a rangy, hysterical eagle who looked back and its eyes tore into him. He felt himself assaulted by a creature who knew its own fate and asked a fellow creature for help. A Hopi man appeared on the rooftop and looked down and Avery moved on.

He passed an old woman with fat cheeks and a shawl and he stopped her.

"Do they dance today?"

She grinned and laughed at him and tiny wrinkles on her face deepened. Avery started to ask again when she spoke.

"Today is last day they dance. They rest and eat now-dance soon."

Avery averted her eyes by looking up. "Ah, the eagles," he indicated.

"Tomorrow in kiva-maybe last day for birds. Pretty soon birds no more fly."

He flinched. To kill eight birds! Then he remembered the anthropologist had said that the transfigured spirit of the birds accompanies the Kachinas to their mountain homes. The spirits only. Their bodies remain behind, dead. It must be so.

The dancers filed in returning to the crumbling plaza from a ravine below. From adjacent areas people flowed into the now active plaza. Avery counted less than five onlookers not Hopi. The dancers came with red, white, green, and black painted leather helmeted masks with tall pointed tablita headdresses, plus moccasins, a fox skin attached to each dance apron, turtle shell rattles tied to muscular calves, and evergreen sprigs and gourd rattles gripped in each hand. A hegemony of gods began to break up the place with sheer power, with religious dedication to the affairs of man-so a bean, a seed of life, will sprout-so a bird species of life will be honored. Men impersonating women kneeled down at intervals and using deer bone scapulars they loudly rubbed wooden rasps with ratchet-like grooves on gourds creating and amplifying a raw, jagged sound. Then the whole group of dancers strung out in a line, revolving, stepping out, opening and closing ranks. The downward motions of arms and legs with piston rapidity and the heavy roll of bodies, all in unison, carried the strength of short, crushing blows. The group intoned a low, soaring guttural hymn that swept over all activities threading the dance like a heartbeat.

The sun traveled in and out of the clouds and Avery felt anointed by the dust and earth and rubble and eagles. Do all paths lead to Hopi? He rejected the idea.

When the dancers retired again to rest he saw the anthropologist huddled in a pose of profundity on a bench at the far end of the plaza. In relationship to the human drama unraveling his advice to Avery seemed trite, as if coming from an uninspired sycophant.

Then he glanced at the eagles. During the dance they had calmly ruffled their feathers between periods of frantic sallies toward freedom. It amazed him how big they actually were–in the sense that no matter how far he distanced himself from them they loomed as dark objects of importance, dense, bulky, and heavy, so easily seen that no one could ignore them. The saying that applied to Christ–He who must die–could also apply to the eagles who must die for the continuance of the Hopi religion.

Avery backed up his car, swung around, and headed out. He purposefully avoided a muddy spot in the road by swerving away and driving between an adobe house and its beehive-shaped oven when a portion of sandy ground gave way and the left side of the car sank to its axle. The car tilted into a soft shoulder of sand. Mired in decay and desperation, Avery knocked at the door of the nearest adobe home.

A thin, ragged little man in Levis appeared and blunted Avery's anger by his docility and regard for his plight. He spoke to a few neighbors who hovered around the stricken vehicle, then evaporated momentarily, and reappeared with boards and picks and shovels. Avery thanked the man and started to help extricate the car when he paused. He asked if the Indian had any old things–pots or baskets. The man said, "Wait." Then he disappeared. His wife replaced him carrying a large orange and yellow ceramic bowl. She extended it to him.

"Too new, it's not old enough–but I think it has a nice design. Thanks!" Avery told her, as he thought the bowl a good thing but not for him, and backed away to the car. Her husband promptly came up and inserted himself in front of her carrying an object. He seemed insistent about what he had.

"This is old, very old," he said slightly defiant.

Avery took it. He held an ancient thick, gray stone pipe bowl, round and smooth and well-executed by primitive tools.

"Where did you get it?" Avery asked.

"Under floor of my house."

Avery liked its heft and size.

"Very old, my father had it–my grandfather smoke it. Old," he repeated.

"How much do you want for it–how many dollars?"

"Five dollars."

"Here you are," Avery opened his wallet and lifted out the bills.

"You got something old," the Hopi man reassured him.

The Hopi man didn't appear to be old, but past his prime. He hesitated while Avery waited. "Near here in shed I have three things," he broke off and nodded to Avery, "and other old thing."

"When can I see them? Now?" Avery queried.

"No, there too much people at dance here. Better tomorrow you come. Be there at my shed," and he pointed, adding slyly, "I have old piece of hide-painted."

Avery's eyes clutched the man with amazement. He said to the Indian, "I'll be at your shed tomorrow morning at eleven o'clock my time."

Nervously elated, Avery debated with himself whether or not he should stop at the store in Polacca. The place would be boarded up today making it difficult to tell if a light shone, and even so, he couldn't determine if the girl who had been inside would be worth the visit. Anyway, he expected the place to be closed. Hungry and excited by the dance he knocked loudly. She opened the door.

He had learned to believe what he saw. No reason for her to be there but she stood before him. He vacillated a second.

She detected his surprise. "Come in, please. You said you'd be back." Her voice quivered quick and soft and thick.

He stepped in, still impressed by her simplicity.

"I didn't see you at the dance," she said pleasantly.

"I didn't see you although there weren't too many people there."

"I was in my grandmother's house looking out," she disclosed, "but I left the dance early."

"To be here," he smiled.

"Yes, I didn't want you to come and nobody here."

"But how did you know I would come?"

"You said you would come," she laughed at his stolidity and he smiled at her sweet credulity.

"Now that I am here I'm gloriously hungry," and he resigned himself to the fact.

104

She continued to laugh. "You're in a store and a store has food." She tested him. "But we don't have hot food."

"Just so it goes down the gullet."

She ran off and brought some tin cups, a pot of coffee, a can of tomatoes, one of peaches, and a tin of soda crackers. She resolutely applied the can opener.

The cracker-jack meal tickled him. The rows of canned food here amounted to what eating is all about–its quintessence. She handed him a cracker with a pile of tomatoes on it and another holding half a peach.

"This is what I've read about what you would typically expect to eat in a trading post on the Navajo reservation. Store merchandise."

"This is not Navajo land. This is Hopi and belongs to the Hopis. This is ours." She seriously reprimanded him.

"What's wrong with Navajo land?" he asked, and she grimaced making a little face. "What happened to you with the Navajos?"

She shrugged. "Oh, I went to the government school with them here at Ganado. It's on Navajo land, not ours." She seemed cold to him.

"Why does it matter whose land it's on?"

"The difference is that myself and another boy were the only Hopis at Ganado school. The difference is that Hopis don't like Navajos and they don't like us. So they attacked us and hit us and beat us, and we fought back. I hit hard pretty well myself," she remembered with satisfaction.

"But why did they do that? Didn't the teachers stop them?"

"One teacher did and he was Navajo. But even if he did try he could not stop them–not Navajos." She shook her head.

"But why?" he repeated.

"They think they are better than us. Navajos own all the land everywhere and try to get from us the little grazing land left around our dry mesas we need to grow corn. Navajos are like you people. They have lots of land but they try to get everybody else's. They are smart but they push too hard and they're greedy. Does that answer you?"

"Heavens, I didn't know anyone could be as bad as us. We swarm the

Navajos and the Navajos swarm you. Everyone has his own pond to lord over except the Hopis and they have the eagles over them."

She pertly cocked her head as he talked and sensed that the reference to the eagles spoke well of her people. She poured boiled coffee from a dented aluminum pot into light, tin cups that instantly took on the coffee's heat.

They drank the hot stuff.

She spoke. "Why are you here at Hopi-to see the dance?"

"I didn't originally plan to come here at all and I didn't know about the dance. I came for none of the good things you have-but by accident," he said lamely.

"Where were you going?" She listened charmingly.

"I was going to a place where there might be material for sale-the old things people made and used, like your sash."

He fingered her sash and its fine weave. She withdrew her stomach suddenly and he heard her short, sharp breaths of excitement.

"Do you like Indian things best?" she asked.

He grinned. "In a way I like them best. I like the religious, generous impulse people associate with the primitive. It involves me because it asks the basic question." He felt foolish for what he said. "Did you know you are called a native aboriginal and you make primitive art?"

She knew what he said sounded complimentary. Her government school had enabled her to understand the gist of most speeches. She gradually inched closer, her breasts free from a brassiere, ballooned out inside her blouse. Slowly she reached somnolently into her bunched, black hair and pulled out a richly wrought silver hair clasp. It shone with stamped designs.

"Here," she barely uttered, "this my grandfather made. He's been dead for twenty-two years. Is this kind of art you want?"

It is doubtful if she had calculated the subsequent effect of her action on Avery. Her hair hailed down its long filaments over her shoulders, around her neck and cheeks. Avery reached out and took the hair clasp and he slid his other hand down her back and inside her blouse.

"Your clasp is better off than on," he murmured.

Her back stiffened and trembled and she heaved forward. His hand slipped around and went between the brown, dilated crests of her body. She let out a cry, a guttural cry, and her body almost snapped in two. She raised herself and fell back upon him. He let her droop and lowered her to the floor. Her skirt went askew and crumpled back over her heaving stomach which set off the brown glaze of her writhing legs. He moved his arm and released the hair clasp from his fingers before he hovered over her.

"Have you ever had a man before?" he asked her.

She nodded.

"How many times?"

She held up her hand, one finger flipped forth and upright.

"How many girls you?"

He laughed at her insistence to be like him. He held up his hand, flipped three fingers. She wouldn't know his lie. In truth Avery could qualify to be more of a virgin than the young Hopi.

"Who was your man?" he demanded.

"He was the boy who fought the Navajos with me. We were hiding from them in one of the rooms and it got cold. We had to hug each other to keep warm. We got warm in our hearts and then we gave in to each other. Only once. That boy always fought for me and I helped him when I could," she emphasized.

"Maybe he should have been your boy."

"No, he would never laugh or joke. He made me sad. He got that way before the Navajos."

He had undone her skirt which lay in a ruffled pile beside a beaded moccasin she had kicked off. She had her hands around his neck and stroked it, glad in her plain indication of love which gave her the support she needed. She watched him anxiously to be sure she pleased him.

"What about a baby?" he demurred. "Can you stop that?"

She shook her head. "I don't care," she said earnestly. He enmeshed her tongue as she flicked it at him, stabbing him, and her head flopped on the floor. She no longer checked his response but her eyes melted and dissolved into her skull-and amid her frenetic movements a rush and quick disintegration receded within them.

After the quieting and a deep lull she put on her skirt and fingered her open blouse. Avery saw that she basked in radiance.

She tried to explain, "It was because you mentioned the eagles-because you jumped to go to the dance-because you didn't mean to come back to the store but, yes, you did. I don't care."

He handed her a cup of lukewarm coffee and he drank his. "No tricky words will work and they sound as cold as this coffee but I've never met anyone who makes me feel so satisfied. You people still keep the dance inside you." He held her in disbelief.

She finished dressing and at quick intervals plunged into him with her eyes, fond and curious.

He questioned her. "Does it matter that you sometimes don't understand me when you basically know everything?" He knew it might.

They had to part, and soon. Her father and uncle would miss her and come looking for her, and besides, he planned to see her the same time tomorrow. They kissed badly as if they were in love.

Sharply at eleven o'clock the next morning Avery honored his rendezvous with the Hopi. He approached the shed but no man appeared. He consulted his watch. He and it agreed that the Indian should be present. No one appeared; the plaza stood empty. How could these people keep time, he thought, when they don't have electricity and electric clocks or telephones? Even if they had watches how would they set them? His man didn't have a watch. He had plenty of turquoise bracelets but he didn't have a watch. He speculated on what eleven o'clock would mean to him. Nothing, he mocked. And yet Avery reflected his own time is store-bought and meaningless-not worth an experience.

He hurried over to the man's house and knocked on the door.

"Come in," the Hopi called out. "I want to get my coat."

Avery obeyed and found himself in a stone house roofed by hand-adzed wooden beams with cut sections of willows placed in between, creating a rich ceiling. The room he found bare except for a venerable wood-burning stove, two box crates, and three children on the floor clutching several Kachina dolls. Avery knew the children regarded the dolls as their play toys and from them they could identify and learn the names of their different gods.

The man scooped something from underneath the floor and stuffed it into a paper bag. Avery stared at the spot in the mud floor. He knew that more objects lurked there. Minor craters in the floor where other heirlooms had been dug up marred a relatively smooth, mud-crust surface. Avery compared himself with the man-they had something in common. The Indian built his functional house over an earlier dwelling creating an underground storehouse of artifacts while he and the blessed Foundation shared a dismal underground vault to house the collection. Good Indian! he thought.

Avery and the man carrying the paper sack came out of the house. The man had no coat with him.

"I waited for you at the shed," Avery fussed.

The man said nothing. "In the morning I brought this bag for you to see some new thing."

"But you said we're going to the shed to get something else," Avery agitated.

"Yes."

As they neared the shed the wan, small-boned man slowed down. "We cannot open shed, my friend. My cousin come to visit me."

Avery observed a young man in blanched Levis by the shed on the edge of the mesa.

"I think my cousin leaves now," he remarked.

Avery looked and the cousin had vanished. But where went the cousin if not to his death on the rocks below? he conjectured. Staring down the mesa Avery saw a pathway of rock-hewn toe-holds for dexterous feet to navigate. The cousin had not perished.

"Do you want use bathroom Hopi way?" his host invited.

"Sure," said Avery, following the Hopi in employing his masculinity and majestically opening his zipper and pouring out his yellow spray that dashed onto the rocks and sandy shallows far below.

The man then opened the shed door padlock and went in while Avery waited outside for the man to make way for him. However Avery stuck his head into the room as the Hopi met him with three good-sized early mineral painted hand-carved wooden Kachinas, displaying simple arms, hands, and sloping shoulders–the old style. They still had their antique color of natural paint. The man beckoned Avery to cover the entrance and conceal them from outsiders while still allowing sufficient light inside.

"You want this?" the man inquired.

"Yes, I like them. How much?"

"Thirty-five dollars each, maybe more."

"Okay, I'll take them."

The man wrapped the figures in some rags and put them in a burlap bag. He asked Avery to carry them.

As soon as the transaction ended he told Avery to get in his car with the burlap bag and wait. During this vigil Avery beheld the man bring three loads of soft drink bottles to the car after depositing the previous paper sack he took with him. Finally he emerged with a fourth box, stopped, locked the shed, and proceeded to the car. Avery had recognized the paper sack, now much amplified in size, among the cartons of bottles. The man got into the car.

They drove down the mesa and Avery felt relieved that he would soon reach the main blacktop highway of Western civilization where he would be free of the village. Just as he had driven down through the steepest part of the mesa the Hopi made a staccato motion with his hand for Avery to veer hard to the left and follow a corkscrew curve.

"On the highway people see us, better we be alone," he advised.

By the time Avery had any bearing he realized that he had moved away from the highway and into a Hopi interior of sand and stone. A few minutes elapsed and he became uneasy and suggested they stop and contend with the paper sack. The man shook his head to the contrary, directing Avery to continue.

The bottom land of soft sand could easily bog down the car, and the road led to an endless confrontation of Hopi dominance without a chance of being rescued. The further he went the more he allowed himself to be in the man's power.

"Why can't we stop?" Avery tersely demanded.

"No, we go on–we get away–no time to stop car."

Fractured by events, Avery began to distrust the man. Where would he take him? Didn't the Hopi ever intend to stop? Why did he carry the cartons of bottles and what had he put in the paper sack? Now he wished he had told Farney where he was going. But then again he remembered he had never put Hopi Pueblo in his itinerary. Somehow he liked the idea that Farney would never find him–know nothing–missing out on events would drive Farney mad.

"We stop here!" Avery said abruptly.

"No, we go on more," the Hopi insisted.

Avery raised his voice, "Why did you bring those bottles in my car?"

"I made old woman that watch us from her house think we go to trading post and trade bottles for money. We fool her."

"We'll halt right now!" Avery said fiercely. "This is enough."

"On that hill. Go there, not much further," and he pointed it out to Avery.

Exasperated, Avery obliged the man who had continually maintained command throughout what Avery now considered an ordeal. When they reached the hill Avery halted the car. "Why this place? Why not any other damn place?"

The Hopi smiled. "We now see five miles around us–everywhere. We try and find hill so nobody can be surprise."

"Alright," Avery went along, but then he bore down, "Now let's see what you have brought."

The sack rested between them but the man did not touch it.

"What's inside?" Avery thrust his hand into one of the sacks and with some difficulty pulled out a large object. Without looking at it he quickly handed it to the Hopi who protested and returned it to Avery.

"You better look."

Avery held in his hand a large, round, painted shield; hardened and thick, it consisted of two layers of hide stitched together, a work he considered extraordinary. He admired it being patina-ridden with wear and handling–in use most probably since the late eighteenth century, and still in relatively good condition.

"Buffalo hide?" he addressed the man, pointing to the piece. "And it's old."

"Buffalo," he nodded, "no one remember how old-before anyone remember."

Avery liked its heft and texture which underscored its wonderfully painted cloud, rain, and sun designs, symbols of the firmament, in reds, yellows, soft greens, and various hues of tan and white. He studied it and decided it could have been traded to the Hopis by the Pueblo Indians.

The man suddenly indicated the other bag. "You look at that."

Avery delved into the quite heavy bag and procured two globular packages, one larger than the other, carefully wrapped in rags which resembled underwear. He took off their wrappings and found two glorious ceramic vessels, an unheard of find because of their rarity, superb execution, condition, and extreme beauty.

"Payupki polychrome jars," he whispered to his soul. He had seen these wares in photographs in a book and he knew they were scarce.

The designs bedazzled him. On an off-orange and yellow cream color base sprang amazing geometric designs-abstract bird, feather, cloud, diamond shapes he could easily detect at a glance-all clustered in subtle patterns and rhythms, yet bold and declarative, an orderly, elegant profusion of forms and symmetry-and genius. Simply masterpieces. The shapes of the jars resembled two truncated cones joined at the base causing a fat paunch in the middle. Like the shield, they exhibited an old style, eighteenth century or even slightly earlier. Amazing-both the large and smaller size vessels comparable to prehistoric Chinese jars.

"I like these, too. They are old pots," Avery broke the silence.

"My grandfather not know pots-he dead forty years; my uncle more old not know pots."

Avery calculated. This man looked easily to be in his fifties and his grandfather and his uncle would be fifty or more years older. The shield and pottery went way back to their early ancestors, and miraculously managed to survive the hammering of time.

"If I would buy the Kachinas, shield, and the pots-all of them-how much would they cost?" Avery calmly sheathed his excitement.

"Museum people want to give me much money, but I do not sell."

"How much?"

The man could hardly reckon the amount. "I want thirty-five dollars each doll and I want thirty dollars for shield-and I dunno for pots right now."

"How about one-hundred dollars for each pot? Okay?"

"Sure."

Avery tabulated the amount and at once realized that the two of them had restricted each other in their freedom to act. The Indian had to sell. He had to sell to him because he did not want to return to the mesa with the artifacts in his hands, even though he owned them and they were his possessions to dispose of as he wished. Avery had become the man's exclusive market. Simultaneously, Avery had to buy because he could not allow the Hopi to be exposed. He took the responsibility. The two of them represented a perfect proof of economics; one had to buy and the other had to sell.

"I will give you what you want and fifty dollars more."

The Hopi waited. "Alright," he said.

Avery gathered sixteen twenty dollar bills plus a ten and a fiver and an extra fifty dollar bill, and gave them to the man.

"How much?" he waved the bills.

Avery explained to him the key: five twenty dollar bills equals one hundred dollars. Sixteen twenties, a ten, one fiver, and in addition fifty dollars.

The Hopi grunted approval.

When Avery started the car he figured it wouldn't work. It would be traumatized by Hopi forces and he would be trapped forever in the Hopi desert. But some Christian God that had stuck to him allied with modern science and together they managed to produce combustion. The engine ignited and Avery rolled down the hill. Guided by the Hopi he reached the highway and at that point decided he had a reasonable chance of remaining intact and getting to some familiar place. When they approached the fork where the dirt road ambled up to the mesa he turned off the road and put on the brakes.

The man scanned the mesa and said, "You go up there? Yes?"

"No," Avery answered, "you walk it alone. Everything will be alright."

"Alright," he said. He shuffled out and waved at Avery as he passed by the car heading toward the village.

Ten miles past Polacca Avery felt in his pocket for a handkerchief and happily fingered the outline of the Hopi girl's silver hair clasp, a clasp that now placed him emotionally in her grasp. He debated whether or not to turn back to see her. But distracted and harried, he had driven by her store and now considered it too late to turn back. He probably made a mistake.

Through his rear view mirror he spied some oddities in the back seat that prompted him to smile off his tension-there lay a heap of soft drink bottles, bagged. When he reached Keams Canyon and Navajo land he had become less involved-the Navajo forces neutralized the Hopis' and he felt at ease. Bless them both.

Avery drove back to Los Angeles and immediately booked a flight for the East Coast. He would soon leave Los Angeles once and for all, he decided. For now he could divide his time between the two coasts as necessary. But on an immediate basis the Hopi items commanded-demanded-his full attention. He placed them in his office as a unit so he could personally commune with them. As an art force they continually pleased and challenged him; they never disappointed him.

Once settled in a nondescript New York hotel Avery made an appointment with Keith Cloudcroft, director of the Connecticut State Museum.

"Even after I left Hopi I felt as if Hopi spirits had been looking over me," Avery joshed and he related his tale in Cloudcroft's office. "I didn't bargain for that trip but I'm glad I took it. After I got back to Los Angeles I beat it here to New York."

"And these are what you obtained?" said the director gazing at three Hopi Kachinas, a shield, two Hopi ceramic jars, and a stone pipe.

"Oh, I got much more but it isn't immediately producible." He pleasantly reflected upon the Hopi girl.

"What?" the director interrupted his scrutiny.

"Alright, what you see there on the table represents what I got."

114

"Oh, I thought perhaps you had something else for me to see."

Mr. Cloudcroft dressed perfectly in a suit and tie. A hat hung from a nearby hook. He had alert, snapping eyes belonging to a youthful frame that had withstood the stresses of some fifty years. A certain aura of exactness and supreme control permeated the man. To him everything had its relative faults and little else, Avery suspected.

"Avery," he deliberated, "I don't know what to say about the articles. I realize you have brought them here as an entertaining look-see and haven't asked for my judgment."

"What bothers you?" Avery asked.

"Well, to me they are sort of a strange crew. They don't exactly add up. Interesting though, and I must say both strangely beguiling and compelling. Avery, why did you choose them?"

"I found them powerful-invigorating and stimulating. They represent a significant culture and they're quite artistic."

"More like artistic chaos, I'd say. But your approach confounds me-a random array of disparate objects certainly strays far from a cohesive, meaningful presentation."

"Just look at them," Avery urged, as he fondly regarded the luminous Kachina figures painted in muted, aged colors.

"I know, Avery, they occupy one's interests but only so far. They don't hold, since to most of us they appear as oddities, actually curiosities, which by the turn of the century they were once regarded. Again, why this miscellaneous selection? Let's face it, the art that definitely commands our attention consists of the pieces that history literally proclaims. Of course that means art such as the Botticellis, Brancusi sculpture, mediaeval glass windows, or Chinese Tang sculpture and painting-the five star items we museum people naturally covet. We can effectively evaluate these in their evolutionary style and context and give them a valid judgment."

"Just look at them!" Avery's tone turned loud and sharp. "There they are, but do you see them beyond your cant and theorizing? You have pigeon-holed these items of material culture to fit your norms and categories, but do you see them? Do you see anything beyond the cliches you entomb them in?

These pieces stand for themselves, each one, because they are intrinsically outstanding and visually rich. Each one. They don't have to be proclaimed by pedants." Avery flushed because he had allowed himself to become emotionally aroused.

"Sorry," he almost whispered.

"As you wish," Cloudcroft rejoined, "I didn't mean to ruffle your feelings. I see I am out of my league here."

9

In New York Avery received a letter from Randolf Farney acknowledging his correspondence about the Hopi articles. Farney waxed enthusiastic about Hopi which surprised him. He even had been there once and he knew the daily spectacle. That's just like Farney, Avery groused, he's been everywhere. Then he mentioned a reference to India, to a collection of a Rajah, a poor spendthrift Rajah who in order to placate the new Indian government, let alone his own subjects, had to get his house in order, and thus wanted to dispose of his collection of luxuries. He may have a group of fine Indian bronzes and stone sculptures. Did Avery want to go? The man lived near Travendum.

Avery wrote back "yes." He rapidly became a global traveler, made possible by the Farney Foundation funds. (Sometimes he found himself thinking irreverently and coining phrases such as the 'Farney Funny Farm Foundation funds.' This seemed to be one of those times.)

Avery's first indoctrination to India centered on Bombay. An enormous city with Indians running it, a bastion of trade flourished in front of Avery. Hawkers and vendors of every description trafficked the streets and boulevards, made splendid bargains, tripled gains, got cheated, hustled to undo bad trades, bustled to compound them: a jabbering, reeling cataclysm of profit-creation. These Indians, shrewd and cunning, became the foremost dealers and traders in whatever colonies they inhabited, while co-mingling with them lingered their opposites, the ascetic, earth-abandoning holy men. Everywhere he had the impression of them both as one statement–glittering delights and richest joys not quite obliterated by the tumors of squalor and starvation. Nowhere did one regard possessions as being so highly prized and worshiped or so lowly spurned and cast aside.

Avery left the airport carrying his suitcase. An official curled his arm up and made a brisk motion over his shoulder. One of the numerous gaunt men hovering nearby jerked forward. "Sahib," he referred to Avery.

"He will take your baggage to a taxi," the official said.

As the bearer crouched there stolidly, Avery noticed that his withered body weighed practically less than the bag.

"I will carry it," Avery informed the official.

"For a few annas it is done. It is the custom here for a Sahib-a right he should expect. It is expected of the Sahib."

"No," Avery said. "I am sorry, no."

"As you wish," the official condescended. "The bearer and rickshaw-wallah cannot eat without annas. Annas are cheap."

"As you wish," Avery countered, "here are some annas for the man, but I want to carry my bag."

The official clipped out a word to the wondering man, gave him the money and waved him away.

The hotel with its white stone exterior blended perfectly with the spacious corridor inside where he stood under huge propeller-driven fans blowing the spirit of Colonial Victorian England. The fans moved the hot air around the guests' and visitors' luxurious saris and white linen suits. Avery liked the fans; in the snug, peacefully heavy atmosphere they symbolized the only revolutionary forces.

In the diningroom Avery encountered a tall, elderly English gentleman whom he had seen lock up a room close to his. The man wore a strange silver ring and Avery asked him about it which prompted him to invite Avery to join him at his table. Gruffly affable, a career soldier, he explained that he had entered His Majesty's army but now had retired. He lived in the Himalayan outpost, Darjeeling, and intended to vacation in Bombay for a spell. Straight, thin, graying, bewhiskered, slow and gracious, Avery thought of him as a colonial knight for the British empire.

His ring proved to be Tibetan, for Mr. Lionel Scott had several times crossed the steppes on a sturdy pony to join the fairs and bazaars of Asiatic nomads and do trade with them. He had brought back with him, he added, a diningroom service set of soft, thick silver, eternally burnished with a muted glow and encrusted with deep red and blue stones, like his ring. Avery could imagine him seated enshrined in his house of long memories perched on the rim of gigantic mountains accompanied by a somber toiling fire that flickered its soul on the soft silver, on the glistening thick tea set and pitchers, bells, and trays.

"You should come to my home and witness the sunrise over the mountains," he advised. "Brandy and the air of Darjeeling mix very well-and the glowing fire . . ."

"And the squalor?" Avery distractedly ventured.

"Not so, at least not to the degree there is in the large cities. In Darjeeling people lead a somewhat pastoral life and there is a free, open spirit. Considering the cool climate it would be impossible to live on the streets-or dirt roads as we have them here."

"What I don't understand is," Avery guided the conversation, "why is there no agitation for change, no explosion of discontent? Fundamental change here is an inching process which is swallowed up and digested so haphazardly that no effect can be noticed."

"You are right in this way," the army man consented. "If we could imagine an open, unguarded warehouse of rice left exposed to the hungry masses of Chinese or almost any other group of people, they would storm it and raid and plunder its contents. But not the masses of India. They would basically resist the temptation and wring their hands and become thinner and expire. This, of course, is an exaggeration, but having made themselves extinct the people would then be entitled to live a new existence in the afterworld."

"If they had a weakness," Avery said, "it might be that they forsake their only real life."

"Oh, I don't know," moderated Mr. Scott. "Perhaps sharing an ideal afterlife while living your present one in hell, like many of us do, is quite plausible and eminently tolerable. Mr. Judson," he bore down grave and austere, "what is your purpose in India?"

Avery didn't feel obliged to answer him, but then the old officer appeared to be so encrusted with justice and benevolence that he decided to tell him. "I am looking for the Rajah Das Gupta of Hyderabad who I understand is staying in Travendum."

"He is, but why should anyone wish to contact that dunderhead? What a vain, witless man."

"He is presumably selling his collection of valuables. I would like to see if they are worth buying."

"He is selling, but who would want any of that claptrap? For years whatever was useless, cheap, worthless, and ugly would be funneled into his muzzle. Although the Rajah bought everything he really had nothing of value. There isn't a better collection of grotesque ivory trinkets in existence, or more toys of pornography. Why, there's a lady friend en route to the Rajah who is staying here at the hotel right now. She is billed as another one of his endless brides to be and is certainly treated as such; she has the best room in the hotel. Since he is adding her to his collection, no wonder he has to sell something."

"Since I must buy art, tip-top art, maybe he will have to sell her as the star of his collection," Avery jested.

Mr. Scott considered Avery. "If you are interested in art I have a friend, an old man like myself, but a respected Hindu, who lives not far from the Ajanta caves in Hyderabad. My friend could be said to be one of the earliest enthusiasts of the caves and one day, sixty years ago, he and a few friends traveled there alone when a thunderstorm broke out. Now my friend's name is Sarath Ghosh, and I can remember him reflecting over his adventure by my fireside in Darjeeling. So when the storm came, Sarath and his party took shelter in one of the caves where he saw a wall painting near the entrance being washed away through repeated buffetings of weather. Sarath, more like an amateur archaeologist, peeled off the layer of painting nearly intact and mounted it adequately and took it away. He intended to preserve the painting until the government authorities would see to it the caves were properly protected and in good hands. However, he became attached to the painting during the long interval, and so far as I know and I'm fairly certain, the painting still remains with him."

"Do you think your friend would be interested in selling it?"

"I do. Mr. Ghosh is ailing and not young; there is every possibility that he will dispose of it. As for the price, that is for the two of you to work out."

"Of course," Avery replied, "and how to get it out of the country would be the next problem."

"That I wouldn't know anything about. Are there export troubles involved?" he asked.

Avery swallowed. Shipping a fresco from the caves which he suspected dated from the second or third century B.C., and harking from the finest Buddhist heritage in India, or for that matter anywhere to be found, would certainly be difficult. He said blithely, "No, it is a matter concerning the customs officials."

"I like your enthusiasm," the older man said, "and Mr. Ghosh will also. When we were young we were true explorers."

Mr. Scott then explained where his friend lived and volunteered to write a letter of introduction to him in advance. "You can tell me about your trip when you visit me in Darjeeling over some of our tea," he chuckled.

Avery genuinely thanked him.

"Just one more word. Be sure to mention my name and our conversation, just in case the letter doesn't arrive. It's quite important."

Forced to wait two days until Scott's letter would reach his friend, Avery waded into the maelstrom of the city intending to visit the ancient sculpture at Elephanta Caves on a nearby island. He watched a group of large crows rim the buildings, perch and hover and perch again as if they had a presentiment as to which one of the unseemly living below would soon be dead. They were waiting to scavenge whoever qualified.

Across the street a taxi bogged down. Hotel-employed drones loaded it with baggage and pretty boxes and flowers, and a number of well-wishers professionally performed their duty of sending it off. As Avery approached a din of honking arose from the thwarted traffic trapped behind. He swung along his suitcase, now safely grooved in his hand as a part of his might, and peered into the cab. Seated graciously in back and dusting off her admirers sat Duskyanne Reef.

Duskyanne!

Quickly, deftly, he opened the car door and vaulted inside just as the taxi spurted ahead into the streaming traffic.

Duskyanne jumped to one side of the cab and at the same time started to cry out when she recognized Avery. She looked at him with a hard-set face. Avery feared the worst. She started to speak and then changed her mind. Avery witnessed her emotional metamorphosis: she began to laugh.

"It's perfect–perfectly perfect. You are absolutely the right one for me at this moment–pointedly perfect," and she sat there calmly, not resisting him. "Extraordinary timing," she continued, and she began to gather her disconnected spirits. "Of course, you always excelled in popping up unannounced, but on this occasion you have outdone yourself. For awhile I have a large amount of time for you–just so you amuse me."

"Like you did at the cafe in London," he bristled. He surprised himself that any bitterness could remain on this historically momentous occasion. Now he could be certain–like a vine he would somehow always be entangled with her. "But I am very happy to be here with you."

"Oh, you have to mention London. What a cumbersome memory you have. That was London and London is over. Perhaps we shall next collide in Tasmania, and I hope you are not going to mention London then?" She puffed at the maverick strands of hair strewn across her brow.

Avery finished summing up her girlish quirk along with a dress of finest Indian silk that caressed the refinements of her figure. "Still, I did get the mask, you know, as I had promised you. And I should be your hero. I also engineered this meeting to thank you." He smiled at his own inanity.

Duskyanne grimaced as she beheld the ill-fated corsage she had crushed while she scuttled away from Avery in the taxi. "It was your coup. On that account I never had any doubt," she said matter-of-factly, "and as for Jabbo and the rest, it might interest you to know that the ruffians have been arrested while working for a neighboring state of my friend the King. And your bravado helped in this case. Congratulations."

The cab driver glanced back for directions, and Duskyanne, resenting his intrusion, waved him away.

"But where are you off to and why the send-off? What a fanfare!"

"It's because I'm being sent off," she laughed, "and you have arrived in time to retrieve me."

Avery observed that she seemed quite comfortable with him now, perhaps flippant, but then that generally had been part of her behavior with him. "I never seem to be 'in time' with you, perhaps until now," he shook his head sadly, "but if I am to play a part in this plot I'd like to know why you are so popular in India. What am I retrieving you from?"

She threw out her voice as if delivering a proclamation. "I am en route to the airport and will fly to Travendum where after a sumptuous marriage ceremony I will be Her Highness, Mrs. Das Gupta. Even more amazing-Mrs. Duskyanne Das Gupta."

"The Rajah!" Avery blurted out. "I know him-or rather about him."

"Then we can be more closely attuned to each other than ever," she darted.

"It's YOU-you who are marrying him! But he is a fool-and continually broke at that. There are those who know him . . ."

She sneered and interrupted him. "With the revenue from his kingdom he had sufficient funds to support me. Remember, there is a royal consistency between an Egyptian king and a rajah."

"Will you stop this insipid jargon! You are about to marry a man-or some facsimile of that-who you don't love and most probably hardly know, and who, if anything, may be distasteful to you. The only good reason to marry him is that you don't have anything else to do and so you want to prove the point that women have the capacity to marry. Who in the hell cares?"

She remained silent for a time. The car sped on and she glanced out but saw only a jumbled flux rippling by her. "I'm in India to marry the Rajah, this time for no other purpose-to marry him," she said fixedly.

"I'm here for the Foundation," he smiled. "I am supposed to evaluate your Rajah's collection but he is bankrupt of good art except for you-his most recent acquisition."

She ignored the last part. "Yes, some of the items he bought from me when he visited Egypt. They were never good in the first place, and he bought anything, by the dozens. Perhaps I can help him now."

Avery adored her when she turned serious, as she did now-very open and alive to what utterly absorbed her, and just a bit naive. "Duskyanne, I have a proposition to make to you. Have you ever been to the Ajanta caves? And even if you have, you haven't been there with me. I have a few days to spare before I attempt to buy a wall painting-a fresco that has been taken off a cave wall and preserved since the turn of the century."

"A third century B.C. Buddha frieze, or those done later by the Jains?" she interjected as her collector's faculties, absorbing random art knowledge, clicked into place.

"Buddhist, the finest. Duskyanne, how in the hell did you get that funny name? It's ridiculous. It reminds me of a Southern belle simmering in magnolia blossoms and crumbling mansions."

She smiled. "I lived in the South until I was twelve, in New Iberia, Louisiana, and I had a cousin my age named Anne who was very fair. We were both named Anne. In order to tell us apart when we were together as babies my mother called me Duskyanne. But-have you given thought to getting the painting out of India? It is not easy," and she became steeped in thought.

"No, I first want to be sure I have it, and if I don't, then there is no use worrying. I'll tell you what. Come with me to Ajanta and we'll survey the place. Then, if your affections doubled for the Rajah, you can go with him. But, if you do, you will marry knowing full well of the greatest lovers in the world painted on the cave walls. Afterwards, if you decide to go third century Buddhist with me we can together finish the business of chaperoning the painting out of the country."

"But I am on my way to the airport," she objected without force.

The driver wheeled about. "Did madam say the airport? We drive around for half hour."

"No! I said, 'nowhere,' and until I say somewhere keep on driving." Her anger jelled into embarrassment.

"We don't very much want to go to the old Rajah rascal, do we? Well then we won't. Driver! Take us to the train station so we can get to the Ajanta caves."

Thoroughly confused, the driver mumbled his consent and steered anew.

"Avery, I intend to marry the Rajah, whether before Ajanta or after Ajanta." She tried to remain stern.

"But how much nicer it is for the lovers of Ajanta to bless you before the wrinkled hand of a dissolute ogre takes over."

"If you don't stop that I will leave now!"

"Alright. For this moment we will clear the deck of the Rajah with all hands."

The taxi swerved into the station, and not until this delectable moment presented itself did a triumphant Avery emerge from the taxi with the girl in hand. They hurried to the waiting train.

Avery bought first-class tickets from the window clerk who told him when he asked what other kinds of tickets existed that he had no other choice because as a Sahib he is expected to fulfill his role and go first class. "Tigers live in that part," he added in benediction.

When they passed the boxcars stuffed with peasants and laborers standing in an almost solid frieze of humanity he realized that outside the protective cloak of his legacy, a "Sahib" could hardly survive.

After a short wait the passengers began to fill the car. Duskyanne settled into a cushioned seat and her whole carriage relaxed and was carried along. It began to get dark outside. She smiled as she observed Avery who became engrossed in absorbing the passengers.

"You never unglue yourself from your surroundings," she teased. "You are in front of every sortie, every twitch and rustle–continually active like a hundred actors changing colors and faces. You actually seem to push events."

So she has been thinking about me, Avery reflected. "Only so far can you push and then circumstances take over and do the work. They brought you here, and I couldn't."

"Like Smedly and the Rajah," she quipped, "and like the Benin mask and now Ajanta. But, Avery, you brewed them. In a way these things never existed before-tangible and potent-until you brought them with you. Even to the Rajah you have brought a change. You are making me see him in some unhappy dimension. You are no doubt correct."

It struck Avery that she had been recreated. A certain warmth and consideration flowed forth. But it also occurred to him that she hadn't changed from being the same female who actually planned to marry the Rajah. "At first I thought you were joking about him."

"No, I am serious," she said candidly. "I've been sort of-restless, non-directed. Not in a good way." She looked away briefly.

Avery wondered if his nemesis, Farney, had anything to do with her restlessness, her non-directedness. He didn't voice the thought, and she continued.

"I had to go somewhere for-reasons-and he, the dear old Rajah, invited me to marry him-a standing invitation. He would provide for me and I would never have to grow old fraying my wits with worry. Oh, stop watching me and stop brooding! He is not that bad. He is funny and sentimental, and when he would go into a pathetic tantrum like a child I wanted to cry or laugh with him."

"But you couldn't talk yourself into joining him. When I found you you let the taxi stall around and . . ."

"It all depends," she interrupted. "I'm beginning to think that the Rajah isn't the man for me. But there have been a few others. And yet, there is only one person-one-who is like you. But there are none with your delightful, unerring meandering. Instead there is sheer dominance, complete and pitiless."

"Farney?" he asked directly.

"Farney-yes," and she nodded her head.

He moved over to her. She cuddled into him and let herself be embraced. "No more kings or rajahs or tycoons," he said. "I'm here."

She remained there a long while and fell asleep under his aegis, and he too dozed off. He woke and curiously observed near-black Indians mingle with those from the north of a slightly off-white color. There existed a sense of restraint, a recognition of a manifest color barrier that plagued both Western

126

and Eastern worlds, but here a fluid courtesy obviously prevailed between them which he liked.

Duskyanne nestled on his lap, over his organ which systematically tensed and jerked. His thoughts focused on the train of Indians in flowing pajamas or immaculately tailored suits, and simultaneously were underscored by her solid supple flesh pressing on his organ sparkling jets of desire. It resembled some order of polyphony where two lines of action are entangled, both clear and delicious and inseparable.

When they reached the hotel they held hands in silence while they ate breakfast, and then boarded the bus to the caves.

"The problem is," Avery mulled it over, "I don't know if the fresco can be bought. My English friend thought I had a good chance."

"Who is the man that owns it?" she asked.

"Mr. Sarath Ghosh."

She smiled. "He is a friend of Das Gupta."

Avery gave a falsetto cough. "End of conversation."

"End of Rajah?" she questioned, but she smiled.

As they rode along she flushed with excitement. "Do you realize that you will be the only one in the world to have a wall painting from Ajanta, the only person to own one-if everything jells?"

"If it does, I'll be the only person to own an original Duskyanne. To keep her I'll put her in a frieze with me and we will eternally love each other. The envious suitors will come and search for you and find only a frieze of figures, and when they are gone we will bloom back to life."

"And the lovers in the frieze always stayed loyal-more so than the boy and girl," she added. "That is the destiny of friezes."

The bus had passed through broken country of rocks and verdant growth when it entered a deep gorge where huge perpendicular rock walls hundreds of feet high swept round it in a semicircle. Immediately Avery spotted the caves in one of the cliff walls. Serenely secluded, they could serve as a haven for Hopis and Buddhists alike, spanned by blood pumped from a kindred heart. Here stood a row of impenetrable cliffs made tractable into a sanctuary by man, aesthetically-religious man. The cave entrances, some simple and staked by columns and others more elaborate with stone grillwork, achieved the balance between man and nature.

Avery took Duskyanne's hand as they descended from the bus and climbed the steps to the caves. The higher up they went the more they sensed the circle of jungle around them exuding an outpouring of flowers and foliage. Only the cliffs resisted the hypnosis of the jungle whose spongy vegetation crept over and claimed each impediment in its course. They could see a torrent of water tumble several levels into the plains below forming a river.

An image of his boyhood on the rooftops came to Avery and he drew Duskyanne to him and held her by her waist. On the neighborhood roofs he as a boy had gazed down at the plaster and cement puzzles of the city. From that vantage point he had maneuvered himself through the maze of human real estate to find his passageway out, never once having been caught down below. Here, he knew that the Buddhist monks had journeyed to Ajanta so as not to be caught at dead-level ground, and had founded a school of living in the caves. They impressed upon the world from a position above or outside; the world did not mold them.

The caves revealed a wealth of stone complexity. Curved inside, Avery and Duskyanne, as lovers to be, beheld gigantic religious shrines along with the monk's monastic quarters. Even though the caves needed no structure or supports the monks complemented them with primitive tools and had laboriously chiseled pillars, capitols, roofs, vaultings, domes, facades, porches, door frames, lintels, elaborate window cutouts, and stone sculpture and bas relief. To Avery they gave birth to a private new world inviolate within the larger one outside, sustained with misery and despair.

"Oh, Avery," Duskyanne cried when she saw on the wall the painting of the great Bodhisattva Padmapani who appeared to move to his own created rhythms assuming the wall as his property; the big charging deity airily emerged in front of them. A necklace hung from his naked upper torso where grace and power became fused to his shoulders. He loomed as a spiritual king, but physically endowed, crowned, holding a lotus blossom as nimbly as a needle. Unabashedly totally masculine, he assumed a graceful feminine trait to complete himself. An ebony princess with flashing eyes gleamed by her sensual lord.

The princesses. Avery watched Duskyanne contemplate them. Statuesque women, instantaneously intelligent and equally sensual, with eyes and brow and bearing exhibiting competence and intellectual power; they depicted young, immediate, joyous girlhood. Full shoulders supported tremulous and opulent breasts that tapered to small wedge-shaped waists, and again ballooned into round and arched buttocks. Avery detected Duskyanne's blood quicken and her face touched with ardor. She quickly glanced down at her own breasts with a smile.

Avery too had been infected with a yearning for the same physical and spiritual satisfaction that emanated from the caves. The insistent surge within him quieted down by the knowledge that he had his own private realm, a hotel room to share with Duskyanne.

Through the columns and porticos wandered Avery with Duskyanne. Elephants, deer, horses, flowers, and geometric designs on pillars, walls and ceilings popped out at them They ran in between columns and flew past a bevy of basking Buddhas carved in a rock slab. Their fingers would run over the sculpture and rivulets of their laughter receded within the caves. Avery noticed at a happy moment Duskyanne embracing a stone pillar and squashing all her consummate softness against the unfeeling coldness. Standing above the cascading stream they watched it perform its seven plunging pirouettes to the gorge below.

Scampering up a steep path leading to the cliff-top they came upon a figure descending toward them. They halted. Gradually an astonishingly handsome girl evolved dressed only in a skirt. They were stunned. For here the past resurrected itself again; the girl could have been one of the stalwart princesses enacting a scene of life in the caves. Her extraordinary figure with its severe waist and high-floating breasts and her great carriage of head steeped with composure were uncanny. Avery and Duskyanne stared as the girl swung away from them and went gliding down to the pooling waters below.

They turned to each other. "The Buddhist monks didn't create in their caves a world solely of their own fiction; the people had been here already," she said.

Avery teased, "I hear that sophisticated men from the cities like to take unspoiled girls from the country and marry them early. The girls are trained to conform to their men's dictates and habits, and that testifies to their noble role in life." The native girl's image still floated before him; her tawny skin color deftly resembled the Hopi girl's.

"But you are not sophisticated enough to lure a country beauty. One of these cultivated men you speak of, I assure you, would not jump into taxis and molest young ladies. You just won't do," and she blew the hair off her temple.

At the hotel, confined to their quarters, they found it difficult at first to adjust to each other. To occupy a room together could normally be handled, but in their case the possibilities so imminent and explosive overwhelmed them. Almost uniquely, Duskyanne smoked nervously until she ran out of cigarettes and refused to send for more. She continually dropped dresses and other attire as she tried to hang them in the closet. Avery watched her and wished for a drink of something but could not command himself to ring the hotel service.

"Are those stylish dresses gifts from the Rajah?" he ventured, needing an entrance which he could find only through discords that would arouse antipathy in both of them, and then perhaps love.

"I told you that I hardly know the Rajah except for our meetings in Egypt where I escorted him on buying trips, on pleasure trips–just on trips. He childishly told me then he would marry me whenever I wished. But he gave that pitch to every pretty girl he met. When I left Egypt I wrote him of his promise and that I had decided to sail to India. When I docked at Bombay he had a whole delegation there to welcome me and proclaim our marriage. He really swept me into all this."

"Would you ever have simply refused him or would you have been so bewildered with modesty that you would have been forced to submit?"

"No, have no fear of that. As you saw and knew in the taxi I was already shrinking from meeting him."

"What must 'pretty girls' perform in order to attract so many potentates to themselves? Does the Rajah receive a 'pretty' kiss?"

"No, I was with the King."

130

"Hah! Hah, I forgot, of course, the King. Kings I believe are higher than rajahs. How picturesque-it belongs on a postcard. The King now clears the deck. And when the King falls, when the kingdom erupts and is on the verge of deposing him, do the 'pretty' skirts that have serviced him flounce up and away when he is undone? What a relief it must be for you that your sweet sacrifice is over."

"You are a sanctimonious, righteous, underbaked dolt!" she cried out and dropped her clothes in a heap. "If you murdered, robbed, or pimped-you would be better than to be so righteous. Do you have that right? Do you have any feelings? Did you want me to cringe before you apologizing that I am not a virgin? Is that what you want to gloat over? I had a King-a human being. What are you?"

"A righteous, miserable sap is as human as a king or an international piece of snatch. You are no better than me either-or worse!" Avery anguished. "I'm sorry. What I did was natural. You've thrown your King up to me so often and rammed him down my gullet that I've vomited him back to you." He pinched his nose and distorted his face. "Ugh, he sure does have an awful taste."

Like a bubble popping she began to laugh and he, infected by it and realizing that he must have been humorous, smiled broadly.

"He does have a bad taste, doesn't he? He's a funny old King now," and she started to be serious, "perhaps a sad dead King. Avery, I did not abandon him because of the impending revolution in his country. THAT I resented most!"

She sank down on the bed where he sat.

"It's hard for you to understand but he once was so different when I first saw him. But you don't know how it was. My family had moved to Egypt when I was a young girl-thirteen. That's when I told you I left the South. Dad had saved some money from the Depression and sold his drugstore. We never felt a pinch of hardship because the town always needed sodas and hairpins and laxatives, and my father owned the drugstore and worked as the only druggist. But he wanted to enjoy his own show for awhile, to wiggle his hips in a rhumba and lie on a white-sand beach and drink absinthe and exchange racy repartee with the foreign colony. My mother had been long bored with growing old and the futility of evoking a satisfying scandal in New Iberia. Both my parents agreed that they would forgive each other their few indulgences which they in turn would now try to enjoy. We had to decide between Majorca or Egypt. Living was so cheap in either that we calculated we were good for five years."

"And it came out Egypt."

"Yes, we arrived in Egypt and it had everything we could hope for. Cairo bristled with bazaars and mosques and included wild scenery and villages in the Sudan and other back country. It turned out to be truly our Mecca. But my father's money ran out sooner than we anticipated, and my mother, at the prospect of working, talked about returning to New Iberia.

"I had finished high school at an English institution and so it was left to me and my father to keep us in Egypt. He started a tourist agency and I scoured the streets to find exotic old objects to decorate the place with. I found items, tourists came, only they did not behave and buy tickets for bus tours, boat trips, or plane berths; they bought the decorations I gathered. I searched and bought more; they bought more, and at least I had found a business while my dad's shrank to nothing."

She propped her hands under her chin and her dress made minute adjustments to her movements.

"Our shop did well; my mother ceased worrying about working and growing old. I learned about Egyptian art, and Near Eastern art, and Far Eastern art, and the various art tributaries that trickle there–from India, Asia, and even Europe.

"One day an official from the National Museum of Arab Art visited the shop and bought a bronze ewer of Sassanian style with the spout in the form of a majestic crowing rooster. He returned repeatedly and soon became our best customer. Then he announced that His Majesty the King turned out to be the buyer of much of the art and would the following day personally inspect the shop's contents.

"Now, the old King who had been patronizing us had just handed over the throne to his son, a young adventurous scamp who it was rumored ate and drank his way though every nightclub in Cairo.

"When the officials arrived we were prepared; my father, mother and I dressed properly for the royal visit of the retired King. My father had been in Egypt just long enough to become confused, and he behaved more like a cross between a Berber and a Louisiana Cajun. Anyway, MY King came instead, the son and now reigning King, and his white uniform contrasted against his olive skin and dark brimming eyes. We were honored and bowed. He was gracious and bought thousands of dollars worth of items. That day my father estimated the amount would allow us to live five more years in Egypt.

"The next time the official came to our place he informed us that the King had actively started the establishment of museums of Arab and Egyptian national character on a level of world significance. Consequently, he would like me to help collect for him and advise him on his museum purchases. His offer surprised me since I had no academic or museum experience. Naturally I was elated and even my parents took delight, although later they were sorry to see me absent so much from the store. My mother replaced me as the shopkeeper. The King issued a standing invitation to my parents to visit the palace. He told them he would allow them access anytime they wished. Sometimes a sweetness came from the King, and doing such a thing for my parents indicated that. He knew the invitation would thrill them and it did.

"Avery, should I be doing this?" She reared up and searched his face. "Is this where we want to go?"

"I want you to go on," he said, "for myself."

She sat up and curled her feet around her, stretching her dress taut in between her knees.

"At first we talked about what his museums lacked and what necessary acquisitions had to be purchased in order to fill important gaps in the collection. He listened in his own way, half wondering why I spouted so many facts as a woman, why I carried on so preoccupied, and didn't laze around and stare and constantly change my costume as he expected of a female. I don't think he knew that I continually did research at several libraries. Actually, he concentrated more on what I didn't say and do, and he was very shy with me. He sensed that my professional pursuit somehow added respect to his kingdom and that pleased him. What I saw was a darling boy my age whose curly hair I wanted to grab so that I could pull down his lips and kiss him over and over.

"Nothing actually changed. He still swam in all his harems and ate and drank himself sick, and he would be absolutely silent during the days he spent with me about any of his nocturnal habits. But a definite element of humor began to engulf us and our suppressed laughs crept into explosions. Then, too, he turned less shy but just as formal, although it was a studied formality following social protocol. I stayed in his service more as a foreign diplomat and not as a dancing girl."

"How did your parents feel?" Avery asked.

"Oh, they were living it up. My mother would say that her life became much more subtle than at the staid old New Iberia Country Club since now it had become so marvelously devious. Mom and dad made it alone and together, and remember, they still made money. They did visit the palace and the King entertained them at a modest party in their honor. They were pretty entertaining themselves. They spoke Cajun to the King and told him they were Cajun royalty. But the King did annoy them. They knew that I had my honor and the King his vice but to them the relationship didn't really jive and simply couldn't be classified. Mom used to call it a perfect limbo.

"They didn't have to be puzzled much longer. The state gave an official function hosting some museum heads and archaeologists and historians of several European countries. A conference took place. The reception included the normal flow of drinks and rich foods, and as usual I drank very little to avoid upsetting social standards–including my own.

"But I had never witnessed my King in his imperial orbit. He drank casks of whiskey and consumed pounds of food. When he got drunk he would eat himself out of that state, and then drink himself back into it, and all the time puffing and sweating and weaving and becoming red and dark like the skin of a plum. I watched fascinated and repelled. He must have known my reaction for he kept away from me and plunged into groups of hulking men who were his companions.

"Finally, I sat wearily down and numbly gazed with wonder at how so many thick limbs and huge soggy torsos could manage to hang there and move without sinking down like a heavy weight at the bottom of a pool. The punch bowl for the ladies looked empty and I started to eat some of the large fruit in the middle of it. The room seemed to be clotted with heat which I imagine came from the steam of our guests' sweat. The silver ladle of the punch bowl clanged to the floor and as I reached for it I saw the King sitting across the room watching me, and not talking so much to the others.

"I noticed the ladies had left without my delivering the usual adieus to them, and then I remained the only woman present. I was tired, yet I seemed to find my second wind. The fruit tasted like an undercurrent of sweet-tangy juices. It had been saturated with potent liqueurs. Although I should have arisen and served new drinks I felt warmhearted for my cozy seat and its soft cushion and couldn't be called upon to leave it. At one point the King got mad at his companions who kept swarming him with camaraderie. I saw him slash his hand, suddenly, against the air like when a king commands in a gesture of dismissal, and I believe he darted a look at me. No one seemed to be cleaning up and the fishbones and carcasses and the heaps of leftovers blocked a clear view across the long table.

"But I saw him, my King, sitting alone, staring at me. He was a man waiting. Just a man. He jerked up and pitched onto the table and knocked down dozens of silver bowls and ladles, causing a noise like the earth fell over and crashed. He stumbled and clutched the table and slowly made his way to me. No protocol could be seen in his eyes and face. That was broken forever. He assumed the royal prerogative. I strangely saw that my gown's shoulder strap had fallen down and I wanted to fix it properly for him–but my hand fumbled around. I tried to scream but my tongue mashed about swollen and I could not. I heaved myself forward and off the couch and he smiled fiercely and tore my dress with his claws as he caught me. Then his paws yanked up my dress and he came down on me. I had what I craved–a royal rape."

Duskyanne rested exhausted from the recollections and the telling of her time with the King. But then she noticed it, touched it. "Darling, you didn't have to take it so–it doesn't mean that much anymore. I was only a very silly girl, totally drunk. It happened many memories ago–now far away from this."

She kept stroking his taut, extended male organ over his trousers. He doubled up and it disappeared. He snapped at the drawstring holding her dress and it billowed out, loose and flowing. She quickly tore at his pants as he broke the snaps of her dress, and they ground into the bed, claiming each other until he turned her onto her back. She lashed out and in an instant she enveloped him with her legs, squeezing against his thighs, putting him off and holding him immobile. Her thighs had an amazing elastic power. He could not, yet, have her. He had to earn her.

He grasped her head and shook her violently. Curled against her neck her hair was cuffed by the breeze he fanned; her head bobbled and slid and made a blur of tiny movements. She surrendered. Her jaw relaxed and lips budded slightly and her breasts rolled and gathered in density. He moved her up and down and to each side by her shoulders. She was breathing softly, her eyes mushy and relaxed with violent expectation. He wondered if the speed of semen he had ejected equaled the speed of light. He had prevailed as her ruling King after a dynasty had worn away, this woman whom he loved.

She lay in a torpor, endlessly, even after he had seeded her liberally with kisses, which gradually drained into the core of her strength as tiny cartwheels of sensations that shimmered on her until she couldn't bear to have him stop. She revived, and they lolled together on their summit. He hovered over her and continually made contact with her long coastline and its port of entry. She asked for her slip and in its disheveled shape she fit marvelously. Not quite delicate and, yet, not really strong, for him she had the right blend; each compartment of her body flowed together. She lay idle and helpless.

"And the King transplanted his pretty flower into his own royal garden and nourished it to bloom." He turned to her.

"Yes, but it didn't occur that fast. I made frequent visits to the palace and stayed longer. The new protocol dictated that I was his subject and should comply to his wishes which I did unstintingly. My parents saw less and less of me and one day I never came home, nor the day after and the days after that. Until my disappearance it pleased my parents that I had a definite, classifiable association with the King which had its points of social prestige, even if I turned into a courtesan. But when I suddenly vanished they discounted everything and feared that I had been murdered, and yet did not dare inform the police because of my connections with the government.

"They went to the palace, passing through the guards who remembered the "Cajun royalty" and they wandered over the palace. They began to open up every room in search of their daughter. They expected to find opium dens and snake pits and belly dancers, I guess, but they ran into a honeycomb of kitchens and servants' quarters and wine cellars–they disturbed people who went howling away. Then my parents realized that it would be best if they returned home to New Iberia.

"The King met them and sternly ordered them out, and reported that their daughter was well taken care of. My stunned parents wanted to see me, but the guards carried them away from the palace. I learned later that they waited around for me outside the grounds, not believing the King and wailing about their daughter's tragedy. They heard rumors that I would not be released but still they steadfastly stayed on in Egypt. Finally, eights months later they sailed for New Iberia and we have never heard from each other. To them I sort of died."

Avery had the urge to laugh at the caricatures she had unwittingly drawn of her parents, but he stifled the impulse. Instead he asked, "Did you care?"

"No, my darling, I was foolish and I guess cruel. I laughed at their middle class exposure. The King took care of my feelings."

"And your King endured until the country had a fit and saw to it that he and his retinue could no longer be endured." Avery kept a straight face but found humor in the comment, although Duskyanne did not.

"No, I told you about that," she snapped. "What happened had nothing to do with his disfavor with the people. We each had our personal fit."

"A royal fit."

"Let's get this King thing out in the open. We had our different interests– and I had been through the first stage of love."

"Could you speak to him? Did he have anything to say when you were not in his arms?"

"It wasn't that. His charm and kindness and happy mood were enough–at least for a long time."

"Could it be because he was notorious for his wealth of women?" Avery rankled. "Even though you were supposed to be totally his?"

"No, then I liked being cherished best and to be able to talk to him while none of his herd could. And of course I kept busy building up his museums and through me he received lots of honors. Every so often I would have pangs as if I was a common housewife and wanted him instantly for myself. Then I would be jealous of the fifty women who could be with him. Which one was giving him pleasure? But that happened very rarely."

"Did the love run out?" He stopped fondling her and the whole room went blank with stillness. She lay there and quietly rolled away from him.

"The love ran out," she said huskily. "That is the poetic expression. Once I said to him after we'd been swimming in the late afternoon sea–'that I just plunged down to its bottom and pushed up so hard that I pierced the sky and broke its egg yolk sun–and it ran all over me.' For a moment only this sun, an Egyptian sun, flooding me. But even then in the water his mammoth bulk floated like a baby hippo. He often had to be pulled out of the water by attendants, and his ankles were swollen, fleshy puddles. What once had been manly, large breasts became monstrosities of bloated flesh. The more affectionate he grew to me the more he devoured and drank endlessly," and she cringed. "When he would lie over me, rumbling in his red, sick-dark color and out of breath–my King knew not the shape of his death mask–he was already dead to me."

Now Avery didn't have to say another word; they lay quiet and he eased over to her and calmed her. She must have slept. Much later he heard her laugh.

"The Benin mask," she chortled. "You have the Benin mask and none of those asses got it. On your own with a vital little piece of ivory you nailed down the mask."

"How did you find out?"

"Oh, among a den of thieves words are stolen as everything else. Word got around."

"But why did you hand it to me on a platter, a silver platter? Why did you choose me?"

"Actually, I attempted to buy it to sell it again. The King was bankrupt and I had long sold many priceless items from his museums–some of his jewels and his collection of weapons which went to you. These sold often at ridiculous prices to defray his expenses which he could never curb. If the mask could not add to the King's coffers then it should not be bought for any money, especially by fools. I like the underdog, Avery, it's my American heritage, and you were certainly far under everyone else. Besides, because you always needed so much luck, I thought you needed my help."

"But," he chided, "wasn't it because of the champion youth who stormed your heart and conquered a ventricle? Didn't I dent you a little bit?"

"Yes, but now you have the whole heart," and she dived underneath the covers and he met her there.

They left the hotel the following day after they had formed plans. She joined him in his desire to try and secure the wall painting and at first she wanted to accompany him to see Mr. Ghosh. But then it struck her that inasmuch as their foray amounted to a business appointment it might be inappropriate for a duo of lovers to appear at the Hindu's door. The man expected Avery alone as indicated in Mr. Scott's letter. Only Avery could strike the right note. So they decided that while he played the roll of knight errant of art she would collect her belongings at her present hotel and move into a different hotel in Bombay where she would no longer be Mrs. Rajah. There she would wait for Avery. Meanwhile, he had time to make reservations for Darjeeling and take her to visit Mr. Scott there, with or without acquiring the painting. At the station he kissed her with the world at his back, oblivious of India and its outward restraint on such matters.

"And after Darjeeling, I would like to show you the States," he grinned. "We would make a team of splendid Americans."

She frowned, but liked that he thought of 'after' and included her in his plans.

"The States aren't so bad," he resumed, "and some of my best runaway friends come back there. And maybe a Baptist preacher from the South will marry us up."

Her face melted into softer and more youthful gradations. She looked away for a moment although he could see her eyes glistening. She wafted her hair from her face.

"You would care for me—always. You have a sort of old-fashioned gallantry, almost like an unformed boy—loyal and sincere. I like that. Avery, could we be runaways to the North or West and hide from the Baptists?" She smiled.

"Yes," he said, "but now better to leave in triumph," and he kissed her again—a sharp, knowing kiss that had a possessory title on it, and he boarded the train. He quickly gave the man his ticket and slid his suitcase out of the entrance. He turned around. She was sitting on the steps crying.

10

Near the town of Daulatabad in the province of Hyderabad Mr. Sarath Ghosh lived in a large white British colonial house. Avery introduced himself as a friend of Lionel Scott to a servant who conveyed the message to Mr. Ghosh, and who as Avery expected immediately came back to fetch Avery for his master. Avery found Mr. Ghosh seated in his study, a short, pudgy brown man, middle-aged, with a head that had the forward thrust and tilt of a pig but which was actually pleasantly arresting. His curved nose tapered, his eyes were small and luminous, his lips puckered like a snout, but brushed exquisitely together with flecks of saliva after each word as if they were slightly stuck. On his small peaked dome straggled a scant amount of dark hair and over it rested a bucket-shaped hat with a tassel.

Everything seemed to be conducted in slow motion in a by-gone era. Mr. Ghosh graciously asked his guest to be seated and ordered his servant to bring refreshments. Avery took pleasure in the house and study lined with books. The establishment had the aura of a library, of sweet smelling, incense-flavored, rich leather-bound books. Mr. Ghosh had long ago wedged himself between his volumes and shared whatever resided in their domain with others.

"Mr. Scott is a good friend of mine," he said shyly. "I have just received a note from him informing me of your arrival."

"He has been very kind to give me your name. Did he tell you the purpose of my coming?"

"No, he said you would explain what you wanted," and Mr. Ghosh accented his coated words so softly and sweetly that Avery felt he could stay forever, which at the same time he considered violently contrary to his intentions.

"Mr. Scott told me that you have an Ajanta wall painting which has been in your possession for a long time. I am a collector and would be interested in the piece. Could I possibly see it?"

With murmuring eyes he spoke. "Ah, Mr. Scott told you. Yes, our dear Mr. Scott. Indeed, he told you. He should pay me a visit. I deserve it before I see him at Darjeeling. Yes, I do have the Ajanta painting you have referred to. It is however unfortunate that the painting is stored away after so many years and we will have to wait for some time before it is located."

The servant brought some gin drink to Avery while Mr. Ghosh declined to take any. With impatient resignation Avery ensconced himself into his chair. Mr. Ghosh pushed a plump finger at Avery's glass and said, "Mr. Scott likes this drink and this is what he serves."

Avery acknowledged this politely and said that he had to soon be in Bombay and hoped there would be no serious delay. He asked if he could send a cable to America which would be paid for by the party called. Mr. Ghosh kindly consented and showed Avery the phone. The cablegram went to Farney. Avery informed him that he had found a highly desirable collectible, and did Farney have a way to channel it out of the country? Did he have any business association that would be an aid to them? Avery could be reached at Thomas Cook, Bombay.

When he returned, Mr. Ghosh announced that dinner would be served and asked if Avery wished to wash up. Avery wished to wash up but could not spare the time to eat, but when Mr. Ghosh said that the wall painting had not yet been found, a disheartened Avery had to consent.

During the supper of roast chicken and curried rice Mr. Ghosh asked Avery if Mr. Scott had mentioned whether the wall painting could be for sale. He was curious as to how the subject had arisen.

Avery answered carefully. "Mr. Scott brought up the painting because he thought that since you placed it in storage for so long a time you might consider parting with it. He thought you might sell it."

"Ah, I see," and Mr. Ghosh's lips gently fleshed together. "You've just recently met Mr. Scott and he told you about this matter?"

"Yes, for the first time when he mentioned the painting."

"You will be visiting him in Darjeeling, naturally?"

"He extended me the offer and I would like to accept but I am terribly pressed . . ."

"Oh yes, after dinner we will attend to the painting. My servant informs me that he has unearthed it. And so," he mused, "apparently Mr. Scott will release the painting. He told you that!"

Avery's appetite suddenly improved and the rest of dinner remained a prelude to the painting's unveiling. When they adjourned into the study once more Avery had never been so relieved. The hospitable Mr. Ghosh became unbearably dull, intractably so, and yet he couldn't find any legitimate fault with him.

The servant had rolled out the painting. Surprisingly, it had stayed in superb condition, its layers backed firmly to a strip of oilskin. Avery couldn't quite suppress a smile. It had been worth the wait. He would bring these lovers, a king and consort, to Duskyanne and lay them down before her as his testament to love, a tribute to her. The painting depicted a complete unit, the king being served food by his queen, in rich blues, yellows, greens, and browns, about four feet in length and slightly less in width.

"I like the painting," glowed Avery. "It's much as I had hoped for."

"How so?" inquired Mr. Ghosh.

"It commemorates to me a special coming advent or reunion," and he caught Mr. Ghosh beholding him with startled appreciation.

"I mean an individual relationship of personal significance."

"Can you fathom that much? My, it is hardly possible," he said utterly astonished.

"What are you asking for the painting?" Avery felt he broke the mood too consciously.

"Oh, asking–well, it has long served my spiritual needs and I suppose I should pass it on to another sensitive soul. Let us say that you owe me storage rates for the painting and that I am lending it to you permanently, since one can't really own something spiritual. A thousand pounds will cover my expenses."

"Excellent," and Avery completed the negotiation of pound notes.

"And now I must soon take leave and be on my way to Bombay," said Avery rather spiritedly.

"Oh, there is no need for that," Mr. Ghosh uttered triumphantly. "There is no train leaving tonight; you had better get a good night's rest and be prepared to leave at seven in the morning. Your bed is ready for you and my servant will wake you in time for tomorrow's departure."

"There is no transportation at this time of night, not even in a private car?" Avery despaired. His plans of seeing Duskyanne that night had been irretrievably stymied.

"No, none. Since I am responsible for you I cannot let you out into the night alone," he said persuasively.

"If you say so. But before I leave I want to crate the painting," he protested.

"My servant will have it packed properly for you in a wooden box. Tomorrow we'll see to that, and I will prepare a paper conveying my ownership to you. Come, let us stop worrying and get some sleep. As it is you won't have much."

The servant launched off with Avery.

"Goodnight," Mr. Ghosh called out.

Avery appreciated the room for its same scholarly ascetic personality as the study. Clean, simple, and staffed with books it could have been a nice monastic cell. Elegant silk pajamas with the initials LS had been laid out for him but he decided to sleep in his underclothes. Although he regarded Mr. Ghosh as the perfect host Avery felt he had a sticky graciousness that covered him like syrup.

As he paused to turn out a small lamp in the corner of the room an old framed sepia photograph attracted him. Pristine and well composed it had the appearance of being in color. Two figures stood in front of a rock opening, and Avery clearly discerned Mr. Sarath Ghosh and Mr. Lionel Scott, and next to them, the Ajanta wall painting spread out. A signed inscription in the corner of the photograph read: "To My Dear Love Lionel, may this fresco, my gift to you as a love trophy, serve as a testament of the eternal bond between us," and across it waltzed the signature of Mr. Ghosh. Once Scott who was the defacto owner agreed to sell the painting it was a foregone conclusion that Mr. Ghosh would agree. It occurred to Avery that he should have associated the LS initial on the pajamas with Lionel Scott earlier. He didn't relish being his host's lover even in absentia.

Avery speculated on what Mr. Ghosh had intended for him to know. The wall painting apparently belonged to Mr. Scott, and consequently it was a foregone conclusion that when he brought up its subject to Avery he was to have it. Only Scott could dispose of this token of their 'eternal devotion.'

So quickly had the servant gathered up Avery and dispatched him through breakfast and onto the train with his newly packaged painting and documents from Mr. Ghosh and Lionel Scott that he scarcely had a chance to scout for his host, although he sensed that he had left the house. Mr. Scott had undoubtedly included in his initial letter to his friend his own legal endorsement.

Avery had decided to first stop at the Cook's agency in Bombay and drop off the painting and pick up any instructions Farney left there for him before going to the hotel and Duskyanne. Since he had lost time he now ruled Darjeeling out. His meeting with Duskyanne would be further delayed because he first wanted to personally dispatch the painting and conduct his business. Once with Duskyanne he anticipated no diversions. The train plodded along and finally jarred into Bombay. From there Avery warded off droves of bearers and rickshaw-wallahs and located a taxi. He held at all times the boxed wall painting tightly under his arm.

He entered Cook's quite late. Almost two days had elapsed since he had been with Duskyanne. He started for the window to check on any messages from Farney when to his complete astonishment there stood Stephanie Farney. She saw him immediately and dashed over before he knew what to do. He really didn't wish to avoid her completely. In fact, he thought it wouldn't be a bad idea to have her around if necessary to complete his business transactions. But he could only spare a brief time now in order to discuss the possibility of having later to deal with the painting at customs.

"Why, Stephanie! What a surprise strolling into you-in India, of all places."

"Avery!" she said with deadly seriousness, and he could foretell a storm impending. "I'm here partly because of the message we received from you-well, at least partly because of that."

"Why, I told Farney to give me any contacts which would help us get clearance for a valuable friend of mine here," and he indicated the boxed painting.

She stood anticipating him, dressed in pearl gray shantung silk, long and elegant. She out-blinked him and hurried to out-think him.

"Avery, Farney sent me to handle the clearance. He told me the correct contact of his to reach, a businessman who manufactures steel. He didn't want our proceedings to be bungled."

"But I just cabled him-only yesterday I sent the wire-he has hardly received it."

"He got it in time for him to order me to intercept you, just barely in time."

"But that is preposterous," he began to quarrel, "I can't operate with all this interference and mystery. I . . ."

"Avery, give me your friend and all I have to do is hand it over to a Cook's agent who is instructed to keep it for the steel manufacturer to handle for us. I have just telephoned him and he'll be here this afternoon. You should be glad that you don't have to fuss with this department of sullied affairs."

He rather begrudgingly delivered the wall painting to her. "I am, Stephanie, but I am not used to these ultra-streamline tactics. Why, next I'll see my mother walking around the corner," and he closely inspected the premises.

She laughed and said goodby to the bank official who deposited the box into the vault. "You see how easy it is. Now where shall we go?"

"Go? Stephanie, let me meet you at . . ."

"No. I don't need to make a hotel reservation yet; we can do that later," and the silence clattered.

He could see her become emotionally undone. She fingered his lapel and trailed her forefinger across the tweed fabric, then dropped her hands. "I don't want to be left alone." She restrained herself. "I am not well."

He waited.

"Won't you please come and talk with me? I have to talk to someone!"

"I can't now-I think I am as desperate as you," and as he looked at her he knew that what he had said had been wrong.

"I know you are going-but I can't let you go!" she said fiercely and without pity for herself. "I didn't come here to do his business-but you can save me-and Farney." She tried to out-brazen the tears that appeared.

Avery realized she knew of his determination to go. He had planned to leave her within the time it took to establish an apology and arrange a future meeting. But it shocked him to see her so wrung out and fallen; all her burning spiritual fire dimmed as she sank to the floor. He encircled her arm and planted his hand firmly on her back. He felt her underclothes and her dress crinkled under his palm.

She was sobbing when he pulled her in front of him and her body, lighter than he had expected, snapped at the shoulder blades while his fingers slipped into her soft flesh. As she arched away from him her chest heaved upwards into small, hard, pitted swells, perfectly outlined now by his fingers catching the stretched material. Holding her for a second, Avery had the sensation that he had recently done this act before, and a tired feeling invaded him. He remembered that different women were convertible, interchangeable-Stephanie and the Hopi girl. Then his spell dissolved when he noticed Stephanie's wanton hair wound up glistening black against his jacket and pouring over his shirt.

"Stephanie, what is wrong? You can't stay here like this. I'll take you to a hotel and come back to see how you are after you have been examined by a doctor."

He struggled with her until they managed to get outside of Cook's, and afterwards he put her into the proverbial taxicab parked in front of the bank. He hesitated because he did not intend to take a place beside her. Now came the opportune moment to excuse himself and break away. She had obviously lied and had secured a hotel because the key to her hotel slid out of her purse. She grabbed his arm and said, "No, please . . .," and he plunged in and gave the driver the hotel address he had noted.

She still could not conduct herself out of the taxi. She had momentarily lost her purse and couldn't remember if she had a coat. She stumbled out and he guided her into the hotel, and still didn't dare let go of her until they entered her room. He sat her down heavily in a chair, and in spite of his chance of leaving her then he couldn't resist the temptation to stay.

"What has happened between you and Farney?"

She lowered her head and spoke as if she disdained all words and reluctantly sloughed them off one by one. "Farney is fine. Farney is fine. Farney is always fine. I am so glad you asked, Mr. Judson."

"Stephanie, make some sense. I am here to try and help you."

Doubled up, barely touching the points of her fingers, she looked away from him and spoke almost incoherently, although he managed to hear her. "Why must I do it? Why? Because he wants it . . ."

"Try to help yourself. Do you want me to call a doctor?"

She turned and thrust her head at him. "Why-you are still here, Mr. Judson? And you know you shouldn't be. Darling Mr. Judson, always so understanding, waiting in the aisle-the helper. Well, the show today is hot and disgusting."

"What is wrong you're wondering? Why, it's simple. Mr. and Mrs. Randolf Farney are running out on each other. The co-founder of our Foundation went to Paris and took a front table at the follies. Three times he made a signal to bid for the elite girl, a golden girl reputed to be a virgin. And rich because of her purity, because like some innocent Little Nell she could refuse offers and collect all the bribe money. But as you know, nothing daunts my husband. He aspires for the best. On the fourth bid he got to speak to her and stuffed one thousand dollars down each of her breasts, and made a date for after the show. He reserved a whole restaurant for her, in fact, offered to buy the restaurant, and they ate alone and danced alone, and he took her into the salon of virgins and he screwed her, and he screwed her, again and again-over and over. And now she owns the restaurant.

"Honest to the hilt, known among business associates as 'Honest Randy,' when he returned he told me how virgin meat tastes and he narrated his exploits-the memoirs of a proud gladiator. But honest again, he assured me that nothing of this scope had happened before, and I was supposed to derive some sort of consolation out of that. Several weeks later my partner for life became sick: he had a rich and glorious case of virgin syphilis, the plebeian disease known as clap, a good old-fashioned dose of it that required hospital treatment. I, as one of his enterprises, sat at home representing all his other enterprises. I, of course, performed efficiently, always trustworthy-his other self. And taking his crap, or clap, whichever way you would have it-and gradually disintegrating.

148

"A week ago he told me all this and he has said nothing else. I am to look after myself," and she launched off the bed and went to Avery, unbuttoning her dress. "Will you look after me, Mr. Judson? Oh, yes, you are already doing that! Then, Avery boy, will you take me, or make me-or break me-the same choice. But first I must let you know-I am not a virgin and I may have syphilis."

She had moved against him so rapidly that he had no time to evade her. She had torn both her dress and slip down over her hips and half fell toward him.

"Suffering virgins," Avery flashed, "I am surrounded by the ghosts of virgins." He scooped her up and pressed her hard, sharp breasts to him and she thrust her hips into him. Avery paused; he gave her a strident appraisal.

Her black hair contrasted against her flawless white skin. Skin only slightly loose and of old tints layered by time, skin when stretched became dotted with porous marks not in keeping with her lean figure. But her breasts were youthfully solid and begged to be fondled, and yet he had begun to lose his desire as he stared bold-faced at her. He asked her to cover herself with her slip.

She said plaintively, "I am sorry. I know how you feel. I shouldn't allow myself to become so rundown. If you want me-I can give you pleasure . . .," and she whirled the slip over her stomach.

Her maneuver allowed Avery to recharge himself. He had a tantalizing measure of insight down a bumptious breast partially covered up. With breasts falling and rolling into the silk cups of her slip he savored and inflated these illusory glimpses into a sensual tantalizing ideal more suggestive than the actual truth.

Also, her pathetic testament made her both appealing to him and at the same time untouchable. Either way he would hurt her. If he did not regard her highly enough to desire her sexually she would be offended, and if he did sexually process her in her disturbed and guilt-ridden state of mind he could psychologically cripple her. In any case, he qualified as the most unlikely therapist to help her.

She suddenly had second thoughts, and fully tried to disengage, but he held her down and uncorked a perfunctory, automatic performance. A minimum performance.

She did not respond, and her eyes grew sad and sadder; she had not enjoyed this act. She had availed herself to no avail. Her eyes looked red but without tears. She immediately put on her dress.

She sat in a chair, so solitary. As Avery watched her he could literally perceive the great grief that came over her. "Why did I do it?" She gently rocked back and forth. "I can never be free from him," she confessed. "I thought I hated him so, and did this stupid act just to spite him. He didn't demand for me to go that far. But I could never really leave him–I was still his."

"Didn't you want me? I thought you liked me!" He felt deceived and hurt.

"You? Oh, yes, you. You are nice. I like you. Perhaps I can learn to love you. But not to sleep with–never that," she said vehemently.

"You said he didn't demand for you to go so far!" Avery flared up, suspicious.

"Yes," she said in an artificial, fluctuating voice, and she paled. "I have done us a wrong, to myself as much as to you. Farney asked me to detain you, to exhibit myself if necessary–but far less than what we did. I intended to do that–invite you–tease–but I am not very good at it. I got mixed up. The thought that he could even further humiliate me–to want me to hold you here so you could not compete with him while he degraded another of his victims is horrible. And so I am further degraded.

"I wanted to hurt him, to punish him badly, but how could I, his dupe, an accomplice, do that? When he sat on my bed and told me that I would have to be the instrument to make his scheme work I knew instantly that I should have to obey him or completely lose him. You can never once cross Farney; you march to his maneuvers and he makes the rules. But I had the one power he could not control, the one freedom that would run counter to his will–I could completely own my body, and if I wished, give myself to another. I loathed doing it–I gave myself to you. But, by God, I detained you, didn't I? He is no doubt finished with his affair by now without you interrupting. Oh, how I have helped and served. And you and I, Avery, are losers."

She twisted her body around at him and a leer crowned her face. "Hurrah for Mrs. Morality! I cannot dare to lose him–yet I have lost him a

150

thousand times-thousands of Farneys lost . . .," and she was left to her bleakest regrets.

Avery had dressed by now and had gone to the door. His face flushed with rising fear and trepidation. The need for great haste consumed him. Detained? Why was 'detained' Stephanie's operative word? He feared the worst, and remembered Duskyanne's teary face in front of the train station. He spoke to Stephanie. "I do not feel sorry for you. Nothing that is basically inert can have the human quality to evoke pity. And yet I do care for you." He almost touched her. "And I know you need very special care. But as you wanted you are in your own hands now. Yes, you have served Farney well, indeed."

As he hurried out and left her Stephanie had fallen onto the floor in a paroxysm of self-inflicted pain. Her nails dug into her hands and had somehow gashed across her cheek, and her wavy, voluminous hair flounced up and down as she repeatedly banged her forehead on the floor.

A taxi providently sped a frantic Avery to the hotel where he and Duskyanne planned to join forces. Her name crowded and consumed his brain. Duskyanne! And again, Duskyanne. He pounded through the entrance doors of the hotel to no avail. He discovered that she had not been there to anyone's knowledge. Certainly she had not registered.

Back he dashed in a taxi a good distance to the hotel where she had her luggage and where he had stayed. A bellboy directed him to her room and as the door remained slightly open he walked in. It had been struck by some holocaust. A lamp had been overturned and the bed was in shambles. Her bed! Half the contents of her purse never made it inside. In the bathroom the water was running and in the cabinet he found a small container which he sniffed. In a panic he rushed to the hotel office and told the personnel what had occurred. He demanded to see Duskyanne.

The hotel official, now quite disturbed, feared that Avery would bring more trouble-trouble enough! Miss Reef had come back to the hotel and claimed her luggage, the man stated. She informed the office that she would dine out and then vacate her hotel room. She returned to the hotel and proceeded to her room, presumably to change and freshen up. Finally, a man called from her room to the office and said that Miss Reef would soon be at the office. For a half an hour he did not heard from her. Finally, the office rang her room and a man answered saying that Miss Reef would be downstairs immediately and that she wished to have a taxi ready for her. Shortly afterward, Miss Reef and her escort descended the stairs. He held her tightly by the arm as he steered her down the steps, her coat tightly drawn across her throat.

The man carried her purse. She did not say a word, and as her bill had already been paid it did not matter. Oh, yes, the hotel owner commented, it seemed as if one of her arms, the one not viced by the gentleman, appeared to be limp and dangled aimlessly. The gentleman looked American, past fifty, and wore a nice blue suit. Because of the circumstances Miss Reef could not tip the porters and waiters with whom she had been exceedingly friendly. He finished his rambling account while hammers peened in Avery's skull.

How could this happen, the manager moaned, when not a sound had been heard? And he continued to worry that if there had been some sort of struggle in his hotel it might receive a bad name, particularly since such a scandal would involve the future wife of His Highness, the Rajah Das Gupta.

Avery brought out the container he had found in the cabinet and brusquely handed it to the man. Couldn't he smell it? Didn't he realize that it smelled strongly of drugs. Did he understand? Obviously, he didn't. It's Farney. The hotel man apologized and disavowed any responsibility. Farney! And that said it all. If Avery could rummage through India's every tiger den and jungle temple he would not find Duskyanne, not if he knew and he knew very well-Farney. Although he had promised a thousand times to weld Duskyanne to his own body he had again let her go and lost her. It would be no easy task to brook Farney, thwart him, let alone kill him. It occurred to Avery that all the things he craved came to him so easily except those that were important. He had the Benin mask and now the Ajanta cave wall painting, and in a way he had little or nothing.

Back in New York he stalked Farney, checked the daily list of passengers entering the States, and lay in wait for him. He even had been accused of night-prowling for pacing his hotel room late at night, and had been evicted from the hotel because of the complaint of the occupant of the room below.

Avery bought a knife, a common, ugly knife that opened up to a five inch blade. It would serve his purpose.

Farney came in on a plane. Avery knew in advance the schedule and watched him land and exit and walk up the ramp. He followed him while he retrieved his baggage and pursued him, taxi against taxi until Farney stopped at his hotel. When Farney went in Avery stayed just behind, out of sight, and Avery observed him check in. He relished the dexterity of his cloak and dagger ramble as he snaked along corridors, sighting his prey to his room.

Farney opened the door and Avery walked in. Farney showed no surprise and he closed the door and faced Avery. Very calmly, as if any sudden move would precipitate a violent reaction from a dangerous animal, Farney walked over to a table and put down his briefcase.

Farney then spoke. "We should have had this talk before about Duskyanne. We both knew that two inevitable results would occur–one desirable and fulfilling for you–or the other your failure with her. You're here because of the other. I don't blame you. It fits perfectly. You've lost, and I'm the one to be censured, oh, for maltreating my wife and abducting girls, and in general, for being grotesque–like that little shuffling motion you're doing with your fist making your hand look gnarled. Well, then use it–stab me." Moderately annoyed and perturbed, he spoke in quiet, driven anger, blistering with burnt out disgust.

His cocked fist checked by his side, Avery stepped up closer.

"It doesn't matter how I murder you, Farney, and I have several ways – whether my arms are crooked ugly, or my fingers wet slugs, they have only this one purpose. Did you have to drug her? Did you have to twist her arm behind her back? Why not kill her? Why not stuff her for the Foundation so you can always gorge on her? Perfectly Farneyesque. A credo of absolute crimes that end now . . .," and he moved menacingly toward Farney.

"Avery, to be born is a crime, in a sense, to be ravaged with waste, boredom and unfulfillment . My 'credo,' you say? My life of short measure–a scientific accident–is how to be done with it. I think I have no choice but to try everything. Every damn thing. Even your being a sort of shuffling pugilist adds a certain dimension to you that I like."

"Farney, nothing you say is getting you out of this. No matter how much you have been steeped in the slime of your own ego you are no better than any of us."

"Too true. I am only one life, and whether you see that I am cut down to nothing now, or it happens later, I can never be satisfied. For all I will know is how much I have missed. And not even that–I will have to guess at that. And so I carry an abacus with me," and he produced a miniature abacus, "and each move I make, each breath I take, and this may be my last, I add to the score one more and go on. Here, take it; you could use it."

Avery fiercely declined. "And Duskyanne?" he growled. "What is she in your pressure cooker?"

"Duskyanne is a relationship–a simply lovely relationship. And I enjoy that too until the workings of each partner reach the best of both, and then I move on. It's a numbers game of illusions. In science it's a mathematical equation with infinite digits. But for me to savor both quality as well as quantity my personal abacus will do the trick. It allows for orderly changes."

"You wouldn't know anything about those qualities you are so consumed with yourself."

"Not quite so. I have been open, even my pores are fully open to it all. Wherever my business takes me, which is almost everywhere, I have quickly closed shop to hear an organ recital in a medieval church or to hear one give a sermon of John Donne's. For an African village resembling a bunch of cupcakes an executive meeting is canceled; for a medieval town tumbled about like cubes of sugar a company merger is forfeited. That, Avery, is my credo, or perhaps my libido," he punned, "but what in heaven is yours? We never talk about that. What are you about?"

Throughout what was an ordeal for Avery there persisted the idea that this blue-suited man was an ordained minister spreading his church. And like a church its idea could not be eradicated since it had already infected him and he had to contend with it. It did not amount to just a case of evil-doing, although plenty of that existed in Farney. But, Avery had to repeat to himself, what WAS his own credo? And did he not sin as much for lacking one?

Avery snarled off his bewilderment. "There is one person that matters to me more than all your rot. What have you done to Duskyanne? Where is she?"

"I don't know. After awhile she went off on her own, just like I did. She is quite capable of doing that. In spite of the brutality that you have accused me of there is no way to keep a woman against her will, as you know. Rape, rope, and reason are but pittances to a willful or a willing woman. That Duskyanne hasn't seen you, as far as I am concerned, is not one of my accomplishments or one of my endeavors."

"No, perhaps not," Avery interjected, "but, still it is rather within your credo to take what you want, Farney. We all seem to exist to fill it out for you. But now I don't think killing you would accomplish anything but to give you a sense of pleasure–that you were worthy to be murdered–that you played high, dazzling stakes and finally broke your abacus and could add no more. Then you would be free from all your stench eroding on you. No, better to keep you alive. My credo is not to kill you but to oppose yours."

"Then in order for you to function properly I had better continually diagram in detail to you whatever moves I make. Avery, do you realize that you are useless? I mean this in quite a complimentary manner for you can trap freshets of beauty where I would fumble. But, likewise, you can't be defined as the average man with his needs, hopes, and purposes; that would completely elude you. You wouldn't know where to begin. Look at your name. Judson! Not some common sense name like Johnson or Jackson. But it has to be Judson. God knows where it came from. This is no fault of yours. After all, Avery, thank God the Foundation eternally provides for you."

It was the blood that dripped from Avery's fist, the blood that trickled into his clenched palm and collected there until it filtered out spattering the carpet that suspended momentarily their duo together. The knife he had gripped so tightly had cut deeply into his hand which now turned purple. Farney didn't react but his gaze glided over the pulpy limb onto Avery himself.

"God damn it, Farney! I nearly forgot not to kill you. I nearly forgot the promise I had made to let you play out your own miserable life and wallow in your own disgust." He paused and considered. Murder reconsidered echoes further revenge.

He said in a high exhilarated voice, "And your wife–your wife, Stephanie? Is she waiting for you?"

"Yes, yes, I know her name," he said annoyed, and then with some reflection he continued. "Tomorrow she meets me and we are taking a short trip to upstate New York."

"Then you haven't seen her since India?"

"No," said Farney emphatically.

"Well, I saw her in India."

"Yes, I know, and what do you want to tell me?"

"That your wife is most enjoyable."

"Enjoyable?" Farney cut the words out of the air. "Enjoyable."

"Meaning to enjoy-that she has the capacity to enjoy-and also to be enjoyed-by me. You know the verb: I enjoy, you enjoy, she enjoys. My credo included her. Stephanie's delaying tactic-yours, really, Farney-worked. It kept me away from Duskyanne while you worked her over. But in opposition to you it worked far deeper than you planned, I'm sure." He liked the sexual allusion. "I couldn't go any deeper with her. I hit bottom."

Farney's personage stood out in relief. The severity of his face revealed the toll taken. His cheeks hardened and deepened the sluiceways rimming them, and a tough, hurt and unlistening face repossessed the old, confident one. He buttoned the coat of his suit.

"Is it true?" His voice winced slightly.

"Yes, delightfully true," and Avery managed to contain Farney's insistent eyes, jolted eyes that begged for the facts with no redemption.

"So, " he said, "we partners share mutually our possessions; we add a twist to Faust. We deal in business, art, and moral behavior. Foundations for our Foundation." Farney stood like a soldier at drill.

"It would be best that we were silent partners," Avery said, "that we do our work alone. I do not expect to see you again." As he went out of the room he felt that even Farney regarded his exit to be a blessing, a concession to their human frailties in order to avoid further 'crimes' against each other.

11

*A*very had no difficulty in circumventing Farney. He divided his time primarily between the east and west coasts, never calling either place home. Avery's affairs did not necessitate Farney's presence and he could purchase and collect what he wished since Avery had absolute authority over each decision. Avery corresponded with Stephanie as Farney's secretary, and although they communicated at such intervals when Avery allowed himself to be located they never dealt on a personal basis.

Obviously, the fact of the existence of Duskyanne, the theoretical idea of such an ideal woman hummed and raced its way under the skin of all those parties affected by her. The wound her image caused Avery he carried with him. It would scab over and heal until he next stumbled over some emotional barrier, and then it would fester and break open again. Work served as his balm, not that he engaged in any activities specially dedicated to good works, but work meant to Avery simply that he excelled at it. His new credo translated to perpetual motion.

The Ajanta wall painting added to the prestige of Avery and the Foundation. Already the Foundation had earned considerable recognition as a floating rib of Adam, alias Farney; a first-rate museum very much to be reckoned with. Since it possessed wealth and astute aggressiveness it had begun to attract the attention of museums everywhere, and their directors greeted Avery with mounting welcome. His name appeared regularly in news articles and museum bulletins, and Avery could no longer frequent his old haunts of antique shops as an unknown prospector. Dealers world-wide endlessly offered him their most prized wares for purchase.

Farney garnered credit too as benevolent–as a farsighted elder statesman and mastermind. Often the newspapers and magazines carried an article on the Farneys and a photograph would show both of them smiling and handsome together, a matched set. Calculated circumstances dictated that the Farneys and Avery somehow never presided over the same forum or viewed an exhibition at the same time.

One problem arose that targeted the Foundation and involved Avery. This had been simmering for some time. Farney had taken an art dealer as a partner into an oil operation deal and the oil did not gel. Relative to his normal successes, Farney considered this an unnatural act of God. But the dealer in question did not come up with his portion of the investment and instead offered as collateral a large art collection he had been in the process of acquiring which would be worth twice the amount of money owed Farney. Although Farney as a shrewd businessman disliked sloppy business affairs, and being owed a tidy sum of money disturbed him as a fiscal aberration, he relished the idea that here he could at least indirectly be a factor in acquiring art for the Foundation.

The fact that the proposed collection could be considered a debtor's gift and as such realistically written off as a donation to the Foundation meant to Farney an unwanted but somehow redeeming accident.

Since the collection's arrival could occur soon Avery decided to immediately prepare for its acquisition and storage. Then Stephanie telephoned that affairs had changed and she needed to meet with Avery. He looked forward to seeing her although he was not altogether ready for her. She acted perfectly proper and pleasant, even infectiously appealing, but something appeared to be missing besides the fact that on his part he continued to hurt. She had not really changed and she seemed to be at ease, yet she didn't seem quite right. He could detect that some little compartment within her, an inner recess, didn't light up any longer or open to receive nourishment. She ran on fewer valves; she jetted less fire power.

Stephanie started smoothly into business. "That Spangle fellow, he continues to be a bother; his case never closes. He has neither transferred the money he owes nor the collection to Farney, and it's been ten months since we began dealing with him. Nothing seems to shake him. Randolf had his mind set on taking credit for acquiring some fine Eskimo, Plains and Woodlands Indian material, plus a smattering of old Australian bark paintings and early wooden masks from Java and Sumatra."

"Quite plausible. And yet . . ."

"Farney wants you to check him out-to see if he's real."

"Farney's will shall be carried out," Avery conceded. "But first I must see some old friends of mine-my parents."

Stephanie looked at him sharply. "Speaking of old friends, I just paid Mr. August Darlington a visit. Actually, he asked for you to see him at his shop, and not me. In fact, he insisted on only you. But as usual you couldn't be reached when you had to be and he treated me with rude impatience. He got quite testy about insisting on seeing someone from the Foundation immediately, even though you weren't there. So he made me go to his shop. It looked strange because black blinds had been drawn over the windows, like the shop had a wake-maybe for the ghost of Darlington who seemed to be dragging his last steps. The old man had too much death in him. He had his lawyer, a Mr. Trumbly, who had brought the proper legal papers in order to carry out Darlington's wishes. Darlington said that he had no time for "just plain affairs" and that you would understand what he meant. He wanted to talk to you about art and he didn't want you to think he still coveted the Scythian gold animals either. He said he had gone above that.

"When his lawyer bragged about how amazing that in such a shop his client had made a fortune, Darlington cut him off and said that money didn't interest Avery or the Foundation, just art."

"What did he want?" Avery interjected.

"He claimed that the time had come for him to assert himself, and his lawyer would explain in terms the Foundation would prefer to hear. Then Mr. Trumbly rattled off that his client had bequeathed to the Foundation the entire shop and all its goods and contents, and he produced some documents which he drew up for my perusal.

"Oh, Avery, even I could tell when I looked around the place that he had stocked it in mediocrity-so dreary. Surely Darlington stood for more than this residue of mistakes. When I drew a blank, because I could see nothing to choose from, Darlington intoned, 'It's for the Foundation' and his lawyer solemnly shook his head. Then, I had an idea that you, Avery, would be proud of. It became obvious that Darlington wanted his art entombed in the Foundation because he felt that he could then lay claim to immortality. Darlington's essence would thus be preserved. So, I thought of a compromise. Alright, I said, let's comply with the spirit of your request. I'll choose one great item, one truly magnificent art object for the Foundation. Wasn't that brilliant of me? But he took it hard.

"He stood there, nasty, and rasped, 'Then choose a great piece.' I glanced around the room and found a charming early music box with a small plumed bird. I turned the key and the bird chirped and sang, turning its head and fluttering its colored wings. Darlington looked aghast and kept on repeating, 'That? Just that!' Despite Darlington's acute disappointment the lawyer ended the meeting by declaring the spirit of his client's contract could be considered fulfilled, and everyone went away and lived happily ever after."

Avery laughed. "Hardly. But now that's settled. Good girl. Now would you like to handle my parents for me?"

"No, I can hardly take care of myself."

"And Farney?" he asked. "How have you two prospered? I don't see him anymore and because of that I miss seeing you."

With all they had both undergone she could be honest. "Oh, Randolf and I travel along the same paths and yet do not bump into each other. I guess we know how to avoid being injured. We have remained friends."

He ventured: "Have you ever thought what it would be like if you were to be without him? No Farney-just Stephanie on her own?"

She looked so pained that he ceased. "No Farney," she spoke softly, "it's impossible. For those moments-few as they are now-I live for them. But I shouldn't-and I can't." She shuddered.

"Even I can't imagine 'no Farney,'" he said ruefully. "It's a notion that's impossible for me to conceive, like losing thunder and lightening. He has formed both of us."

"The way you described him is not what he thinks of you," she answered. "He feels beholden to you as you indicate you are to him. He has told me so-that you are vital to him–that you had to exist or had to be invented. So you are also some kind of structure to him."

"Pure Farney," Avery replied. "We serve only as supportive beams to hold up his edifice. But thank you anyway. I feel better. I am a noble cog. But if I am not the balance wheel to his watch, or some jewels, at least I would like to think that I'm the mainspring. So, Stephanie, I appreciate your kind defense of me."

She arose. "It seems like Farney has as usual usurped our conversation," she noted. "He has certainly kept me on a tight schedule. I am to meet him tonight. But I am glad that I could be of help to you," and she mustered a laugh, "even though you really don't seem to need it. Now that you are a model for people to aspire to–poor old Darlington."

And they both laughed, were happy to laugh, as they went out together to go their separate ways.

He waited in front of the Golden Heights Country Club, surrounded by the lush, cultivated ambiance overlooking Beverly Glen, until his parents drove up. Appraising the luxurious Cadillac, Avery chuckled that the old fellow still enjoyed a fine lifestyle. Then the old fellow got out and came over to him. He looked older and thinner but scarcely different from his usual well-groomed and precise self. "Let's go in," he said dryly.

"Avery, my son," and his mother moved quickly toward him. "I am so happy that you're in Los Angeles again, regardless of how brief your stay may be. It is so good to see you." She had prospered less well; it had been harder for her to maintain her brittle, nervous prettiness. Now she looked too thin. Her expensive, silk sheath dress emphasized her boniness. "I've missed you," she fluttered. "Your father and I often talk about you."

"She does most of the talking," Mr. Judson quipped and led them into the diningroom.

As he entered he noticed the elaborate buffet and ruefully worried that the dinner would be a long affair. His mother started to direct the conversation as if it could only be safe in her skillful hands.

"I wonder if you would like our apartment. Your father is retired now and we thought we didn't need the big house since you were not with us. Besides, I never did like the neighborhood, especially now; it never upgraded itself."

Mr. Judson detached himself from the table and announced that he intended to go for his food. His mother detained Avery by pressing his hand to the table. "Your father didn't want to sell the business. He saw no reason to let it go when it could operate practically on its own."

"Perhaps he meant for me to operate it?"

"I am glad you didn't. You are completely different. You are more like an artist. Anyone can be a businessman."

"But not me, mother. Remember, I was the one who couldn't make it."

"No, don't be silly. Your profession is distinguished. Fascinating. I wish I could have watched you while you were receiving all those honors. However, I suppose I shall be happy in the new apartment. You know something strange? Your father didn't want to sell the old house."

"Why not?"

"I suppose he was used to it. He said he didn't see any necessity to move; he was perfectly comfortable. Even I have fits of nostalgia. Avery, do you remember how you used to make special spears out of a special bush of palm root? When you had pulled them all out of the ground you went everywhere to find more, but you never did."

"That was long ago and I'd rather talk about . . ."

"And you used to practice dying-a hundred times a day. It took you the whole length of the livingroom before you finally clutched yourself and died."

"Mother!"

"Do you remember? And the rooftops? Do you . . .?"

Mr. Judson had been standing with his plate of food in hand a few steps in back of her. "Will you quit whining over him?" and he sat down at the table. "He doesn't like it and he never will. You tell yourself you must achieve the perfect understanding. You hope-hope-that he will change and be your boy again. But that will never happen."

"Alright, we know what you think." She resented what he had said. "Let us hear what Avery has to say."

"Well, what does he have to say? I'd like to know."

"I am glad to see you two. I don't want to be the cause of any friction between you. We have for a long time established our own lives. Father is right; years ago I stopped being a boy. I enjoy my profession just as you did your business," and he turned to his father.

"My business, you say? You put everything so neatly. You defamed my business—my business and our lives you deride."

"I have a great deal of res . . ."

"Your profession, hell!" he accelerated. "What is your profession? Still a glorified window dresser. Window dressing the world with rubbish. Have you ever had a decent job? No! Why, that precious Foundation of yours has put you on perpetual dole–a foundation fed by a sex maniac millionaire. To me you're Farney's pimp–pimping art for him."

He had already considered that and rejected it. Farney had alluded to the same thing. Who pimped for whom? Sometimes he thought that Farney got the shaft. He got up.

"Stop it!" she glared at her husband. "I have listened to you for forty years and you are a bore. And you are now driving him away from me." And she added ominously, "But in spite of you someday I will have my son back."

Avery stood transfixed. She pathetically would be the one less durable. Her frail charm burned in anguish and despair and by degrees would become eradicated into a face of crinkled blank paper. He nodded his head to them, and at that moment they ceased fighting and remained still like figures in a wax museum. He found his way out without having eaten any dinner.

Avery slipped away early the next morning before sunup. He had a whim that kept percolating until finally it possessed him. He drove into the Southwest and stopped at the great churches at Laguna and Acoma Indian Pueblos, and as he fathomed them he knew he could be comfortable here within the huge, thick adobe walls and under the long, rough-hewn log rafters leading to religious altars. The adobe churches offered a comfort he had not known since the caves at Ajanta. He plunged further into Navajo land and here and there he could see horses tied up, sleds, blankets drying outside, shacks, cabins, and groups of hogans. When a modern schoolhouse popped up it astonished Avery. Where did its students come from? Then he remembered the random sprinkling of hogans he had seen. The scattered settlements had added up miles later to a school.

The terrain changed from the flat desert to the higher, cliff-rimmed desert. More clouds whipped up and so did doubt within Avery. Should he be there on impulse? He took a bead on First Mesa, and soon arriving at its base where the road coiled to the summit he swerved away into Polacca. There he saw the trading post after some years; trading posts rarely grow older; they are already old to start with.

He ringed it now with increased apprehension. Unbelievably, he could spot her through the half-open door at the counter; she stood with a customer. Encouraged by her physical fact he invaded. In a flash she saw him and flushed with poised excitement, but hardly discernibly. She rushed to conclude her enterprise of selling and yet remained reluctant to dispose of the customer as her means of shielding the two of them from being alone together. She looked considerably better, actually striking, much fuller, more shapely. She moved proudly and her movements were strong and sure.

He out-waited the transaction, waited through her packing the gift and sorting the change, and at last she had to confront him She even allowed him a shy gesture of delicate restraint that he wanted. She didn't appear awkward and she sweetly went to him and extended her hand to him as a friend.

"I have thought about you; many times I have done that–but it's funny. We do not even know each other's names. We should have a new meeting. The time is new. My name is Katy."

"And mine is Avery Judson, and I've always wanted to meet you. You have been in my dreams too."

She gathered in the minutes slowly and smiled warmly. "You have kept your habit of coming at closing time. We can lock up and go somewhere." She did not raise a question or give a preference but rather she offered a tentative possibility.

164

"Store's closed; ring the cash register," Avery proclaimed. "I would like to go with you anywhere."

She closed the door and outside they hesitated.

"Where do you want to go?" she asked.

"Oh, anywhere-up there," and he flicked his hand and realized that he had marked out First Mesa. "Yes." He showed his eagerness. "Let's go up there."

They drove up past the structures of stone and twisted up higher until they breasted a level nest of houses and people, an extended backyard and playground. They drove along the rim engaging dogs and disturbing chickens and parked near the edge where they could peer down its side.

Avery smiled inwardly. "Now I have my ideal rooftop."

"We have ladders to the roofs of our houses," she tried to enlighten him in her sensible manner.

She pleased him. "Your ladders often stick up above the rooftops and it seems they continue like invisible tracks to heaven."

"They stick out because they have to and there is nowhere else for them to go," she said rationally, drifting with the space-enfolding space concept. "Why did you come back?"

Avery avoided her consuming stare and set his sights on two distant mountain peaks. "Because I have to . . ."

"No, I don't think you came back because your heart could not go other places-any place if you want to. You did not have to come here."

He did not contest her; she had hold of the truth.

"I came here because I thought of you and wondered how you were now."

"Yes and no," she corrected him. "You do not want to quickly swallow up everything in front of you so much now. And you have slowed down and come back here. You are not the same. I am that way, too. I am different." She waited for him to respond.

"Katy, we both are different now. No, I'll use your words-have 'slowed down.' But you are a lovely woman. You have not lost anything."

"You have come back," she said, content with such a singular occurrence and trusting in it. "I remember you asked many questions. You talked about

165

the eagles. You talked about me, and I told you things no one else knows about me. I like to think about what you talk about-I have lots to do then."

He made a movement toward her.

"No, not here! Not now," she said.

He knew so-in Hopi, and he hung back. "We could go somewhere-to Chaco Canyon-or somewhere."

"Yes," she said, thinking out loud. "Maybe I could go there with you. I must tell my parents something." She pierced him with a look. "I want to do this. Even if it makes no sense. You are here. You came back. I will meet you at Keams Canyon Post tonight. Take me back now."

He viewed her with awe. "I am glad to be back-even if nothing like this happened-I would be glad to be here."

He drove her to Polacca and she jumped out without a word.

At ten o'clock she waited at the Post where he picked her up. A little black suitcase nestled in her hand and she had on a coat over a white blouse. The blouse shone immaculately clean and black braids swung behind her.

"I told my parents I will be back in three days."

"I am thankful for three days, but what did you tell them?"

"Only that I need to be away for three days or I would be very sad. They don't want me that way. They let me come."

On the highway they talked little. He put his arm around her but she sat stiff and straight, yet within her self-controlled composure she relaxed. He didn't have to talk to her; she was there for him. He drove into Gallup.

"We had better stop here for tonight," he said. "I understand the road to Chaco is poor and will be hard to follow."

She didn't hesitate. "Alright. It's more pretty to see it when there is light."

They stopped at a nondescript motel and she carefully emptied her little metal suitcase and put everything tidily away.

"You can't go to bed," he bantered. "Even though you have a toothbrush, you don't have a nightgown."

"I have my best slip," she said seriously.

"But that won't allow you into bed," he smiled and brought her over to him. "Were you faithful to me?" he asked her.

"I was," she answered, "but you men shouldn't ask that-you are not faithful-you said you were with three ladies first."

"I said it, but I didn't tell the truth. I was embarrassed. You were my first woman-really."

"I knew that. You were a poor, nice boy," and she lay on his lap, "and I liked you because you said that but didn't mean that. I was first loved before you were, I guess."

He laughed. "I was a virgin. It seems that I must always first bring up that subject."

"Like our Virgin Mary we have in church?"

"Yes, like her, only she had a baby who became famous."

"I had a baby."

"What? With me? My baby?"

Avery sat there in a daze. "Are you alright?" he asked her.

It struck her as funny. "Oh, it happened some time ago."

"No wonder you look different," he said admiringly. "You had a baby."

She was puzzled. "I am glad my baby helps me be different."

He couldn't explain to her; he hardly knew himself. "You are prettier," he told her.

She liked it, and lying in his lap she watched him preside over her. She closed one eye, and then closed the other.

"What are you doing?" he asked.

"I am seeing you-two of you. They are different."

"You are the Hopi psychoanalyst-very magical."

"One of you jumps to this side when I close my eye and there's another you jumping away when I close my other eye. They are afraid of each other."

"One of me likes to be here with you in an ugly motel and talk about a baby and our first loves and do nothing in particular but everything in reality. The other self . . ."

"Goes far away," she interrupted.

"Floats away," he added, "to snag wondrous art items all over the world."

"Well, we're here," she said.

"Yes," he agreed and they slipped into each other, "fantastically here."

He kept on thinking of the baby while she warmly caressed him and firmly, deeply met him halfway. Her breasts were bigger, he thought, because of the baby, because of the milk she had to feed it. Her waist and stomach and buttocks were broader and more womanly because of the baby, because it had pushed through her making her all over again. Making her all over to love him with an insistent yearning desire which she fully displayed that night to her second lover.

Katy took care not to wrinkle her cheap cotton blouse that stayed so white. She laid it neatly on a new flimsy purple table that supported a hideous lamp emblazoned with black and gold plastic spangles. Love against a mucous-hued wall and over a chartreuse gold-threaded carpet and witnessed by cheap off-violet drapes. To Avery it seemed sad and humorous, and he detachedly considered it marvelous. He missed the Gideon Bible.

She cherished further endearments, hugs, cheeks closely pressed, and eyes staring into each other's only inches away. When they slept she wanted his hand draped over her waist or chest, claiming her. She could be at ease only if she pillowed on him and he, in turn, felt at ease for the first time in his life.

It stayed simple. They dressed after she used the shower which she didn't have at Hopi. They chose the nearest cafe, a rundown one with sawdust on the floor–but no chartreuse or purple. At a seamy counter they ordered their breakfasts, he a green chili hamburger and she a red chili omelette. They drifted out with strands of coffee-gulpers rushing to their work, the abject bums, and the Indians–Navajo Indians everywhere.

"Now you are outnumbered," he kidded her. "Gallup is a Navajo town. They better not know you are Hopi."

She smiled, but still did not like meeting Navajos everywhere. "Are there not Navajos in other countries?" she asked. "I know they will not be at Chaco Canyon. Only our ancestors are there."

They walked past pawnshops and across the railroad tracks which partitioned the town into good and bad. Freight trains lay stacked about. They all defined a Western town, an Indian town, and a railroad town. Avery witnessed the daily scene. Where he and Katy went Indian traders and their wholesale stores thrived. Cheap grocery stores and tattered shacks selling odds and ends and drunk Indians frequenting doorways created a curious, somber atmosphere. But the Indians preferred to be quiet in their dealings, whether of the old or new generation. The turmoil of these people who now depended on the city and who had been weaned away from their giant, open homeland now channeled their dejections privately inside rooms or meeting places or in their hearts.

Rough and circuitous, the dirt road to Chaco lived up to Avery's expectations as they bumped and jarred through barren dry stretches until they finally arrived where Katy's ancestors had lived.

The canyon had been gashed by a sunken river long dried up. The ancient city lay beyond revealing citadels of large rock dwellings. Huge complexes of houses, once many stories high which enclosed a group of ceremonial kivas bloomed from a now existent no-man's land. The two of them stopped and reviewed the tribute of work in stone. Masonry, fitted tightly together into patterns with rocks as tools, formed enormous walls conceived by an ancient communal mind.

She pertly said, "I'm glad there are no Navajos here. You can feel a nice spirit-a spirit that's peaceful. Navajos only build dumpy little houses that look like mud pies."

In a way her delicious pride could be historically verified; the Navajos as nomads and raiders continually roamed while her forebears as sedentary farmers organized this complex city.

"Yes," he acknowledged, "this is the place where maybe your grandfather's grandfather and even further back-where they lived as farmers and artisans. He helped build a city and happily started what many, many grandfathers later sprouted into a peaceful, kind Katy."

She shrank into shyness at his words. She took his hand. They climbed over serrations of rocks onto a long wall and gazed down at circular kivas and narrow passageways opening up into larger rooms-spacious and comfortable.

"When the river once was full this must have been a lush valley for growing crops," he called across to her as each sat on walls opposite each other, dangling their legs over the rims. Even the space between belonged to them both.

They camped out in the night. She had provided for it and brought some meat and a grill and coffee. He had brought a coffee pot and blankets in his car anticipating an overnight camping stop. He had not expected the night to be so warm, and entwined with him she created more warmth. She patiently watched him light a fire, a feat he accomplished without mishap.

"Prehistoric man couldn't start a fire better," he half joked.

She replied, "Maybe he lit it much faster."

He liked her quip.

"What kind of meat?" he asked.

"Mutton."

"Mutton-old lamb? I mean old sheep. I know about mutton," he said assuredly.

"Sheep about one year old-just right. We eat it at Hopi lots. Makes good stews," she said.

"The same way the Spanish like it, and I think as good as lamb if cooked right." He finished eating it before she had hardly begun which tickled her. "My first real conversion," and he licked his lips."You know," he decided to rile her, "Navajos eat lots of mutton."

She tossed her head. "Try to find a Navajo here to sleep with."

"I guess a Hopi will have to do," he answered.

She cleaned up by the stream and they stretched out on the blankets. She sat up and smothered the embers with handfuls of sand and remained there after the fire went out.

"What does the fire think?" he asked her.

She pivoted toward him.

"Thinking about the baby?" he continued.

"No," she grinned, "I have not thought about the baby. He is happy-I know that."

"He?"

"Yes."

"But you were thinking about something."

"Yes," she answered, "I have to go back home tomorrow. It makes three days."

"I am sorry," he answered, saying the meaningless.

"Yes," she said, "I wish I had as many days as you have for me. The little presents you bring me I like-like when you show me things I do not understand and I learn them. All the things you say and do-you make presents out of that."

They stayed in silence until she approached him. "I have been faithful," she said, and in the fullness of her body she proved it again masterfully.

The morning woke them up, found them in a tight grasp as if they feared its rays of ultimate revelation. She did not wear her slip and tiny beads of sweat ran down her breasts and his chest as they broke apart. She fetched her white blouse whose whiteness still remained undiminished, and put it on. They had a breakfast of more mutton and coffee, and ran down the canyon. Avery saw the morning cruel in leveling its theatrical blast on them, revealing their plight of having to leave their sanctuary. They left the golden ruins, hurrying away from them in the sunlight.

When they drove away Avery felt relieved. No obstacle prevented him from establishing a reunion with Katy.

"Do you need anything," he asked her, "for yourself or the boy?-think of the boy," he mused.

"No, we have food and a house and I have work."

"Could I help you in any way?"

"You have already helped me much."

"I mean can I do more?"

She did not answer and Avery knew she would not take his money.

"Are your parents good to you?"

"Yes, they love the baby and are nice to me. They are sad sometimes."

"Do they know about me?"

"I think they do. I had to tell them. But they say nothing. They try not to get me hurt."

"I know I have hurt you."

"No, not that. It's the right kind of hurt. You are like my uncle who was a medicine man and a little crazy. He was serious about what he sees-sometimes many magic things. Sometimes not. When you see that way sometimes in your eyes you dance. You are very wise then. But in between you are silly. You are wise and silly. I like you both ways. I didn't wait for you, though I thought lots about you. So I guess I waited."

When they reached Hopi he stopped a little before the trading post to let her out. He ached to stay, to talk more with her, to explore her feelings and his. He had never discussed Duskyanne and Stephanie with anyone. For a brief moment he entertained the notion that he could tell this trusting, straightforward young Hopi about the other two women who had been so frenetically in and out of his life, but the moment passed. He extended his hand to her and she took it. She clasped his hand in both of hers. She released it and severed their physical connection. In Hopi he certainly could not kiss her. He took one deep look and hoarded her image.

"I would like to get you more white blouses," he said.

She concentrated on him as if trying to store him in her memory, and stepped back to leave. "Then bring them!" She flung the words at him and turned toward the trading post.

12

Jim Spangle lived in New Orleans, Louisiana, and Avery hastened to the historic old city to check him out for Farney. Spangle, a leading dealer in primitive art, had emerged quite suddenly to the forefront of the field from an uneventful and obscure background. It had been rumored that he had found backers to support his advertising and publicity campaign which appeared in every major magazine. True to his name he seemed to be a bit of a bright spangle and caused Avery in his role as the entrusted corporate dignitary on top of a lofty foundation to raise his eyebrows, if ever so slightly. "I'm Farney's toy," Avery muttered.

Spangle's shop, located in the middle of the financial district, did good business, and as far as Avery could ascertain the banks loaned him money and gave him credit. Investment circles considered him a young, enterprising "comer" who if realistically appraised had too many questionable projects going for him. There lay the rub.

One art dealer in the city with whom Avery had done business summed up Mr. Spangle: "He seems to obtain lots of collections. They just seem to come to him."

"From whom?" Avery queried.

His friend didn't know, but the word circulated out that the man gobbled up collections, buying and selling them.

Avery telephoned a collector in Saint Louis and explained to him that as a personal favor he wanted him to offer to buy from Spangle a primitive art collection-whatever one Spangle came up with. He need not explain his actions any further; Avery would take charge after that. His friend in return notified him that Spangle currently offered a mixed bag of rare and choice Eskimo,

Plains, and Woodlands Indian art and some fine Australian bark paintings. He claimed that soon he would obtain another collection. Avery told his friend to decline the offer and that he would contact him later. After making a date to see Spangle in his shop, Avery pounced.

Spangle did not recognize Avery even after he introduced himself. The shop swarmed with art items of high quality which Avery had not anticipated. When Avery asked if everything could be bought the stout, burly man, sporting red hair and a beard laughed. "If you want to buy the whole shop it is yours; just take it. Of course, I would just have to buy a new collection, or maybe I just wouldn't open up again."

As the man affably rambled on Avery pondered over the scene. Spangle had fine taste and seemingly a legitimate business to boot. Then why his penchant for buying collections he never seems to obtain? No sooner had he conceived of the thought when the gentleman mentioned he had negotiated to buy a "new collection."

"If you would rather invest in a collection I'm about to purchase, mostly Eskimo, Plains, Woodlands material, plus a few items from Australia, I can also arrange that for you."

Avery closely regarded the dealer who played the role of cordiality itself. "There is no reason to go on," he said simply. "You should be under arrest. In the vernacular, you have been found out."

"Are you insane? What are you saying? I do not have to put up with this crap."

"Do you want me to call the police?"

"Where is your badge–your search warrant?"

"I don't need one. You've been caught."

"Get the hell out of my place!"

Avery started inspecting the art displayed around the room. "You owe my partner a large collection which you claimed you owned. I happen to know that you are selling the same collection to other dealers and collectors. Have you received a check for it? If you want to go to jail, just stop me now."

He picked up and examined a prehistoric black-aged Eskimo ivory Okvik woman. "Most probably from the Saint Lawrence Island of Alaska," and he deftly put it in his coat pocket. "And this I also like," and he scrutinized a Chumash California Indian dark steatite stone swordfish and likewise made it disappear. "With a rich patina-an excellent example, and I must say to your credit, a real one. In fact, I have to say you have fine judgment, at least with art," and he snatched a rare old Kickapoo Indian wooden prayer stick with incised carved lettering which he tried to put in his coat pocket, but thought better of it. He opened his briefcase. "It fits comfortably in here."

All the while Avery continued to define and appropriate various eclectic delights. Mr. Spangle, his fine show of humor now dissipated, looked on glumly, totally at a loss. Occasionally he put a heavy hand over one or the other eye as if to be sure he correctly witnessed the destruction of his shop.

Avery, all but finished, paused to consider a Northwest Coast Indian carved wooden pipe bowl inlaid with abalone shell. "No, I don't think so. It's attractive but a little late. It's not good enough for the Foundation."

He turned and faced the owner. "You have swindled a good number of people by selling the same collection of material over and over again. By now all of us own that collection and I guess it would be reasonable to say that the collection is oversubscribed. In order to avoid being arrested you will have to close up your shop and tomorrow be gone from this city. I thought it would be prudent for my partner and me to take our share of what we are owed. I will spread the news so that other suckers will wise up and help themselves to your cache. At least I got the pick of the crop."

"You can't prove a thing. Now get out!"

"Thank you. I will. It's nice to find one who has a selective eye-about the pieces, anyway. But it hasn't applied to your dealings. My name as I told you is Avery Judson-with the Farney Foundation."

As he reached the door the man began to shout. "Well if you must piss on my parade at least you've said I have good taste, whatever good that does me. Now that you have ruined me I might as well jump in the Bayou Teche at New Iberia."

"Holy cow!" Avery exclaimed. "New Iberia-that's the place she told me in India. This is HER country!"

He took a short drive to New Iberia and found it easy and uneventful.

When he arrived there he had to inquire at a drugstore whether the party he sought lived in the area. He felt as if by invoking the names of Mr. and Mrs. Reef he would make them materialize, and to his dismay he learned that they actually existed. Told to him in Ajanta, affairs that originated in New Iberia and continued in Cairo coincided with a measure of truth. The Reefs, a policeman informed him, lived slightly out of the center of town across from the old cemetery.

The house itself appeared Southern Victorian, good and solid with a regional airiness made for graceful living. Avery walked under the slender columns and detected a light on upstairs. With considerable trepidation he intended to call on the Reefs. Both he and the Reefs had once played such a tenuous role with Duskyanne that he wondered if he would now appear to them as a lost, wandering shade come to haunt them. Why did he come here? he pondered. He rang the doorbell. Everywhere he saw signs of careful maintenance: a small but lush garden, a trim white gate, and a freshly painted house. A man opened the door who admitted to being Mr. Reef. Somewhat bewildered, he stood rather plaintively in the dark, and after Avery gave him his name he paused a moment and invited Avery inside.

Mrs. Reef called down the stairs, "Who is that, honey?" As soon as Mr. Reef repeated Avery's name she hustled down, buttoning a wrap around her.

"Come on into the house," Mr. Reef assumed a casual, polite tone, "and meet my wife." He escorted Avery into the sitting room.

"Excuse me if it is late. I can drop by another time." Avery sat down, then awkwardly got back up; he would have been delighted to go.

"No. Don't mind Mrs. Reef. You haven't disturbed her. She sometimes never puts her clothes on all day, and even in the night," he said benevolently. "It is an old custom she acquired during her Arabian Nights period when she played the role of a mere dancing youth performing a hundred and one solos," and he twinkled good-naturedly.

She rejoined, "Mr. Reef, whenever the weather permits adorns himself with the Bermuda shorts he is wearing, and in fact he has worn them far beyond Bermuda-worn out dozens of them in the darkest casbahs and the meanest bazaars."

They finished their routine: "Thank you, Mrs. Reef, you never looked younger," and "The compliment is returned, Mr. Reef."

They were jolly, fleshy, and still vigorous people in their fifties. She retained a soft, charming femininity and he unfurled an unflagging whim to shamelessly cavort at any cost. He wondered where Duskyanne fit into these non-sensible people. This woman, he thought bemused, in some insane dream could have conceivably been his mother-in-law.

"Now, about you," she directed her attention to Avery. "We adore having perfect strangers startling us."

"Yes, we love unresolved mysteries," Mr. Reef added.

"Your daughter is . . .," Avery weakly began and stopped when they both bolted upright as if they had been gaffed by the tops of their heads.

"Our daughter?" said Mr. Reef.

"Whose daughter?" uttered Mrs. Reef.

"Your daughter . . .," Avery faltered.

"If we had a daughter we would be more fortunate, but I am afraid we don't, or don't know if we do. Or if we did, when did we, dear?" she asked her husband. "Oh, it's all so bewildering."

"Well," he collaborated, "we once celebrated a birth certificate that had baby teeth."

"And we did receive one postcard sent from India indicating a visit would be forthcoming, perhaps from a ghost. There is only this dab of evidence," she added.

"From India?" Avery blurted. "A card sent from India?"

"As we said, we know less than nothing about this mythical daughter business you speak of." Mrs. Reef continued in her vernacular. "We have a dog, a female dog. I think you said your name is Mr. Judson—an odd name."

"Strange," Mr. Reef relayed, "but now that you have brought it up we have even heard from a friend of ours who has just returned from Spain a day ago and who manufactured a daughter for us. He said in a letter that only yesterday some offspring had strayed to Santander who he had recognized as an apparition purporting to be a daughter. Very odd."

Avery gulped with astonishment and jumped off his chair. "I must be going," he sputtered.

"But Mr. Judson," she reminded him, "did you intend to speak about a female sibling? I believe you did."

"No, madam, my apologies," he said conscious of his formal rhetoric. "No-no-my regrets. Maybe we'll meet another time. Glad we met." And he fled.

In New York a cablegram had been waiting for him from Spain, from Barcelona, from Stephanie Farney. It read: "Dearest Avery, I have done what I should always have done, since I could not ignore the situation or accept its facts. By now, it is done. My vacation in Spain has ended in my being the matador, only turned against myself. I have tried to give myself the plunge of straight mercy. Randolf has been called, only I wish to see you once more. Once more. Just once. Stephanie."

Avery re-read the message and blinked. Could it be a hoax? It apparently had been sent from a hospital or she gave the hospital's address. Anyway, it pointed in the right direction–where he planned to go regardless. He wondered where Farney lurked. If his wife had gone alone to Spain on a vacation Farney could very well be nearby.

He flew to Spain and on this trip he thought his bones rattled and his flesh loosely shook. Now, as his temperament changed he saw not what vividly attracted him, but in many instances what did not actively disconcert him. He sank further back into the seat and he could not control his daydreaming as surely as he once did. The various cracks and uneven transitions of his life became part of the dream itself.

He tried to fix an image of Stephanie in spite of Duskyanne's resurrection. He had been unfair to Stephanie and yet he hadn't. Perhaps he could partially blame himself for the impasse between them because he basically presented himself as a supportive friend on the one hand, and a suitor who desired her on the other. Consequently, she felt divided as to which role to assume. But throughout her assorted ordeals she stood as the moral, self-effacing one who tried desperately not to injure another, and when she did, Farney or himself, she went to pieces. He felt kindly for her just then, perhaps sickeningly so. As for Duskyanne, she stood out as a different breed. In art and out of it he could not string together the beads of her life, not yet.

In Barcelona Avery sped directly to Stephanie's hospital. He presented his name and asked for Mrs. Farney. A nurse telephoned someone and another nurse came and met him. Although a native Spaniard she emphasized to Avery that she had married an American diplomat and through her husband had become a friend of Mrs. Farney who hired her as a special nurse.

"How did you know to be here?" the nurse interrogated him.

"I just knew."

"Her husband has not yet arrived although he has been contacted. But you? You nearly wasted your time. It was bad."

From her telegram he had feared that she might not hold on long enough for him to see her. "What do you mean 'bad'?"

"She bloodied everything. She did not just sever her wrists. She had to batter her head against the floor. When I found her I wondered why she didn't take drugs and do the job more effectively."

"Be still!" Avery said firmly. "Enough of that."

"But she did mention you-Avery Judson. Why, I will never know. Yet, Mrs. Farney wants to see you, and if you will, please follow me."

"Wait," she barked as they neared a special ward partitioned off, and the nurse slipped alone inside. Then she waved him in and vacated the room.

Avery squinted against a hard dart of light from a slightly open window although the rest of the room remained quite dark. In the corner of the room she lay on a bed with her forehead bandaged. He could not see her wrists because they were under the covers. He imagined that the bandage on her head could still be wet from the blood he could see. He edged closer, and leaning over he kissed her.

She smiled and a spirited gleam swept her face. "I guess what I have done is rather unproductive," she said to him, as if they had already slipped into full conversation. "Avery, why do I think one mess gets me out of another?"

He could love her, he knew he could, out of compassion or otherwise, and he believed she could love him. Not that he had to have her, possess her, but if he had the chance he would slowly and calmly fall in love with her.

"Well," he smiled as he saw her relishing the insoluble muddle she threw at him, "one mess gotten out of is one mess disposed of–even if you have used another mess as your lever. Once you are out of this one I think you have definitely cleaned your slate," and he became serious.

"You came," she said. "I sent you that cablegram not knowing which way I'd end up –but feeling I would be here to see you–because you'd be here."

"It was pretty mixed up–that wire," he conceded, "but I figured that we–you–had a good chance."

"I've been lying in my bed pondering what would happen–would I die and how would it feel, my dying? I don't mean the pain–they've stuffed me with too many drugs to feel any of that. But I've laid back and tried to experiment with myself–to discover its shape or approach, or to think of a good literary line about it, or even to sing it in a song. Then I noticed my nurse–my friend's forbidding face she made at me for not being a Catholic and for breaking her laws–and mad at me anyway for being idiotic.

"I watched the light crawl in here. Oh, they have tried so hard to stamp out the light! To close up the room. But little feelers would burrow through–would corkscrew through the most unimaginable surfaces. You can't repress light. And I discovered a collection of almost hidden little runners of the sun's rays; I found them out. And I played with the kind of expression that would be on your face if you would make it here to me, and how they would find Farney. I didn't want to die. I couldn't."

"A good dose of selfishness would not hurt you. It's a particular kind of medicine that I prescribe for a person in your condition. Use it to assert yourself."

She looked remote, but clear. "Do you mean Farney? Free myself from Farney? To still that surge sometimes between us–no, nothing else is like that–beyond everything. He can be harsh but not always," she said plaintively, "and I must learn to live with that fact, too."

"Will Farney come?" asked Avery forthright.

"Yes, they have reached him. Soon he'll be here. And I am tired." She was honest.

"I know that," he said, "and I will try to see you again." He went to the door and signaled goodbye to her. As soon as he touched the handle Stephanie's nurse opened the door for him. He walked out and when he went down the corridor she hissed, "Now don't you come back."

In northern Spain Avery found Santander. Once there he knew where to find Duskyanne, just as he would have known where to find her somewhere else at the special places that draw curators, collectors, lovers of antiquities-those who chose to haunt the repositories of the finest in art-just as she would have known where to find him in Santander had she been seeking him.

As he paid his admission to enter what he considered a holy Mecca he remembered it being midday. He entered the caves at Altamira and broke into a perspiration of agonized prayer. It would be the last one of infinite possibilities of finding Duskyanne. He looked obliquely. She stood alone, drawn with excitement, closely inspecting the eternal beasts of Altamira. He had captured luck. He saw her waiting there-precious, amazed, half crouched, her hair down her forehead, her sensual quest unquenchable. He gazed at her gazing at the pantheon of animals, and then she became aware of him.

"Don't you think this is one of the best?" she asked quietly, and then stared ahead. "All eighteen thousand years of ultimate sophistication from our endless mind." Turning to him she said, "Of course, you would meet me here. Did you sniff me out? You must somehow have found out about me in Santander. Wherever we are we meet at the centers of art-it's our network of power, true power."

The charging animals or the standing animals, expending energy or storing up energy, lay before Avery almost life-sized on the stone surface. A wild boar stretched running; an emerging bison curled into a charge; a deer, perhaps pregnant, extended poignantly her long, vibrant form; a lowing bison with head and tail uplifted-all brimmed on the cave roof before him. Duskyanne wavered as she beheld the figures. If the beasts could magnetically attract her, he thought, then he certainly would be part of her quest-even the quest itself.

"You had to be here-where else could you go?" he said with an afterglow of amazement in his voice.

"Only here," she said.

"When I heard that you were in Santander, actually through your parents, I knew unquestionably you'd be here," and he helped her stand up. But his hands did not let go of her waist. He felt to the center of his being the touch of her flesh through her dress.

"Boo," she said softly, and he let go of her. "What will we do when we still meet once more? We just drift and meet as if this is an ordinary day. Darling, I am screaming in my toes!" She squeezed his hand hard.

They lapsed into the same haphazard rhetoric of their earlier meetings.

He looked up. "Let this pagan temple bless our union of stray souls. Oh, great bison, witness this, our seasonal reunion . . .," he babbled, letting the strain and excitement get the better of him.

"Let's skidoo," she said.

"Let's split," he chimed in, and they made it out to the entrance.

For the night they stayed near their temple at Santillana del Mar. "Let's chuck our past," she said in a toast to Avery, and she emptied her glass of wine.

"Glory to our future," he toasted her back. They leisurely finished the bottle of wine until she became sleepy and he lifted her to the bed. She bounced gently on the mattress as he released her. Before she relaxed into its depths she threw him her shoes. And as before with her he captured her surprised, flushed, pain-triggered joy, and traced her hand as it unconsciously flopped around beside her ecstatic face.

He stayed in delirium. The great bison had indeed blessed them in bed that night. They considered the trip they embarked on as a personal sojourn especially designed for their passage into love.

It turned cold as they went into the province of Asturias. Even though they traveled in deep summer the vastness of the mountains held a damp greyness. The car they had rented sped them through unbelievably green fields and slopes, made greener by the veil of grey cold that also greyed the rocky patches between the trees. Water sprung in little gushings that sprang from every source and gathered into agitated streams. She told him that she had always planned a pilgrimage to Altamira, not to buy or sell anything but for the caves themselves. They passed by rude stone shelters with balustrades. Some had wooden square structures with stubby pillars perched on top which in turn flared up and into stone disks.

"The round stones prevented the rats from running up to the second story huts which farmers used as granaries," she explained.

The air fizzed with vapors over this ancient land and it seemed to congeal in darkness when a sudden twilight fell on them making them feel beautiful.

Duskyanne had counted on reaching Oviedo and that evening she seized the day. In the heart of Asturias they drove into the small town and settled in a hotel. Then she declared to Avery that she had reserved for him a surprise-the flawless gems among churches. She avidly told him about the scarce little Visigothic churches that thrived in Asturias and its environs.

"Visigothic?" he uttered. He simply showed his ignorance, and she excitedly elaborated on the perfect blend of the Eastern Byzantine and Latin and local traditions never again duplicated.

"Visigothic Christian churches?" He still doubted her. "It's an oxymoron. Aren't those guys, the Vandals and Visigoths and Ostrogoths the ones who tore down the last bastions of western civilization and ravaged them? A period called the Dark Ages."

"And roughly became Christians in the process-our great, great, great ancestors," she exaggerated. "And, of course this period should be called the Light Age."

"Hell, every ancient group of people in history naturally becomes our ancestors."

"And so they are."

"All except the Visigoths," he teased. "They couldn't adjust to being good Christians and so they bowed out to a little bit of Saracen here and there. I know the Muslims conquered Spain and flattened out all Christians."

"Yes, seven hundred years after Christ the Muslims ran them out but their churches still greet us and even influenced early Muslim mosques styles."

"But God does not live in them; He won't enter them."

"Listen, you stupid clump, I would like to marry a Visigoth in one of those churches."

"I know," he mocked and shook his head with sympathy. "But come, let me give you a Visigothic back rub."

He liked the frivolously serious ways she treated the little areas that so enamored and possessed her. Within her passionate nature they grew like vines and became entwined around and within her; they could no more be removed from her than her bursting lungs. Not that Visigothic churches in Asturias did not matter; of course they vitally mattered and everyone in the world agreed. However, since Avery could not buy them nor collect them he would not especially dwell on or in them.

Duskyanne did not err in her Visigothic connection. San Miguel, Satullano, resembled a domestic church-bright, warm and personal, and he spoke his approval and gratitude and she licked his ear in assent.

Before Santa Cristina de Lena they cast their shadows on the slender, compact stone building and were directed into a small but deceivingly spacious nave, a playroom of delight where steps led up to the chancel of a gaily incised stone altar. He stood peering through delicate columns down at her in the sweet nave. "My friend," he said, "I dearly love you."

The church, San Miguel de Lino, proved even more impressive. This small yet high edifice was full of consecrated leisure. It had tall, straight buttresses designed with deep flutes and tiny windows carved in the geometrical traceries of pierced slabs of stone. Here, adding proof to his love for her he found a piece of string and tied back her wandering, amoral strands of hair with a knot under her chin.

The best they found to be Santa Maria de Naranco, a long, rectangular stone house ribbed by lean, slender buttresses. Located one hundred meters from San Miguel it originated as a country palace overlooking the valley and the towering mountains which dominated it. Within, the handsome, dark gallery exhibited an arrangement of barrel vaults and arches and spiral columns. It could be anyone's house-their house. The columns directed their sight through the windowless nave to lighted rooms beyond. In her future house, Duskyanne argued for some windows to let in more light, while he, the adamant purist, reasoned for the dark, long room before him.

"My funny old parents like light," she jested. "They don't like to think darkly. And I can't see the dust unless there is a wee window," she complained.

"If it's old Visigothic dust, anything old," he said, "then it should not be removed. Besides, it might add a special patina to the house."

"Bah," she retorted. "You can have one room as you wish and then we can live in the rest of the house."

As they steered back toward Santander they jointly took away with them a profitable new idea: to write Visigothic fiction.

"No one knows about it," she said. "It's absolutely a virgin market. The Visigothic novel should replace the Gothic novel which is now passe."

"No one cares," he said, "not even the virgins."

"You're bad," she said.

"I'm glad," he answered.

From Santander they boarded an arthritic bus to Barcelona. He told her about Stephanie and his wish to call at the hospital once more before she joined him at their hotel. To this she heartily assented.

"I know I would like her," she said.

"How do you know? You haven't met her."

"From what Farney isn't-she must be good."

He did not consider her reasoning a theorem which had general application. For example, he felt what Farney isn't doesn't necessarily mean that Judson is.

She shut up about Farney and he shut up about Farney since his lingering clutch would have consumed them both.

"Avery!" she cried, "I didn't know you were here," and Stephanie delightfully and obviously attempted to straighten out her hair but abruptly gave it up. "You've seen me at my worst so I guess it doesn't matter, does it?"

"No," he smiled. "The nurse seemed to let me right in. How are you?" He could tell that she looked considerably better-very much alive.

"I wasn't expecting you-and yet I guess I was. I've been reading insanely everything I could get a hold of and found that I had already read much of the fine old enduring stuff before–and forgotten. I must have had a spanking good education. I remember my German nurse called me a precocious child while she shook her jowls and ate apple dumplings."

"Do you know what you need?" he paused a moment. "There is no question of it," he smiled. "You need to be more of a pig-dog. As a little boy my friends called me that. It means a person who eats so much he gets sick. And he eats so fast he can't enjoy his food. His life is over-hung with fear that others will get more than he or that he will miss out on something. As a painfully shy boy I didn't know how to handle women and now I am a pig-dog about them to make up for lost time. Especially women like you."

"Here, here, the many women filling the life of Avery Judson," she intoned dramatically.

"No. But, yes, seriously, for you to be a little bit pig-dogged is a good thing. You will be so involved in stuffing yourself with life that you will forget to give it up."

"Speaking of good things, Avery, did you find any art goods in Barcelona? I've been to the early Romanesque churches at Tarrasa nearby. That you would like." She showed a genuine interest in his interests.

"No, I didn't find any art–although in a way I did. Sometimes I don't know what art is and I think everything is art."

She laughed. "It is."

"Yes, I know," he said. "Art comes in many colored surprises."

"Well," she mused, "I have certainly not conducted my life that way- as sacred."

They both felt amiss on the matter of life and realized that they didn't consider themselves authorities. The conversation adroitly shifted to pleasantries and her getting well. When he left he promised to see her in the States, and Avery had already envisioned introducing her to Duskyanne.

As he knocked on Duskyanne's door he heard an erratic shuffling. After waiting for what he considered too long she called for him to enter. She was lying on the bed on her side distantly observing him. The upper part of her brown suit was unbuttoned and her hiked up skirt pressed a tight rolled

186

band against her stomach. She leaned over and her body skimmed over the bed. Her hair was down again.

"What is wrong?" he asked. "I got caught up with Stephanie who's seen the Romanesque Tarrasa Church with frescos and capitals."

"You got caught up, I got caught up," she sang in a sing-song voice. "My Romanesque Love bumped into a capital. How arty," she snickered.

"Are you drunk?"

She shook her head, no.

"Then what is this about?"

"I broke down in your collection-my patina rubbed off and I was not of sterling merit. Not sterling silver. I am your fake," she laughed.

He saw everything in slow motion now, grotesquely swinging around his own stolid bulk planted in the middle of the room. "And the King's original and Gupta's possibility? Why do you want to wreck us? Don't do it, Duskyanne. It has been so hard to get us started. And it is so easy to cut us off. We and us-that is what we have. I do not believe it, unless you are under a spell . . .," and he suspiciously ran his eyes around the room.

"No, Avery," she said with heavy foreknowledge and sat up holding her jacket together over her shoulders, "there are no real caves for us and none of them are brightly painted-that is not the world-it devours our priceless havens and we get routed. Every item in our collection has a price. And I am not sure it is not better to avoid growing old in boring familiarity . . ."

"Is that you? You haven't been drugged? Warped by someone?"

"No, I have never pretended to be any different. I am just myself."

From an adjoining room Randolf Farney stepped out. He wore an undershirt which revealed a beleaguered scruff of hair under a thin, almost scrawny neck. Avery had never seen him without his suit.

"Avery, she wanted to leave the hotel to avoid you but I would not let her. I value you as highly as I do her and I regret being estranged from you. Duskyanne, tell him the facts. That you saw me at a hotel where I stayed and invited me for drinks. Three drinks. But it doesn't matter; no one's drunk. That you were not tortured and never really prevented from doing what you wished, but enjoyed torturing yourself with ambivalence. And your conviction that you must have your freedom to remain free-to be able to throw yourself in and out of any relationships, no matter what. Tell him about us long before-in and out of the King. Tell him, Duskyanne!"

She slowly nodded her confession to Avery, "Yes, yes . . ."

"So," Farney declared, "Avery, define the devil as me but allow him his own self. I am sorry that I have not had your friendship for so long."

"Is that the case?" Avery demanded from her. "The coin has been flipped and landed on its other side and there you are sleeping in its shade-any coin, any flip, any side, and you have squatted around somewhere as long as you are comfortable, of course. We live dangerously but we always live comfortably." He knew that he was being enveloped by his own rage and grief and that what he would say would be his way to fight back and not what he wanted to believe-or else he could squeeze the lovely guts out of her and end it. Before, he had once reserved a knife for Farney. "But I gather you have settled here for awhile. Certainly your ass is well grooved and by now your royal doubts are financially cured. But you can be sure you have handsomely given in return for what you have gained. For yours is a glorious cunt, a patina-ridden pussy, Duskyanne, a literal masterpiece, and what else is a masterpiece for but to be shared. You have the great gash. There's no price too great for it-a country, a family, a dozen Benin masks, a life . . ."

He couldn't speak further; his life stood before him as unformed and mushy as ever. Somehow the notion took hold of him that he and Duskyanne were doing each other favors by exchanging blows as gifts. And as if his people stood as myopic visions before him he confusedly surveyed all around them, over them, and swayed back.

"Thank you, thank you for the dance," he said, and was gone.

In a Belgium hotel he counted one, two. One two, button your shoe. An abacus adds one, subtracts two. That gives him a minus screw. All he started with was one, two. He pictures himself hanging onto the parallel rods of a gigantic abacus, forced to swing monkey fashion between one parallel level to another because giant counters slam back and forth across the rods smashing into fingers and causing him to lose his grip and fall far below.

Farney and Duskyanne, Duskyanne and Farney. Damn it! He is still playing with these his prayer beads. Or, is he now actually attempting to clear his battlefield of charred debris? In Antwerp-he is still in Antwerp-what else has he lost? He thinks of his failures-all the art objects that managed to elude him; these prickle his awareness. But not all is lost. He feels better. He can lay claim to the treasures he has assembled. The Benin mask. The Scythians. Gradually his horizon expands and other interests invade his barren landscape. There's dumb Mr. Dalton Smedly-and the eagles, the dark bunch of them. The battlefield finally becomes repopulated and new contestants begin to occupy the field. At last one person emerges stronger than the others and routes them all away. But does he have a home? He isn't sure where that is. He can no longer remain in this place. Fact number one. He can no longer rely on being near Duskyanne, near wherever she is, within some radiating tangent from her. He can never re-hope and have that insane, sudden exhilaration. Fact number two. It is not easy for him to gather his clothes and belongings and locate his suitcase. But he does so. Once airborne, he sleeps long and deep. Without dreams.

13

*A*very met Katy at Hopi land. She greeted him warmly as if she did not expect any explanations and the two of them would never again need to hurry their affairs. Or so Avery believed that to be her attitude. He then presented her with a number of white blouses of different materials and she immediately selected a particularly pretty one and put it on. Katy beamed happily and Avery felt glad to make her so delighted. His single, simple act of offering himself to her had accomplished this.

It came immediately to him that they would live alone. Katy's parents withheld their blessing since they did not understand their daughter's behavior. However, they realized it would be best for all concerned that she be allowed to follow her own heart without censoring her. Her son would be raised by them. It had been decreed. Avery understood and agreed. But where to go after that? Not to resume his former course of activities he considered his only choice. To disengage. To reinvent himself. But as he would no longer traffic in art he likewise could not live on the mesas among the Hopis. He could never be Hopi or go Hopi. And what would be the use?

Katy wanted to be close to her family, but not that close. So they stayed in Hopi but down below on the flat land in Polacca where they could glimpse the outlines of the dwellings on top of the mesa that housed her parents and son. Katy's house had been fashioned of stone, stones to rest in, that formed the endless calvary of life, and he wandered among their shapes and harsh-cold colors and they grew warm to him. Within the stone walls she kept a good house, clean and well-ordered.

Katy turned the gears that structured Avery to his firmament. She arose early in the morning to light the wood-burning stove and prepare for the day's meals, and in the winter the stove plus the adobe corner fireplace glowed with heat.

Avery gathered and chopped the wood. This started out to be an onerous chore but because he performed it so often he made a ritual of it. He first carefully selected the mellow, dark-grey and brown wood antiqued by the elements. The tinder-dry wood would burn instantly. But not so the white-yellow wood which he considered the hardest to cut down since these trees grew vigorously and could not be toppled with one axe stroke. The newer wood would be better after a year's stay outdoors. From his chopping Avery hoarded the pinon and cedar chips and shavings for kindling. When the rhythm of the axe stroke smoothed into his system he began to like it.

Water he hauled from the well outdoors and Katy would heat it on the wood stove and cook or bathe with it. Between hauling water, gathering wood, and chinking the loose stones of his house Avery kept busy. The fireplace had to be cleared of ashes, sometimes several times a day. The well had to be cleaned out, and the roof as well as the walls had to be patched and made ready to drain off and reject the infrequent rain showers. From river stones inset into the ground he made a stone path to the outhouse clothesline and the horno where Katy baked her magnificent bread. He fed much of the garbage to the chickens and two ducks, and the unassimilated trash he hauled away and buried.

The ducks he delighted in. They constituted pure goodness compared to the snake-eyed, savage hens. The ducks became associated with a waft of water where no water existed along with the suggestion of cool shade where a few trees grew to provide shelter. The ducks, affectionate to each other, as melodious in form and motion to him as they appeared to the Chinese Tang painters, became instead the flowers in the garden of necessities he cultivated. Growing corn, beans, peas and squash mostly occupied Katy's attention, although Avery's interest flared up when they ripened and could be picked.

Many times, even for days, they rarely spoke, and at first he minded it. Katy, herself, spoke more often with her hands, or head's degree of tilt, or the crouch of her small, alert body. He could accept silence, but then she did not read as he read, and it took more work to explain his ideas to her than he perhaps wanted to expend.

"Do you ever read books?" he asked her.

She said, "One, two–not many. I like to watch you do it. You think hard."

For awhile Avery intellectualized the impasse, and although he had a fine sactuary did it satisfy his needs? Katy as a person elicited a spark wondrously aesthetic to him, like a lissome animal, but then again animals don't talk or read and that's partly why they are not people. But Katy always let herself be known and he never had a doubt as to what she meant. When he didn't let her drive because he thought she looked tired, she insisted upon it and declared she wanted her rights. When he wanted to relocate an anthill to see if the ant community would return to its former location or thrive in a new habitat she disapproved. She didn't want to make the ants further tired with extra cartings and haulings.

He criticized her for having no curiosity and not caring to innovate, and yet he found her rerouting a course of water to see if the land lay level and if it would go uphill. She personally planned an irrigation system for their garden. She pointedly liked him to conduct small scientific experiments and to explain them to her which gave her great pleasure. Why does fertilizer make crops grow better; how come a caterpillar becomes a butterfly; why do rattlesnakes and king snakes fight when other snakes don't? And she would like to think an eagle flying high above could sense an earthworm turning inside its hole. He would explain to her, often drawing pictures which she kept as great creations. Underlying all his explanations she maintained her belief that he really didn't know very much, although far more than she, because the essential importance of everything and all relationships could never be known and would remain correctly and hauntingly unfathomable. "We must not spoil what we have by pretending we are smarter and more important than what happens around us. It is only pretend. We make little games," she would say to his sallies of rationality.

She had decided opinions. She wanted to pick up every hitchhiker on the road and yet decided to be quite reserved in speaking to people who she met as casual acquaintances. She had intense compassion for the needs and suffering of others and would share with her neighbors her most highly regarded possessions, and yet she would harden to the needs of the prosperous who if they suffered any ills or misfortunes she considered them weak or incapable. The well-off, she believed, should at least be able to take care of themselves. However, she completely catered to Avery in respect to the arrangements of objects in the house and instinctively adhered to his desires in those matters. He was the curator–he placed things right.

Occasionally Avery felt she spoiled him. She would over-nurse him when he got sick and she always arose in the morning before him and tried to let him sleep and be at peace. Still, he did not feel unmanned by her attentions and in turn he would chide her good-naturedly about why she had to wake up the rooster and why she talked to the corn. He would read to her out loud over and over Norse mythology and the exploits of King Arthur's knights until they became practically senseless to him, and his reward would be the drama unfolded in her face. He could not tally up their days, each and every one of them, since they did not have that kind of collective import, but they resembled his emissions with her, good and even in their regularity. Only with her did he feel that he added up to something as a person. He could stop and think about himself, and each time he stopped he made healing connections with his psyche that made sense. He could carry his roots farther with each step he took.

Although he thought about the subject Avery did not miss the art world he had known so well. To him it boiled down to the matter of translating different orders of phenomena. A dance, a storm filtering in. Children running wild and naked. The rhythm of running and walking and talking projected on real dirt. Dirt and stone buildings against the spectrum of distance and sky. The fresh food tasting good and feeling good to touch and to the eye, and back again to the dances. The myriad dances all through the spring and summer and fall. The masked dances on top of the flat hills of dirt with long-haired old men and brilliantly witty and vulgar clowns smacking of Roman poets, and the lilting women's basket dance could all stand side by side with Japanese Nara wooden figures, Chartres, the early tithe barns of Europe, the Fauve Derains, and the sculpture of the East Indian city of Konarak.

The moments and touches of magical excitement continued to reach out to him but he interpreted their qualities on a different scale, huge and unbounded. No longer did his senses become cloistered and surfeited with art material as they had been before Hopi. So, he made the transformation. He now viewed the new and varied galleries he experienced as loosely displayed, but nevertheless he converted them into a living tableau of surprise and profundity.

Even so, occasionally a mental picture of a Norwegian Stave Church or a Minoan wooden figure would strike him. He resembled a cured alcoholic who after occasionally taking a drink to some degree revives his former disease. So Avery too would be caught up unbalanced by mainsprings of his past world-flashing images of disturbing ideal forms-when he turned the channels of his mind to former frequencies.

The natives always had a degree of curiosity about him, and by instinct Hopi curiosity meant hospitality. If he would be meandering around a village to gauge the sizes and shapes of old stone houses or just loitering pleasantly in the sun a woman's voice would invariably drift out to him, "Do you need anything?" He would answer that he had what he needed. To say that would be fruitless against his potential friend's insistent urge for a gathering of souls to chat-a chat that he would later discover to be mostly silence. The family that he would now be technically visiting had no deep Christian precept of helping one's neighbor or suffering the consequences for those who neglect to do so, and thus would not be under the discipline of Christian charity. But rather it harbored an itchy, instinctive compulsion to drum up new interest and to snare the different facets of news that abounded-which amounted to having a good day. Household stewards passed around stews of posole or the finest grated potatoes with meat of every kind and description-without the use of napkins. Unless Avery pressed a point, his host said little that was verbally directed, complex or profound. The wonder arose when various people came together, not agitated but content.

Above all he felt that he could sense a completeness in the elements and events that surrounded him at Hopi. There sprang a lilt and lift among people in their honest dealings within their space-filled, undiluted homeland. At times his village meant the most to him–the people in it, the houses of chatter and laughter, the peaceful pauses among serious, aware friends, and the ragged stone walls enclosing them all. This realm he inhabited had its own special lineage which tuned him to it, and in turn brought out the best he had to offer.

The time arrived to pick the corn, but this time Avery went out to the little field for once without Katy who had severe stomach cramps. She begged him to allow her to accompany him, but he told her to rest. Even the species of small corn specially engineered to grow with less water had to gestate quickly during the short rain-parched summers. Planted on a wedge of stone-gashed ground the corn still managed to flourish. To pick corn without Katy amounted to mortal sin. She always looked forward to her little triumph with no strain or worry, and she would almost pat the corn, even rub it with encouragement-her embryos of life. As he contemplated corn Avery heard a rustle at the end of the cornfield. Someone skirted around it and approached him. Avery swung back and met the intruder. He faced Farney. Four years had passed and Farney came.

"I saw you from over there on a rise and I find it incredible seeing you there. Avery Judson among the corn. I had a hell of a time finding you.You just disappeared into nowhere, and I mean nowhere. Your hut, I guess, is over there. But even so, the country's worth every inch of the labor it took to get here. But, Avery," and he raked him over with blatant disregard, "come come, it's rather childish, the whole setup here–playing Indian."

Neither man offered his hand to the other. Farney perspired a lot-hardly older and blue-suited.

"I didn't want to get corn today anyway," Avery stared at Farney and the corn. "So Farney, let's go to my place."

They trudged to "the hut," as Farney called it, and while Farney crossed its threshold and went in he modified the harsh, unfeeling words he had just uttered about Avery's present scene to now being "a romantically rustic and childish excursion." He took in the elegantly peaceful atmosphere. Katy with some apprehension had seen them approach and ducked into the other room as they appeared.

Farney sat down. "Actually, Avery, I am here at the direction of the board of directors of the Foundation and not by my own wishes. As you calculated the Foundation has been unable to fill your shoes; that I've always known. In a sense, I've resisted this meeting, to see you in your act of hibernation, but unfortunately or not you are permanently one of the two Presidents of the Foundation."

"So what? You may get the hell out of Hopi! Farney, your visit here is no blessing. If one of your monuments is tarnishing don't bother me with it. As President of a clump of immortality, I resign."

"But you can't resign–no, it wouldn't stand up in court. You are not free, any more than I am. What makes you think you can shuck your background and your career at a whim? Just waste your talents? That is a sin. Sin is when you don't burn out every damn chromosome in you–using them to the hilt. What do you do here? You posture. You play with the trees like a dog and talk to the corn because there's no one else you can talk to and who would understand you. And, of course, you can do the bit with the fig leaf–nature's sweet incarnation. Aren't you starved to use your real intellect? Resign you say? Why not kill yourself, incarcerate yourself, and be done with it?"

"Alright then, as President I choose to vacillate, to be riddled with indecision–to pass up the whole show. I'll be President of the trees and Chairman of the rocks, thank you, Farney. I'll have my brand of corn and you can have yours. Shit! Farney . . .," and Katy joined Avery.

Farney's eyes grew shrewd as they clamped down on his resentful partner, tarred with sun and swollen larger with muscle, and then focused on Avery's acutely silent and vastly foreign wife outwaiting him. United, the two of them formed a solid block of obdurate obstruction.

"No–Avery–you started what only you can finish. Something of magnitude depends on you."

Avery laughed harshly. "Farney, you can be here in Hopi and yet be so blind as to see only yourself bloated up as 'something of magnitude.' Farney, this is my wife, Katy."

"Katy-how do you do? I'm here partly to meet you. Just simply to see you. And I can see much good-but Avery, I expect you to come home-bring your friend and children if you have any-bring all of Hopi-but take your rightful position in what you have pledged to undertake with me. You will say no to me now, so I won't stay to hear you out. Thank you, Mrs. Judson. Goodbye."

As Farney departed he glided a look at Avery who intercepted it and said convincingly, "No, Farney!"

Farney's visit came and went but its effect on Avery lingered in his thought, weighted the steps he took, and perverted what he saw as he honed his eyes on the already honed countryside. He didn't feel unhappy, but . . . Katy did not comment on Farney because she realized that Avery regarded him seriously, and if she cast her negative, albeit partially defensive feelings upon the man it would give him more substance in Avery's mind. "Better leave him alone-that one," she muttered to her maidens of corn.

But Avery now saw his world differently. The clouds blurred a little, the dance lasted slightly too long, the wind rustled annoyingly petulant. And what had once been charming-when the Hopis made fun of themselves and said, "We dumb Indians"-became trivial instead of endearing. Even their humorous idiosyncracy of putting a price on a favorite article and immediately removing it from sale when anyone bargained for it he regarded as a defect. And the silence of the land and its people turned into precisely that, a void of silence, no longer tinged with subtle connotations but now laced through with the presence of Farney. Moreover, he could not wait until the end of an event or situation to unfold. He would abruptly leave before the sunset fell or Katy took bread out of the horno, and he would convince, or better, cheat on himself to believe he had actually perceived with full satisfaction their conclusions. He saw that he had begun to close down within himself devising a separate reality from all outward occurrences. He no longer could witness the ripe and full climax of countless matters to resolve themselves.

In the evening, mesmerized by the inner life of the fire, Avery would unbraid and comb Katy's long hair and watch her say goodnight to her small pet turtle after rounding up all the dead flies she had killed to deliver to its snatching jaws. When the fall cloaked the terrain and the high gleam upon the earth lessened and the shadows thickened and darkened Avery told Katy about the letter he had received-several days ago-and had kept from her. He had waited for the right time, but the right time in fact never came; everything seemed wrong. The letter came from Stephanie who wrote that Farney had taken ill and was quite sick with something-he didn't think she named the illness-but it added up to a sick Farney and a grave situation. Would Avery come to New York to see Farney? Was it a trick? Avery conjectured. Farney did not send the letter, and that alone constituted the letter's veracity. Stephanie wrote it and he didn't believe she could actually be capable of performing such a ruse for Farney. Not Stephanie, not now. Not anymore. Then he had to go. Maybe he had already wanted to go before the advent of the letter. No matter now.

"So, you go. You come and go," she told him. "This is your home to come back to. If you return, I will never let you go away again. I promise."

Then she pulled something from under her pillow and gave it to him. "Here-this you owned before you gave me those white blouses and it is still yours when you leave."

She produced her turquoise and silver hair clasp, actually given to him on the occasion of their first meeting. It was his.

He said a troubled goodbye, and yet a clean, well-resolved goodbye. He acted as if he had continually forgotten something he had left behind, and if he could retrieve it and add it to his person he would be able to complete himself. Avery kissed her once and kissed her twice and almost kissed her thrice. He said, "Piss on Farney," which he deemed convenient but he knew his indecisions could not be entirely attributed to Farney.

As he glanced back he thought that she might not be so sure of him this time-that he might be irredeemably gone.

14

*A*very proceeded directly to the hospital and found Stephanie presiding over Farney's welfare, his personal secretary until the end. Enormously pleased to see him she unabashedly gave him a hug and couldn't believe he had arrived so soon and just in time. Her hair had become a dark gray but its thick profusion still attracted Avery. She acted obviously depressed; her voice kept dropping.

"Farney?" he inquired.

"Yes. He wants you. He has an order out against all the orders of his doctors that if you should appear you should be instantly sent to him. He is still remarkably clear. He says that he wants to have one last run-around with you."

Avery shook his head. "I am still no match for him and once more he will know the great secret before I do."

An orderly conducted Avery to Farney's room. En route, he saw Stephanie signing papers, scanning reports, and sending out orderlies. "He shouldn't talk to you more than five minutes," the orderly said.

"Hell, no," Farney bawled out.

As Avery approached him he started off. "My wife wrote for us to come and be with her in Barcelona when she was wrapped with death, only she didn't die. And I thank you for your support of her. But I can't get out of this death thing-I have less than six days to live." He rested his hand on Avery's arm, a thin, bony hand attached to a thin, bony body. The touch from this man who had in effect leveled a total onslaught against him deeply affected Avery; after all, even Randolf Farney now lay before him painfully vulnerable.

Farney resumed. "Once I had a little girl cousin-I talk now with the past tense of performance-a girl who was making a disturbance at a party of grownups. So I said to her, 'Sissy, stop that noise; you don't count.' And she answered, 'I do count–one, two, three, four . . .,' and she peeled off her fingers to six as far as she could count. Avery, I don't count now, except a handful."

"But you have counted already, counted a lot. You have had one hell of an effect on others, on me and others, and places and things–like a glacier covering everything in sight. With me, you busted me up, but in the long run I got patched back together again. My head is attached to the same body. Because of you I still work at what I do best."

"Perhaps to you and my wife, yes, I should have regrets–and you most probably do have regrets. But the Foundation is in your hands now. Do you recall my telling you–there is a will to be opened upon either of our deaths? But I don't want to talk legal rot."

In his blue suits Farney's hair had always a tinge of dark solid color but now had a grey-white hue. It seemed strange to conceive of Farney supine for any length of time, Avery reflected.

"One more thing," he said. "While you were at Hopi Pueblo I started to build a building to house all the material stacked away in the storerooms. The Foundation desperately needed a home for all its art. Since you couldn't do it I took over as a businessman to build it. But I kept my part of the bargain and did not buy one particle of art. The museum building will be completed in six months, only I will not be there to see it."

Avery began, "Farney, you are incredible. You started out by being one up on me and I never really caught up with you. I hope by now you've brought my Dunn and Bradstreet record you once compiled up-to-date. But even at this moment you'll have the advantage of knowing something ahead of me that I'll know at some point."

He moved his head slowly, but impatiently. "Yes, yes I know all that. Like blind, intractable constellations we have senselessly navigated around each other for so long that the course of one determines the other's. What a waste. And now that I will no longer be here to turn you away from me, Avery, I would like you to see the Foundation building completed and open to the public. You are the only one left to do it. Will you consider this, not as a favor to me, but as our pledge to each other?"

"Yes, Farney, I'll see to it that the collection is displayed in the museum for everyone to see; that much I will personally supervise. But I do not promise more. I have made no plans."

"Fair enough," said Farney. "Nothing could be fairer. I have no plans either."

"Avery," and he smiled to veil his fatigue, "I am going to leave you a personal legacy of no great importance-something I created."

"Alright," Avery acknowledged. "I would like to have a Farney creation."

"And Avery," his voice took on surprising authority, "you understand about Duskyanne, don't you?"

Avery shook his head. "Don't tire yourself, Farney. There's nothing to understand."

"Yes, there is. You should know this. In the first place, I knew Duskyanne before you did. I had to- after I met you-be best at something. Better than you, at least. It couldn't be art. And it couldn't be taste or sensitivity. I made money-better than you-better than almost anyone I know. But you don't care about money so that didn't count. However, there could only be Duskyanne that counted to both you and me. I could best you there. And that I achieved by playing on her weakness involving wealth-a thing you never would consider. I bested you at the Duskyanne game. It's no great comfort now. But you needed to know."

Avery turned away from him. The nurse entered to fetch Avery and Farney did not resist. "Avery, I'm bushed. We'll have to talk again. But the next time it'll be in the Collector's Lounge where all the artists hang out. It's out of bounds to the rabble of angels and a few devils. Our group will be by ourselves putting cloud paintings and star art in our collection. You'll be there. So long."

"I'll be there. So long." The nurse escorted him out and closed the door.

Stephanie was attending a meeting with a staff of doctors. Avery didn't want to see her anyway.

For the next week Avery saw little of Stephanie. He immersed himself in the Foundation's business. He talked to her on the telephone but the conversation concerned Farney. He met her at the hospital but she told him that Farney lacked the strength to see him. Literally, he felt that some invisible cloak of Farney protected her. And Avery admired this-her devotion to Farney to the exclusion of everything else in her life. He wondered what she would be like if she remarried. Could she forget? Could she be so involved, perhaps, with a lesser man? He cut himself short-just fantasies.

On the sixth day Farney died. Stephanie could not be reached even by Avery. She conducted Farney's funeral as a private affair, open only to members of the family. As Farney stipulated Avery would be delivered the deceased's 'personal legacy.' It turned out to be a poem typed on paper and at the bottom Farney had scrawled out in pencil, "For Avery." Farney bequeathed him only a poem but Avery felt honored. Almost a poem to him. A memorial.

On the strength of the day he trusted;
seeing with film-flicker depth
he ran each frame on.
Color tracks, old towns
tumbled like sugar squares,
textured scent, sun glazings,
storied his days tangy
taut, and they were bested.
He told his love in Paris
that she was one of numbers
to have until their workings
reached the best of both;
when he would abacus -
add her to the score
one more and move on.
On the strength of the day he crested;
trying to stake down the minute's spine
he thrashed sprawling hours
and lives leaped in pores.
He flung the finery and filament
of his life's spray
across ancient sea-backs and land-legions
so he could be like sun
and run all over.

Avery liked the poem. He thought it a good one. He conjectured, though, why Farney had written "For Avery" across the bottom. Perhaps Farney wanted to be bound up somehow in Avery's dubious immortality, to continually be a reminder of his far-reaching tentacles, even now locked away. Avery had no wish to be bound up in Farney.

Stephanie continually went on trips tending to the business of Farney's personal estate like in the early days when he first began to know her. Avery watched for her to roost near him. He in the meantime plunged into coordinating the display of art works for exhibition in the new galleries rapidly being completed. Final acquisitions had to be made as well as contacts with museums and collectors throughout the world, and although Avery preferred a low profile the publicity accorded him grew and his name became part of the shroud itself that enfolded the creation of the museum.

In the final stages of finishing the edifice he toyed with a phrase he coined that pertained to Farney-Farney's overwhelming "edifice complex." Then he ran into Stephanie occupying an office in the museum. He found her working after the building had closed. She appeared tired but relaxed, and in keeping with her taste dressed immaculately.

"Come in," she invited. "I have been waiting for you."

"And for some time I have been waiting for you. We have both been so mired in this gigantic maw of construction that I have neglected to ask how you are?"

"At times I am depressed by all this." She looked out at endless unfinished corridors before her. "But, Avery, every day I am conscious of you. In fact, you continually cross my mind."

Her remarks pleased him. "It's a wonder you can even find me among the crates of art items I'm unpacking. I can't believe all this is becoming alive just as planned and hatched from his original brainstorm."

"Yes, a brainstorm that has practically overwhelmed both of us. More like being crushed by an imponderable weight."

"Call it what you will," said Avery, "but whatever existed in the past is something quite different now. Somehow I feel as if I am much freer-that I can feel better about my past experiences. And above all, I had great ones-great in their own right. They are what counts-because I will never forget them. This museum itself has little to do with those rich moments-to be truthful-anything really. But I suppose the art objects need a home. Anyway, I am no longer intimidated by the museum; it can't make me feel identified with Farney even though I am his willing pimp."

"Maybe you have a constructive attitude, Avery, but not me. I can only feel I am some flaw frozen in this concrete maze-that those bleak corridors are my unfinished life. What to you is mostly a museum of good memories-is to me my husband's mausoleum *ad nauseam*-his public funeral for those to distort out of proportion the man I now crave to forget. Right now I am working for Farney as he would want me to. I am his good girl but I so ache to become a woman once more-my skin's young still . . . but," she corrected herself, "I suppose it's not right for a wife recently bereaved to solicit a man for her own. I think I will feel as unidentified as you do after the Foundation's opening sends Dear Randolf off into immortality to dwell among the gods. Then there's a fine chance I can really be free of him."

Avery laughed gently, "Perhaps 'Dear Randolf' will sometime meet Darlington in the Collector's Lounge among the throng of the elite, each presiding over their own bailiwick-Darlington sitting in the simplest Windsor, and, of course, Farney on the tallest throne. Please excuse my silly notion. But more to the point, I have always known about your tantalizing skin and I would like to collect it. But to observe all propriety we shall proceed on your terms. We have a date then-after the museum opening-and the ghost of Farney walks no more. Agreed?"

"Oh, yes, let's go on a trip, a long trip and get entirely lost."

Avery gallantly kissed her, kissed her deeper than he dared, then helped her close the office and saw to it that she took a taxi home. A trip, he pondered, which trip? Two were possible, but he didn't know which one to choose.

Later that night, quite late, Avery received a telephone call.

"I can't sleep," Stephanie's voice tingled excitedly, "I feel a new woman all over again. Alone in my bed doesn't work anymore."

"Is that an invitation?" Avery queried.

"Almost. Not quite. But in two days will be the opening-if I can live waiting that long. It's like ages."

The invitations reached far and wide. Ambassadors, cultural attaches, heads of state, diplomats, great collectors who dipped into their reserves and made splendid donations, museum directors, philanthropists, notable art historians, art critics and reviewers, archaeologists, university pundits, and eclectically selected members of society rolled out of their humble digs with their Joseph's coat of many colors for the occasion. Even Dr. Artin Pasha was present, appointed as the minister of culture to a newly-created African nation, and Avery saw Dalton Smedly in the crowd looking quite important, but still in a dither. No Hopi Indians attended.

Stephanie assumed the role of supreme hostess and greeted the guests personally. Although Avery tried to be with her she got tied up with Farney's people and only occasionally did Avery come across her. She dressed in a canary yellow, long-sleeved gown with quite a low neckline, now piquing Avery's attention. At these brief intervals they would abruptly stop and behold each other as if they had new eyes, and then awkwardly try to carry on their normal routines. Once Avery caught her, girlishly and audaciously, winking directly at him.

The throng wended up the steps and through the wide portal; above inscribed in marble it read: "Man offers Art To God And Nature To Atone For His Own Intrusion."

"It is all amazing," said the cultural attache from Holland as he flicked his head toward his fashionably attired wife, "this collection." They gazed at the museum showcases, one after another full of exquisite rarities of art revered by man. The Dutchman nudged the French Consul and remarked heartily that the Eastern colonies were well-represented.

"And yes they are," the Consul crisply observed. "Astonishing for an untrained American amateur to secure works such as these when even in the forties we could have plucked the same items at will from our own territories-but no longer. Well, whatever the facts, the man knows what he's about-and knew it years ago." The Frenchman joined a leading male art critic whose tallow, ruffled hair, tinged with grey lent distinction as he promenaded down the museum corridor in conversation with a host of distinguished followers. "Almost great," he pronounced.

A museum director whispered, "There he is. I didn't see him enter." An eminent anthropologist reacted, "How can one man do it even in two lifetimes, really?"

"Karl," the Austrian ambassador overheard the conversation and addressed the museum director whom he knew well. "Do you mind, gentlemen, if I join you? Remember, this is not the work of only one man. What would this Judson fellow have done without the old man, Farney? They both conceived the institution and Mr. Judson had all the financial assistance and opportunity possible–including the erection of this building."

The museum director gazed hungrily at the grand array of flawless art and reflected, "Still, any collector or director of a museum like myself that has the finest assortment of early Japanese antiquities will realize that although you can have a grand building to house material you must have great art to make it come alive. Even in my field he has preempted us," and he stared wistfully. "What he has put together testifies for both himself and itself."

Avery, flanked by his museum curator and staff, started down the long gallery and paused at the first exhibit. At the far end, Stephanie stood with her hands stretched out to receive him, eagerly waiting for the Director of her husband's museum to move through the art pillars of his accomplishments.

A banker whispered to Avery and he nodded. The Foundation did not need the money he offered since it continued to be sufficiently endowed by the Farney Trust, nonprofit in design, but he would gratefully accept the grant.

Avery detected the Egyptian cat with pleasure. As a young man he had obtained it aided by a measure of luck and had been fortunate enough to start out with an outstanding piece. And he continued to be lucky and still young when he topped the cat with the exquisite Benin mask–less than a dozen in the world, as anyone informed knows. To keep the mask he got Farney. Of course, the Scythian beasts lurked in their cages seemingly ready to whirl out and face the doting audience. And indeed, the Ajanta wall painting did hold up the wall; he would give instruction that it should never be removed. This is my life, he thought, paraded before him. But was this a life–worthy–his? He faltered. Three Kachina sculptures and a hide shield faced him. Opposite stood the ultra-elegant fat-bellied ceramic jars equal to the best Chinese vessels. Hopi. Yes, Hopi.

He started to continue on, but he could not–he could not move. He clung there and stared. His aides began to push on, bypassing him and leaving him alone. He veritably remained alone. An insistent urge plagued him to turn around and face the unseen force that inexplicably pulled at him, badgering him, forcing him to come to a halt. He quickly wheeled around but saw no one. He faced a disturbing nothing.

He looked back and swore that the tallest wooden Kachina had turned ever so slightly. He wondered if it had moved. In his growing awareness of a different reality Avery believed that the wooden figure took on human dimensions. The eyes of the Hopi sculpture took on depth and locked on to his own, and he did not, could not, break the connection. Through the free-standing glass case that enclosed the figure he could see through to the other side a relaxed, smiling Stephanie Farney beckoning him to come to her, her tantalizing, silver figure shimmering through the prisms of light that infracted on the glass. He squeezed his eyes tightly shut in an attempt to sever the linkage to the Hopi statue. He opened them to catch a stunning view of Stephanie through the layers of glass. Avery glanced about him, his eyes darting without focus on the other figures of museum art, all antiquities of compelling beauty, but he could not fathom them. Their eyes stared without expression. Only when his gaze reconnected with the benevolent eyes of the Hopi Kachina did a measure of calm return that soothed him.

It didn't worry him. The Kachina came from far distant Hopi mesas along with the gleaming white blouses of his remembrance. Stephanie, behind glass, gestured to him and her gown swirled as she arched forward to peer through the case. Avery smiled at the Hopi figure. He remained safe as long as he did not proceed down the gallery, did not move to the other side of the case in Stephanie's welcoming direction. He began to perspire. A flashbulb lit and a reporter adjusted his camera and shouted some gnarled words. Avery reared his head, bewildered, hapless. He glanced at the Benin mask, secure in its display case. Did he, himself, wear a mask? He wondered which one he might have on. Could he change it? He turned his back to avoid the photographer.

He could move. Suddenly all corridors opened to him. He felt revitalized; he innately knew so. Avery turned once more to the Hopi figure, threw back his head and laughed. He started to run, actually run. In a happy, obsessed mania he whooped an exultant cry and exploded out the museum doors.

Ending his journey Avery arrived and greeted her with a warm embrace. Tears clouded their eyes. Avery shed his old scars. He was home at last.